A DANCE OF MAGIC

CAROLINA CASTILLO

CREATIVELY UNWRITTEN LLC.

Published by Creatively Unwritten LLC
Copyright © 2023 by Carolina Castillo

First Edition: April 2023

Ebook ISBN: 978-1-957534-05-3
Paperback ISBN: 978-1-957534-04-6

Cover by Moorbooks Designs
Interior Design and Formatting by McKayla Boyd

To my loves, the OG Series. Thank you for loving
all the parts of me.

Content Warning

The content warning below may contain spoilers.

Content warning includes:
- Graphic depictions of panic attacks and extreme anxiety
- Depression
- Mentions of suicide
- Mentions of weight loss due to under-eating
- Death of a parent(s)
- Murder (off page)
- Drug use
- Mentions of past sexual assault (off page)
- Explicit sexual situations.

As always, I urge you to take good care of yourself.

A Note From the Author

A Dance of Magic was a surprising thing that came out of my first love, A Song of Magic. I never intended to continue writing in this family, but Julia wanted her story told, and who better to do that with than Lucas.

Lucas, formerly Jay (I had to change that shit from the first edition of Song), is honestly my favorite dude. He's so patient and sweet to the grumpy gremlin that is Julia. I love them so much and hope you do too.

For playlists and other bookish goodies, visit my website: carolinacastilloauthor.com

This book contains common phrases in Spanish, and they're not always translated.

Enjoy!

Carolina

1

The guilt came without fail. Sometimes, it was smooth and sneaky, sliding in like dark clouds on the horizon. Other times, it came on hard and fast, like a baseball to the face.

And it always, *always*, followed the grief.

It had left her sleepless last night, lying in her own cold sweat, and she felt the exhaustion in her bones.

Julia Candela sat in her car, swallowing bile, and telling herself that she had to get out or she'd be late to her appointment. Her visits with her therapist weren't a luxury, but a necessity. Both, really, if one sat to think about it, but she would've gone mad by now if it weren't for Mariana.

Counting in her head, she calmed down her shallow breathing, and the knots in her stomach subsided. Somewhat. They never really went away. It was just like her to be fighting a panic attack over getting out of her car at her therapist's office. As if that wasn't the whole point of being there in the first place.

Clearly, she'd learned nothing in the last year.

Everything pointed at the lack of sleep, which everyone in her life kept reminding her that sleep was important, like Julia was a child. Or stupid.

She steeled her spine and pressed the ignition button to turn off the SUV. Keys in hand, her tiny wallet in her hoodie pocket, she locked all doors and walked up to the short building. It was one of those places that housed many therapy offices. A tall cherry tree in the front was full of white blossoms, and though she didn't do it, Julia had the urge to reach for a tiny flower on her way to the glass double doors. Sunshine streamed into the lobby, where a woman sat behind a desk. The tiny blonde woman smiled pleasantly and told Julia to sit until Mariana came to collect her. It was the same every single time. Down to how it made her feel when Mariana finally came out, only a few minutes later. Julia fought the urge to look down at herself and compare. Sadly, she failed.

Mariana was beautiful, her hair dark and curly around her narrow shoulders, and her skin a deep gold. She wore a perfectly tailored pencil skirt and a tight blouse, and she smiled brightly as Julia walked up to her in sweatpants, slippers, and a hoodie that she'd spilled toothpaste on that morning.

"It's good to see you, Julia," Mariana said with a kind smile, and took the lead toward the office. Where the hallways were mostly bare, only a piece of generic art here and there, Mariana's office was cozy. It had no business being this homey, with its bright blue sofa and colorful pillows of Incan fabrics. Instantly, her nervous system calmed down.

Julia pulled one of the pillows on her lap, so she felt less frumpy in front of this woman who seemed to have it together in ways Julia couldn't even imagine anymore.

On the orange, flowered chair across from Julia, Mariana sat with a notepad and a pen, her cute red glasses on her nose.

"How've you been?" Mariana asked, and Julia lost the ability to talk.

She didn't even know how to start, or what kinds of things she could say without sounding like she needed to be institutionalized. How did she tell her therapist what was happening inside her? How every time she woke up in a cold sweat in the middle of the night, something heavy and alive wriggled inside her, wanting to come out.

Julia cleared her throat. "I've had trouble sleeping."

No shit, Julia. She had to hold back the urge to roll her eyes, but Mariana's expression didn't change.

"Any idea what's keeping you awake?"

Oh, gee, I don't know. Even her inner monologue was filled with sarcasm these days.

"I keep having nightmares," she told Mariana. The truth, just not the whole thing.

"You want to tell me about them?"

She'd rather not.

"Dreams can be a good indicator of what's going on in your subconscious," Mariana added, as if Julia had said it out loud. Like she knew that there was turmoil in speaking about these things.

Of course she knows, you dumbass. She's seen your mess for almost a year.

Julia let out a shaky breath. "I was in a room and there was blood." Everywhere. It had been at her feet, inside her shoes, and on her hands.

"What was the room like?" Mariana asked, confusing Julia for a moment.

"Um… it was the attic where my mom died."

The attic where her mother had been *murdered*, but she didn't have to clarify that part. Everyone knew. The media had called it a tragedy, and it was, but none of their reports had ever expressed how horrible it had been. How Julia had believed her whole life that her mom had tried to run away with her lover, just to find out that was a lie. That her father had killed her mom and her best friend in a jealous rage.

Julia fidgeted. "There was blood everywhere," she continued, sniffling, fidgeting with the colorful pillow. "My mom used to have this old table in the attic." Where she used to do magic, but Julia wouldn't be telling Mariana that. "And all the things she used to have on it where still there, like when she was alive."

She looked up to find Mariana's dark eyes on her. The woman knew Julia's entire story, but these nightmares she'd kept to herself for a long while.

"When she died, her stuff disappeared. Not completely, since my sister found my mom's journals about two years ago."

"Have you looked at the journals?"

"No." They terrified her. Julia knew the story. Was there really any need for her to read them? Sophia, her second youngest sister, had said in the past that it was good to see those things, but Julia had to disagree. Her mom hadn't had the best upbringing, and those journals would only show that and make Julia feel even worse about the fact that for almost twenty years, she'd convinced herself to hate her mom over something she hadn't even done in the first place.

"Why not?"

"I guess it makes me feel guilty," Julia said. No way to run from this conversation now. Mariana would keep asking until Julia said what she was actually thinking. "And I know we've beat this dead horse for almost a year, but I don't know how else to feel, to be frank."

"You don't have to feel any one way."

"But I also don't want to feel guilty anymore."

Mariana nodded slightly. "Can I tell you what I think?"

"Of course."

"I think you did the best you could with the information you did have back then." Mariana laid her hands on her notepad, the pen between two of her fingers. Her nails were short and unpainted, but neat and well-groomed. Julia looked down at her own bitten nails, then hid them away as Mariana continued, "You couldn't have reacted any other way when you had nothing else to go by."

"Yes, you've said that before, and I get it, but…" Julia swallowed, frustrated, the words leaving her brain faster than she could even form the thought.

"Tell me what you're feeling right now," Mariana prompted quietly, taking notes.

According to her, Julia would do best to work through every emotion when it came, but sometimes, Julia had to remind herself that Mariana was full of shit. She didn't want to feel anything.

Still, she said, "Frustrated."

"Why?"

"Because I would have thought that after all this time doing therapy I would have made some progress."

"You feel like you haven't make any progress?" Mariana asked.

No, I am falling apart.

"I think you've made a lot of progress. The evidence is right here," Mariana gestured toward Julia with a narrow hand. "You're here, when you don't have to be."

"I do have to be here."

"But you don't. What's keeping you from just staying home?"

Julia had no words. She leaned forward, elbows on knees, and pressed the heels of her hands to her eyes so she didn't cry. She was so sick of crying.

"Unearthing trauma is traumatic on its own," said Mariana.

Lifting her gaze to Mariana's, Julia said, "How fun for me."

Mariana was smiling a little when Julia removed her hands from her face.

"There's a processing time for everything, and those bigger things will take much longer to deal with. Given your history, I think you're doing really well."

A processing time… like ordering a dress off the internet. You pay for it, and the shipping, then you have to wait for delivery. It was absolute bullshit.

"I'm glad you think so," Julia said, "I just don't really feel like I am. Every time I have one of these nightmares, I wake up feeling guilty. Like the spill of that blood is my fault."

"Is the guilt in the dream too?"

Julia shook her head. No, the guilt was reserved for her waking hours. It was like a nightmare that she couldn't ever wake from.

She told Mariana that and Mariana tilted her head.

"Why do you think you feel guilty?"

"The grief," Julia said, unwilling to fight against it anymore. She looked anywhere but at Mariana now, ashamed of the words she was about to speak. "I just want to hate him for what he did."

"Your father?"

"Yeah. I gave him everything, and he was lying to me that entire time. When I confided in him about my anger toward my mom, he knew all along."

Mariana's expression was sympathetic and it made Julia's stomach wriggle unpleasantly. She didn't need pity from anyone; she just didn't want any of this shit that she couldn't seem to get rid of. The pain in her stomach that was always there, the tension on her neck that left her stiff and miserable, or the sharp ache around her heart.

Whenever she visited Mariana, Julia left feeling slightly lighter. At least some of the time. Today, she left with the same heaviness with which she'd arrived. It stayed with her all the way to the house in the city she called home. Sophia had graciously offered for Julia to stay there when she'd decided to leave her ex, Harold.

Another one of the big liars of Julia's life. Harold, who she'd never considered the love of her life, but had at least respected for his role in her life. Until she'd started to notice how rude he was to the wait staff and the people who worked for him. And when he ended up sleeping with her best friend, which Julia hadn't even found out until after she'd left him.

She parked in the garage of Sophia's street-facing house. It had been their mother's once upon a time, one of those extravagant gifts she got from Julia's dad. Sophia got it in the will, and had lived there from the moment she'd turned eighteen and left their childhood home outside of Seattle. Now, Julia lived there, like she'd been meant to all along. At least she didn't have to live in the mausoleum she'd shared with Harold.

A single door in the garage led into the house, right by the entrance. It was an interesting floor plan, not really what Julia would have chosen, but the house had been built decades ago. A narrow hallway led toward the kitchen, which sat to the side, before a simple archway opened into the dining and living rooms. Half the room was windows, which made the light bounce off the light-colored walls. Sophia wasn't one for luxuries, only the essentials. A sofa, an armchair, and a fuzzy rug under a marble coffee table. The dining room had a simple, round, wooden table with chairs.

Julia's eyes fell on the wooden box by the window. It held everything she needed to forget that she was sad and panicked. Whatever was happening inside her wasn't only related to her depression. It was so much heavier, almost oily. As if she'd drank too much the night before. Except it was every night.

She opened the window to let in fresh air. Clouds were rolling in as she climbed onto the windowsill, opening the wooden box.

The click of the lighter was so familiar now, the weight of the joint between her fingers comforting. One long drag, and Julia blew out a cloud of white smoke, then watched it disappear into the sunlight. She hoped it would take the awful feelings purring inside her with it.

But it didn't work right away as she'd wanted. Her tolerance was too high now. So, when she brought the joint back to her lips, her fingers shook as her stomach seized. Her mouth and eyes watered with the acidity.

The feelings were still there after two more puffs, and so were the racing thoughts. Her failed marriage, her dead mother, and the disease that had almost killed her. As if the universe had thought that Julia's life had been far too easy and chose to dump everything on her at once.

When it rained, it poured indeed.

And there it was, the grief. It had been almost a year; it should be a little easier now. But of course it couldn't be as simple as her hating her father for what he'd done. The grief came anyway, even though she did hate Conrad Montgomery with all her heart.

The pain in her stomach spiked, and a tremble in her hands traveled up her arms and spread through her body. It was an ache inside her bones, one that had nothing to do with Julia's emotional turmoil. She pushed off the window ledge, and her nose started to drip as she panted. On her hands and knees, the tears finally came, and this time, she let them.

"I don't want this," she whispered into the empty house. "I don't want it. I don't want it."

She held her breath, squeezed her eyes shut as the wave of heat came. So hot that if she hadn't experienced it before, she would have been convinced she would combust.

A gasp tore out of her at the familiarity of the sensations.

It brought her right back to when she'd fallen ill with a magical disease Grey had called the void. Something that should have only affected witches, but had almost killed Julia. It didn't make any sense. Magic wasn't hers.

"I don't want it," she said, her voice still shaking, but her nervous system calmer as the joint had its effect.

Not the magic, not the feelings, and not the memories.

Because it wasn't just that her father had lied his ass off to everyone who had ever known and loved her mom. That he'd killed her in a jealous rage, convinced she'd been cheating with her best friend, Will. And that when the truth came to light, when he'd gone to jail to pay for his crimes, he hung himself before his trial.

2

The club was loud when Julia arrived on Monday morning. It was inventory and rehearsal day at Nowhere, Sophia's club, and because Julia had nothing better to do with her life, she helped where she could. It kept her mind busy, so she didn't have to deal with her own shit.

Her heels—too high today, if she was honest—made a satisfying clicking sound on the tile floor as she made her way down the long hallway. It was lit by a bright row of overhead lights. Posters lined the dark walls, pictures of every current employee and regular performers. Julia loved this part—how Sophia and Victoria, their childhood best friend, had created a place like this. A family of people who got along well, fair wages, and a club where people could come unwind.

Sophia and Victoria didn't need anyone's help. Nowhere had been popular and lucrative well before Julia had come in, but she was glad she at least had this.

Once, she'd been invaluable–her father's words. She'd been COO to his empire, and she'd been damn good at it. Then, in the blink of an eye, everything was gone. Her life was purposeless, cast adrift, and she'd had to reevaluate everything she'd ever known.

At least helping Sophia meant Julia was somewhat in her element. In fact, she'd hoped to meet with the owners of a building that was for sale next door, which Sophia and Victoria wanted to use as an expansion for Nowhere.

Julia could already see it. A themed dance club with amazing food and entertainment. There was enough demand at Nowhere that Julia thought it was a great idea to expand, so she'd jumped at the chance of procuring that building for them.

Business was her thing, always had been, and getting into what would surely be a bidding war, according to their realtor, was exactly what Julia wanted. Maybe it would bring her back to life. Because one thing she wasn't good at was staying still, and this depression had done nothing but stop her in her tracks.

She would get that building if it was the last thing she did.

At the simple brown door, she stopped, bracing herself for all the questions that would surely come. Why do you look tired, Julia? Are you not sleeping again, Julia? Have you eaten, Julia? Would you like us to get you something, Julia?

And it wasn't that Julia didn't appreciate the concern; she wasn't made of ice. It struck her that what bothered her most was that everyone in her life was aware of her struggle. Sometimes Julia felt like everyone was just waiting for the moment when she broke, and it pissed her off. She was still hanging around, wasn't she? Quite the feat.

Bronze knob cool under her fingers, Julia opened the door and found Sophia sitting behind one of the two desks in the small office. A big blackboard took over one wall, and the week's schedule was written neatly in colorful chalk. Sophia looked up, her hazel eyes brightening when she saw Julia.

Damn if it didn't warm Julia. As much as she didn't *want* to need anyone, it felt nice to be seen.

The last year hadn't been the nicest to any of them, but Sophia seemed to be handling it well. She looked happy, which relieved Julia, who was always worried her younger sisters needed something she couldn't give them.

"Are you ready to meet the owners?" Sophia rubbed her hands together.

Her excitement made Julia lighten a little. It wouldn't be so bad.

"I am, and I'm getting that building if it's the last thing I do." She sat across from Sophia, who typed something on the laptop in front of her.

"I have no doubts you will." Sophia twisted her long curly hair into a knot at the top of her head and secured it with a pen. "Meanwhile, I need your opinion on food."

Julia felt the usual pang, waiting for Sophia to harp on her about not eating.

It's not that I don't want to—

"For Latin Nights," Sophia added before Julia could go into a full-blown anxiety rant about not being able to eat anything. Her sister turned the laptop so Julia could see the spreadsheet. Julia blinked at the screen, frozen in confusion for a moment. Sophia had detailed all her research on ingredient prices, quantities, and pricing for a variety of Caribbean foods. "It's five dishes to start, and I think they could be really popular. With the rise of social media and the ease of access to so many foods from so many amazing places, I feel like this could be a good idea."

Julia looked at the pictures of gorgeous Caribbean dishes Sophia pulled up; mofongo, rice with gandules, stewed chicken, and several other delicacies graced the screen.

"They look amazing, Soph, but are you offering new foods for every single theme, or just Latin Nights?"

"We haven't gotten that far yet. We're discussing the possibility."

Julia bit her lip. She hated having to be the one to say it, but she had to be the voice of reason. What if it didn't work out and sent her sister to ruin?

"From a business standpoint, it seems like a big change to make in one go. Drastic changes to menus can cause issues with your regulars."

Sophia's shoulder deflated a fraction.

"I thought about that."

Julia's heart dropped at the disappointment in Sophia's face.

"It's not that you can't do it," she added quickly. "I wouldn't be me if I didn't ruin the fun with business shit."

Sophia's expression softened. "Julia, your input is extremely valuable to me and Victoria."

The words made her skin itchy. She'd lived for the praise and people asking her for help; the way they praised her work ethic and her smarts in a boardroom. She'd been the highest powered woman on her father's payroll. To be fair, he didn't have a lot of women working for him, which should have been red flag número uno.

But did she even think about it? Not until it affected her, which made her some type of person. She didn't even want to think about what that was.

"I'm just trying to bring more of Mom's culture into this place," Sophia continued, knocking Julia out of her spiral of self-loathing.

"Our culture, you could say," Julia said, though she didn't believe it. There had always been a disconnect with that part of her heritage, and now that she'd had time to sit and think about it, she regretted not knowing more. The music had always called to her, as well as the food, but her mom was gone before Julia could appreciate those things, and life had taken her through a different path. What that path was supposed to teach her, she had no idea.

A 'no sabo' kid was what they called people like Julia. Someone who didn't quite belong with the rest.

Nausea swirled in her stomach. Drinking only a black coffee that morning was coming back to bite her in the ass.

"Maybe I can add a dish here and there?" Sophia asked quietly, and when Julia looked at her, she realized how much Sophia wanted this. Julia softened, and even her nausea let up.

"You could have a provisional menu, specials, and see how they do," Julia added and Sophia grinned.

"I'll chat with Victoria about it."

"Chat with Victoria about what?"

Julia turned to the door, where Victoria was standing with arms on her narrow hips. Her tight curls were pulled up in knots, and her green eyes were bright. Like always, her dark skin gleamed like a mirror. Victoria's willowy figure was clad in blue jeans and a simple hoodie.

"Adding Caribbean dishes to the menu provisionally," Sophia explained. "But we can talk about that when we meet with the kitchen staff later."

"It's a yes from me, but sure," Victoria said, smiling brightly. She gave Julia a tight hug, and when she pulled back Julia had the thought that preparing for her wedding was making Victoria even more beautiful somehow.

Meanwhile, when Julia had married Harold, she'd been so stressed out, she'd puked into a trashcan right before walking down the aisle. Maybe her gut had been trying to tell her something all along. Not that her gut was telling her anything now, so maybe it never did.

"How are you?" Victoria asked.

"Fine." Julia gave her a smile that felt unconvincing to her, so it probably looked that way too, but Victoria didn't say anything. Bless her. She was far less pushy than Julia's sisters, especially Amy, the youngest.

"Helena will be here in an hour for rehearsal," Sophia said as she typed on her phone. "The dancers should be arriving soon."

"I thought you were singing this weekend," Julia said. According to her notes, Sophia was due to sing. It'd been months since her last performance.

"I was, but I asked Helena to sub. I have things to do with Grey."

Conflicting emotions arose. On the one hand, Helena was good for business. But on the other hand, hearing Grey's name always made Julia cringe inside. Not because Grey was a bad boyfriend or person. On the contrary, he was good to Sophia. So good that Sophia had moved in with him within the first year of their relationship, and things couldn't have been better since. It was the guilt Julia couldn't stand. The fact that her father had killed his... How could she live with that? The nausea started building again, so she shut down the line of thinking.

Not today, she thought as she turned to Sophia.

"Helena's great." She smiled, but it felt like a grimace. Not that she didn't like Helena; the woman was a genius. An incredible singer, Helena came with a built-in audience, since she was internet-famous for singing covers of popular songs and arranging them herself. She'd been singing at Nowhere for well over a year, and though she was excellent for business, that wasn't the sole reason why Julia liked her.

Helena was the only other person who understood what it was like to survive a disease like the void, a magical disease that took the lives of countless witches and had put Julia in a coma. When Sophia had met Grey, he'd been searching for a cure for the void, desperate to save Helena's life, along with many others. It was what ultimately led them to discover what Conrad, their father, had done.

In all that, Helena had found her way into their hearts, and she was the only person who understood Julia's struggle. Everyone else thought they got what it was like, but that wasn't true. They were all watching from the outside, imagining that they could, while Julia and Helena were alive to tell the story.

Trauma bonds for the win.

And Helena being a witch had nothing to do with Julia at all. Sure, the void only affected witches, but Julia was not one of those. That was Grey's issue. And Sophia's.

Sure, keep lying to yourself. That's going to help.

But no. She couldn't allow her mind to go there. If she did, then it meant that what nearly happened last night was supposed to, and it wasn't. She didn't want it—there was no room for it in her life.

Julia shook her head, forcing herself to pay attention to what she was doing here. Her heart was pounding now, and she wanted to go home more than anything else in the world, but she had things to do, like meet with the realtor.

Though her heart raced, Julia was the picture of calm to the other two women in the room. "The realtor should be here any minute."

"And we love you for doing that, Jules."

"Oh, it's my pleasure!" Her voice was a little shrill, but that was only because Victoria always made Julia feel like she was being read like a book.

"You know, Latin Night is happening soon," said Sophia, leaning back into her chair. "I think you should come."

"I don't know about that." Funny how she'd never shied away from doing things and now it was an impulse to stay home. For a few reasons.

What if she had a panic attack? Crowds and noise would only make that worse.

"Come on, it's been so long, Jules," Sophia pleaded. "I really want to spend an evening with you. We can drink and you can dance with strangers. You used to love dancing."

"I did love dancing, but I just can't right now."

Sophia's expression turned to one of concern.

"I'm fine," Julia added quickly. "The nightlife just isn't for me. It's never been." *And I'm a coward of elephantine proportions, too.* The disappointment was pointed in Sophia's face, but she didn't push.

"Well, the invitation's always open," Sophia said softly, then went back to her computer.

"Make the nightlife your thing before my bachelorette," Victoria said, never looking up from her screen, and it almost drew a laugh from Julia.

"Of course." She chuckled and looked at her phone when the alarm went off to remind her of the appointment with the realtor. She'd one business with Charles for many years, but she hadn't seen him since she separated from Harold. Since those two were still in business together, Julia thought it best to stay away until now. With a wave, she left and exited Nowhere through the back door, and walked down the wet alley between it and the building they hoped to purchase for the expansion. As she rounded a corner to the front of the building, once a cowboy bar, her stomach fell out.

Because it wasn't Charles waiting for her, but Stephen Belvedere. Tall and lean, with dark hair he'd slicked back from a handsome, angular face. Stephen's suit was fitted to his frame perfectly, and he walked forward smoothly with a smile on his face and dark eyes assessing.

"Julia," he said as he leaned forward and kissed her on the cheek, like they used to greet each other before they'd found out their spouses had been fucking each other behind their backs.

She wasn't even shocked when she found out—it was like Harold to do something like sleeping with not only her best friend, but his childhood friend's wife. When Julia had told Stephen about it, he'd already known and had chosen to file for divorce. They'd reconnected one night six months ago, and after a few too many drinks, she went home with him.

Not her brightest moment, but Stephen had been sweet and decent in bed. Just not mind-blowing. Though, what the hell did she know?

"It's been a while," she said, her voice a little too bright. She refused to be seen defeated, like the last time when she'd been a damn mess. How else did she explain having sex with him otherwise?

"I tried calling," he said, his voice a little tight.

"Well, I've been busy."

What a lame-ass excuse, Julia Candela.

"I can imagine." His tone wasn't unkind, just a little hurt. But what did he expect? She wasn't going to get into anything serious with him. That night, though she didn't entirely regret it, should have never happened.

"Not that I mind you being here—" Oh, she did mind a lot, "—but why did you come instead of Charles?"

"He had a last minute meeting to attend to."

She doubted that.

"And you happened to be free to show me this place, even though you don't work in the field anymore?"

"What can I say? I wanted to see you." He smiled down at her. "You look great."

Julia fought to urge to look down at herself. Was he blind? She was wasting away. Julia had lost quite a bit of weight in the last months, what with the nightly vomiting and lack of appetite. It wasn't pretty.

Instead, she gave him half a smile as the owner showed up with his realtor, a woman who was thankfully as short as Julia so she didn't have to walk around feeling like a little kid. The owner, David something-or-the-other, was an older man who looked down at Julia with an appraising eye.

She took his bony hand when he offered it. "Julia Candela."

Stephen gave her a look, but she ignored him as she established a conversation with David and the realtor, a dark-skinned woman named Sasha.

The former club was one huge room, and it needed a lot of work, as there was debris everywhere. A thick layer of dust covered what was left of the old bar, and one of the windows was broken, glass everywhere.

"How long has the space been empty?" she asked, knowing perfectly well what that time was.

"Two years next June," Sasha said.

The back had a tiny office they'd have to update, and there was no kitchen, which would have to change since Sophia and Victoria wouldn't have a place without food. No wonder the last one hadn't survived.

Her checklist out, she and Stephen asked all the appropriate questions of the other duo, and it was the first time in a while that Julia felt more like herself. Negotiating, assessing the things they were told, scrutinizing every wall and corner. She could almost see it. They'd have to paint the dark brown walls, section the area in a way that made sense, add a better, newer stage. Julia imagined VIP booths, potential for more privacy than Nowhere could offer. Not that she knew much about clubs.

As they finished the walk-through, Julia knew she was going to make an offer on behalf of Sophia and Victoria, and with Stephen and their company behind the negotiations, she would get it. There was no doubt about it. If she had to offer up some of her own money to help her sister, she would. It was the one thing she had the most of. Money that just sat there because she didn't want to touch it. Because it came from Conrad.

Outside, Stephen walked her through the narrow alley toward the parking lot.

"You're just as sharp as ever," he said when they'd stopped beside her car.

"Did you doubt I would be?"

He smiled. Stephen was in his forties, the heir of a realty fortune, and he was handsome. If only their pasts weren't so intertwined, not that Julia had the energy for anything resembling a relationship at the moment.

"Not even a little bit," he said.

Julia nodded. "I can trust you'll get us that place?"

"Expect an email soon." Stephen kissed her cheek again, lingered a little long. "Or a call?"

Suddenly, they weren't talking about the building anymore, and Julia wasn't sure how to feel at all.

"About the building, of course," he added, as if he knew what she'd been thinking. "I had no idea you'd changed your name."

"Yeah, a while back," she told him, needing for this conversation to be over immediately.

"It was your mother's maiden name?"

Anxiety tightened in her chest and she nodded, waiting for him to mock her for suddenly wanting to connect with the mother she'd hated all her life.

"It suits you," he said with a kind smile, and as she looked up at him, she saw the sadness in his eyes. Regret squeezed her heart that it'd taken that long to see it.

"You okay?" she asked him, briefly touching his elbow.

He sighed. "You know how it is."

"I do." She nodded eagerly and got a rumble of laughter.

"I heard those two are looking to buy a house," he told her, and she was both surprised and not.

Julia had gotten the house she'd live in with Harold in the divorce, thanks to a clause in their prenup about infidelity. Harold had tried to hide the fact that he'd been cheating on her with Kate, but Stephen had come to her rescue with proof that Kate and Harold had been sleeping together for years.

Julia didn't even like the ridiculously modern house, but Harold loved it, so she fought for it, and now it sat empty and gathering dust. Harold could suck it.

What would Harold do with it anyway? Move in with Kate?

Julia would rather stick needles under her nails than to ever let that happen.

"Good luck to them," she said, though the only wish she had was that Harold's dick fell off. She gave Stephen a quick hug and turned to go back to Nowhere.

Back in the office, Julia told Sophia and Victoria her thoughts about the place. With every positive word, Julia watched two pairs of eyes become wider and more hopeful, and she knew that she'd do anything to make sure they secured the building.

"So, I guess the first thing we do is price out a kitchen," Victoria said.

"The first thing we do is get the building," Sophia said. Victoria stuck out her tongue at her business partner.

Laughing, Julia said, "We're getting the building. I have people working on it." She didn't have to say who 'people' was. The girls knew about her tryst with Stephen, but it wasn't something Julia wanted to get into right then.

Victoria and Sophia turned to her with hope written all over their faces.

"You really think we will?" Sophia asked.

"Hell yes," Julia said, confident that she could at least pull that off. Sophia and Victoria had the funds—they were smart with their business—but Julia knew she'd do anything to make it happen.

Amy burst through the door moments later, a huge black bin in her arms.

"What's going on?" her youngest sister asked. Amy's hair was dark, when before it had been different colors every two months. She was taller than both Sophia and Julia, and she wore a loose romper and sandals. Her blue eyes were as bright as the sky.

"We're putting an offer on the building." Victoria grinned, and Amy's mouth opened in happy surprise.

"You're totally going to get it," Amy said with a huge smile.

"If Julia has anything to do with it, we already have it," Sophia said, kissing Julia on the cheek, just as her phone went off with an alert. Sophia went back to chat with Victoria as Julia grabbed her phone from her back pocket. Her heart sank. What a familiar sensation that was these days.

She'd have thought the internet would have moved on about it, but no. That was way too easy. There was always an article popping up out of nowhere about her father and his crimes, especially now that people seemed to be obsessed with true crime entertainment. It was annoying how some random person could hear about something tragic and got attention for telling the story in the most salacious way possible.

She closed the article when she saw her father's name, hands shaking.

Mariana had told her that having alerts on for those kinds of news wasn't helping her, but Julia didn't know how to stop looking. If she didn't check, how could she know what people were saying?

"Everything okay?" Amy asked, her blue eyes sharp.

"I'm fine."

Amy's eyes narrowed, then rolled.

"You're not sleeping again."

Julia counted backwards, exhaling slowly.

"You're having trouble sleeping still?" Sophia asked, worry marring her brow.

"I woke up very early," Julia lied. "I'm okay, I have coffee."

"Hot bean water isn't going to fix anything," Amy said. She also looked tired, and it irked Julia; Amy throwing stones when she lived in a glass cottage.

"I can take perfectly good care of myself, Amy, but thank you."

Amy didn't add anything else and opened the bin she'd brought, her mouth tight. She owned a boutique, and because she had a lot of contacts in fashion, she was going to dress the dancers for one of Helena's shows soon. Sophia approached her.

"Are you sure you don't need any help?" Sophia said quietly. "I have potions."

A conversation they'd had many times, and one that Julia didn't need to have again. She'd been having such a good day.

"I'm fine." The lie rang loudly in her ear.

"I didn't ask if you're fine," Sophia said.

"Let's not do this again, please."

"Not do what?" Amy stood again and crossed her arms.

"Amy, I can't do this right now." Julia had only come here to talk about business, not to be interrogated and treated like an incapable child.

"We're just concerned for you," Amy said.

"Amy," Victoria warned softly.

"No, it's time to stop tip-toeing around her like she's incapable of understanding." Amy's voice rose with every word.

"What are you talking about?" Julia asked them.

The three shared looks between each other, and Julia had a hard time not storming out right then. They were going behind her back.

"We're worried about you," Sophia said softly. "You don't come out with us anymore, and we barely ever see you unless it's about the club."

Julia fought back the tightness in her throat.

"I'm doing the best I can." The tremble in her voice pissed her off, so she gritted her teeth against it. "I'm sorry if I'm too busy to come hang out at the club, watching people dancing in their underwear—"

"Oh, busy with what?" Amy snapped. "You don't have a job anymore, and you're obviously a fucking mess."

Julia felt the anger start at the bottom of her feet, like an electric current.

"I'm aware that my life is a mess, Amy, but thanks for the reminder," she spat.

"Don't do that," Amy bit out. "You won't talk to anyone, won't come out to brunch, which is the only tradition we have left, and now you're trying to tell us you can't because you're too busy when we know better?"

"Amy—" Sophia started, but Julia stopped her.

"No, let her say what she wants to say." Julia crossed her arms tightly around herself as the chill started to spread. She wanted to go home. "What, Amy? Want to tell me how I'm not doing well enough for you?"

"You know that's not what I mean." Amy's voice shook.

"Then what do you mean?" Julia had to control her volume because all she wanted to do was shout and rage. "First her husband cheats on her, poor Julia. Can't keep a husband—"

Amy looked stricken. "I would never throw that in your face. I hate Harold for what he did to you and you know that."

"So what is it? Going to therapy once a week isn't good enough either?" Julia asked, throwing her hands up. "Is it that I'm not handling it well that our father, my own personal fucking hero, turned out to be a murderer? How are *you* handling that, Amy?"

She struck a chord. Amy's chest inflated, and her face turned bright red.

"You think all this shit only happened to you," Amy snarled.

"You guys, please let's not fight." Sophia's voice trembled, and if Julia had looked at her, she'd have seen the tears gathering in her eyes. Victoria tried to take Amy's arm, but Amy moved away and came closer to Julia.

"You act like you're the only one traumatized. You know, you're not the only daughter left to pick up the pieces. He was my dad too, and she was my mom. And Sophia's, whose boyfriend is also affected by all this crap. No one's sitting around acting like a fucking victim."

"How dare you?" Julia's voice broke, and she hated herself for it. She was desperate to keep herself from crying, but the tears were right there, hot and annoying. "You have any idea how much I've sacrificed?"

"I didn't ask for your sacrifices!" Amy yelled, her eyes full of angry tears.

It was a slap to the face. Julia reared back with the force of it. Sophia brought her hands to her brow, pale and close to crying herself, while Victoria looked around at all of them, as if she didn't know what to say or do.

Without another word, Julia turned and left. Her throat was on fire, and as the door slammed behind her, she heard Amy's sob. But she wasn't going to turn back to console her. It was true, they hadn't asked, but how unfair. As if Julia'd had a choice.

Outside, it was warm, and she stood by the door, feeling like she couldn't breathe, before she headed for her car. Amy had no idea what Julia was going through. Let them talk about her behind her back some more. She didn't fucking care.

Not true. She cared. Too much.

She drove home in silence. Even the radio didn't turn on, as it normally did, and she couldn't even remember if she'd had it on while driving here.

But wasn't Amy right, too? Two things could exist, as Mariana liked to remind Julia.

She could be right, but so could Amy.

Julia hadn't gone through all of it alone, and when she'd needed her sisters the most, during the ugliness of her divorce, they'd been there. No questions asked. Ever.

The blow up in the office echoed in her head, and the guilt came with a vengeance. It was like one of those unexpected ocean waves that knocked you on your ass.

Julia went straight to the shower, walked into it with her clothes on while the water was still cold. It was the only thing to help her panic sometimes. Or maybe it was a punishment.

Both things. They were both true.

She would never understand why this was the only way she could feel something other than this horrible guilt and despair, that confused feeling she didn't know how to explain. She missed her father for the things he had taught her, which led her to become successful and smart, a woman very few had dared cross. No man could walk over her.

Unless it was Conrad Montgomery himself, or Harold Houghton. The two men in her life who had hurt her the most.

Her stomach swirled angrily, with grief and pain and humiliation. But the other thing, the one she didn't want, wriggled inside her like an awakening creature. Julia held her breath because she didn't want it, her body shaking with the effort of keeping the fire from spreading through her.

She stood under the spray of the shower until she was shivering and couldn't feel her hands anymore. And that living thing that was inside her no longer moved under her skin.

Afterwards, wrapped in a fluffy robe, Julia found her way to the windowsill, a joint between her fingers. She allowed the smoke into her lungs and held it there until she was coughing so much, she almost threw up. But when it had its effect, the haziness removed all the trembling inside her and quieted the beast that wanted to awaken.

All magic did was bring pain and loss. Death. There was no place for it in her life.

Slipping off the windowsill, Julia put what was left of the joint away, and went to bed. Nothing in her mind, she succumbed to the blissful darkness.

3

Julia sat in the bath, her hair piled atop of her head, slimy with a masque. She almost felt human again. Her joint lay on the edge of the tub on a tiny glass plate. The sun hadn't fully set, but the moon was high in the sky already.

Tonight was Latin Night, and her sisters, Victoria, and Helena were blowing up the group chat with excitement for the evening.

The first text was from Sophia—a selfie on a full-sized mirror. Her voluptuous curves were in full display in the fitted white dress. It tied behind the neck, and it had big red hibiscus flowers across the body. Her hair was down, a mix of waves and curls. Julia'd never been able to wear hers like that. Granted, her hair was mostly wavy, not curly, but her father had been very strict about appearances in his companies, and Julia quickly learned that her own wavy hair was not professional enough.

Julia: You look amazing.
Amy: HOLY SHIT!
Helena: So hot. I'm wearing red tonight!
Amy: I'm wearing black. Should I change???????
Victoria: You can match me, Amy!

Julia watched as the chat got flooded with pictures; fierce dresses, bold makeup, all gorgeous and captivating. Suddenly, she felt it; that dreaded fear of missing out.

Her stomach felt like lead as they talked about shoes and dancing and the food they'd order once they were there.

Sophia: I've even stopped minding what a terrible dancer I am. Latin Nights are my favorite.

Helena: You're way better now than a year ago!

Sophia: Sure, but not by much. There's just so much Lucas can do for my two left feet.

Victoria: It's not that bad!

Amy: Oh, it is. We can't all be Julia, the Dancing Queen.

Julia laughed when Sophia sent a middle finger emoji.

Sophia: Julia, are you going to make it tonight?

Victoria: Please, please, please!

Helena: The five of us haven't hung out together in so long! I'll even buy you drinks and flirt with you, if it helps you decide…

Julia snorted.

Amy: It's going to be so much fun. You should come.

She stared at Amy's message, her heart fluttering. Did Amy really mean that? They hadn't talked since their blow-up days ago.

Unbidden, a small, half-smile twisted her lips. A part of her wanted to go, allow herself to relax. But her stomach clenched when she thought about being around that many people.

Julia: I'm sorry, guys. I'm exhausted.

Clicking the send button, regret immediately surged through her. There was no reason why she wasn't going, other than that she was a coward. Crowds were hard these days, though.

Amy: You love dancing, Jules. Please come out.

True, she'd always loved dancing, and she used to be good at it. She'd even taken ballroom dancing classes in high school and college, but that didn't negate the anxiety it brought her to have to brave crowds.

She pulled the plug on the tub and got into the cool spray of the tiled shower, to rinse out the hair masque. Sophia had done a beautiful job updating the house when she'd moved in years ago. Now, Julia got to enjoy it. Or survive in it. The walls were light like the rest of the house, with white cabinetry and porcelain sinks and tub. A big window in the corner, above the tub, allowed in light during daytime, so there was no need for turning on lights.

She jumped when the doorbell rang, the sound startling in the deep silence of the house. Grabbing a robe and a hair towel, she rushed to the front door, dripping water on the wooden floor.

Helena stood outside, her form-fitting red dress hugging her like a glove down to the knees. Blonde hair down and curled perfectly around her face, Helena had kept her makeup understated and sophisticated with a simple cat-eye and nude lips.

"You look incredible," Julia blurted.

"Yes, and so will you." Helena stepped into the house, her smile starting in her bright blue eyes. She removed her heels in the entryway, where protective crystals hung to keep out anyone Julia didn't want in the house. Literally. All gifts from Grey.

"I don't know, Hel…" Julia followed Helena through the dark house and back toward the bedroom, where Helena stopped and turned to her.

"You don't know what, Julia?" Helena put her hands to her narrow hips. "That you'd rather stay in here and isolate yourself instead of coming out and having fun with us? We *miss* you."

Chagrin and disbelief warred inside her. After her fight with Amy, she doubted that. They hadn't talked about what happened at all, just moving on and pretending nothing happened.

Helena stepped forward. She wasn't much taller than Julia, only a couple of inches, though her figure was more toned than Julia had been in ages. Her hands on Julia's shoulders, Helena looked straight into her eyes.

"Amy's not upset about the other day, and you shouldn't be either," Helena said.

"Of course they went and told you about that whole thing."

Helena's brow rose. "And *you* weren't going to tell me?"

Of course she was, they just hadn't talked in a few days, and Julia would have felt bad going to Helena just to bitch about Amy.

"Look at me," Julia said instead, with a long sigh. "I'm a mess and I don't even know if I have anything I can wear."

"Are you kidding? You have one of the best wardrobes." Helena left Julia standing in the dark hallway and went to the closet where she turned on the light and started rummaging through the clothes. Her wardrobe was good, some top-of-the-line designs, but it struck her how neutral everything was as Helena went through everything. The entirety of Julia's clothes collection was mostly professional-wear and pieces that Harold had considered elegant. Dresses with simple silhouettes, and pant suits. There was a colorful piece here and there, but the rest was every spectrum of neutral.

Helena made a small, approving sound as she pulled out an A-line dress Julia completely forgot she had. It had a pleated skirt in an off-white color. The top was fitted, sleeveless, with a square back.

"This is cute. I want you to wear this." Helena grinned.

"Are we really doing this?" Julia deadpanned, but something like excitement fluttered in her stomach.

"Fine. You can get dressed and come out with us and have fun, or we can talk about your feelings." Helena held Julia's gaze steadily. Her heart suddenly pounding, Julia took the dress and, with a grumble, went into the bathroom to change. At least she'd already bathed.

"Not bad," Helena said with an appreciative glance when Julia came back out. Julia's face heated. "Now, your hair."

"I can do my own hair."

"I don't doubt that for a minute, but let me." Helena moved forward and started opening drawers, where Julia kept her hair products and makeup. Hair dryer in hand, Helena dried Julia's hair with a round brush. Julia had worn her hair short and straight for a long time, but neglect had allowed it to grow out, and she didn't hate it. It was past her shoulder blades now. She used to be envious of Sophia's long curls and Amy's adventurous color choices, but she'd shunned the idea of doing the same for herself. The idea of walking into her father's office with blue hair almost made her laugh out loud. The fit he would've thrown.

"Penny for your thoughts," Helena said as she plugged in a curling wand when Julia's hair was dry.

Julia heaved a sigh. "Nothing important."

Helena made a humming sound, but didn't push.

After her hair was falling softly past her shoulders in soft waves, Helena applied makeup expertly onto Julia's face. A little concealer on the bags under the eyes, a swipe of a neutral shadow on the lid, and a simple cat-eye. Mascara, a slick of pink lipstick, and she was ready. It was similar to what Julia herself would do when she had the mental capacity for it. She looked at her reflection and almost felt like herself again.

At Helena's instruction, she slipped on a pair of nude heels, which she was glad for. Heels were her thing. They always had been and always would be. They made her feel powerful when everything else was shit.

"You look hot," Helena said, putting her hands on Julia's shoulders, their eyes meeting in the mirror. Julia nodded, taking a deep breath to encourage herself not to take everything off and go back to bed. They left together after their rideshare showed up, since that was how Helena had shown up here in the first place. Julia pressed her hand to her racing heart. It had been so long since she'd been out, it all felt like a weird dream.

In the back of the car, she looked out the window at the sparkling city pass by. Her stomach was in knots, her chest heavy and tight.

"It's only Nowhere," Helena said.

Julia turned to look at her. "I know. I can't help it."

She didn't have to spell it out for Helena, who reached over and took her hand between hers.

"Then let me help you."

Julia's heart sank. She knew what Helena was asking. She wanted Julia to let her use magic to help her relax. It was Helena's special kind of magic, a soft thing that could calm the entire energy of a room with a mere thought.

"No." Julia cleared her throat unnecessarily. "I'll be okay."

Helena smiled sadly, but didn't argue. She knew Julia couldn't handle magic in any way. Not even soft magic like Helena's.

When they arrived at Nowhere, they headed toward the back door, bypassing the long line. Music leaked through the walls, muffled to the outside world, but louder as they opened the back door and walked in. Anticipation made her heart race as she remembered how much she loved Latin music, even if she didn't listen to it much these days. She rarely ever listened to any music at all, which was sad, now that she thought of it.

The music that greeted her was sultry, the rhythm almost shy, though its dance was anything but. Bachata was one of her favorites. She loved nothing more than watching people dancing to it, losing themselves in the music. Sometimes it was sexy, sometimes fast and vigorous. And it always seeped into her bones, the dueling guitars and rhythms.

To her left, all tables and chairs that usually sat in front of the stage were gone to open up to a dance floor. Couples moved together, though not many, since the biggest part of the crowd was still outside.

Soon, the entire place would be full of bodies moving along the sweet melodies like ice skaters.

Julia swallowed as she took in the colorful lighting above, the deafening music, and the tables that were starting to get occupied by patrons. Helena took her hand, squeezing it as if she could sense Julia's mounting anxiety. Julia squeezed back as she allowed herself to be led through to find the others.

Sophia rushed toward her with a squeal, arms outstretched, a huge grin on her face. Julia's heart filled, and it filled more when Amy did the same, and everything seemed right in the world for a moment. No one was mad; everything was okay.

"I'm so glad you came!" Sophia yelled over the music. She looked lovely, her eyeshadow bright and sparkly, which complemented her hazel eyes. "Come on."

She pulled Julia past the bar to where Victoria was sitting at a round table. As Helena and Amy started chatting about costuming, Julia sat between Victoria and Sophia, allowing herself to relax. She was here to have a good time. She *deserved* to have a good time, damn it.

"Let's get you a drink," Amy said. "Did you eat?"

"I did," she lied. Of course she hadn't eaten. "I'd love a drink."

Moments later, a whiskey sour in hand, her favorite, she got into Amy and Helena's costume conversation.

"The theme is diamonds and glamor," Helena explained. "I want curtains of crystals everywhere for that night."

"And I was thinking she could wear red," Amy said. "Helena looks very good in red, as you can see."

Helena waved her hand down her own body. "Case in point."

Julia laughed. "You look good in everything."

"Not yellow! I look sick," Helena said and finished her drink, a whiskey neat.

"She does look sick in yellow," Grey said, sitting by Sophia on Julia's other side. Helena threw a balled-up napkin at him, which he caught.

"Jerk," she said, grinning.

"You said it first," Grey protested mockingly.

"You're my best friend," Helena said over the music. "You're supposed to tell me I'm being too hard on myself."

"You want him to lie to you about wearing yellow?" Amy asked with a laugh.

Thomas, Victoria's fiancé, showed up then, dressed in a blue shirt and slacks. He was just a little shorter than Victoria in her heels, and his almond-shaped eyes sparkled when she stood up to greet him with a kiss, her hands in his black hair.

At that moment, the DJ said something in Spanish that had the crowd going wild, and Victoria screamed and dragged Thomas to the dance floor as a new song started playing.

"Come on!" Amy yelled over the lively merengue, and pulled Julia and Helena to the dance floor. Sophia and Grey were there moments later, but they didn't make much of an attempt to keep the rhythm, just making eyes at each other. Helena and Amy were laughing as Amy explained how to move one's hips successfully to this kind of music. She seemed to have it down, but Julia was frozen on the spot, unsure of what to do. Amy went into a flurry of instructions, but Julia barely moved, her legs leaden, even though she didn't need the instruction at all. Merengue wasn't hard to begin with, but she swayed from side to side, suddenly feeling like every eye in the house was on her.

Victoria came toward her and grabbed her, as Thomas joined Amy and Helena. With Victoria leading her, Julia let out a laugh as her feet began to move.

"Are you okay?" Victoria asked. "You look a little overwhelmed."

"There's a lot going on at the same time," Julia admitted to her friend, but continued to allow herself to be led.

"I know. I'm really happy you came."

The brass instruments buried themselves into her, and the percussion matched the beats of her heart as she let Victoria twirl her around.

Julia's brain reached toward the lyrics, a pull deep in her chest to sing along to words she barely recognized. Victoria pushed her away, then pulled her back, only to make her turn away once more. Their hands slid apart, and Julia found herself in the middle of the dance floor, alone and breathless. A smile still stretching her cheeks.

Time stopped.

Her laugh died as the music muted, as if coming from far away. Everything became silent when her eyes found him.

Juan Lucas Dolores.

His name echoed in her head, as a whiff of his scent found her nose—whiskey and tobacco and something else warm and sensual. But she knew it couldn't be his actual scent, as he was too far away for that in a crowded dance floor. It was in her head, like it had buried itself in there so she could access it at any time.

He was so tall, his body lithe and hard under a black button-down and slacks.

Her face warmed when he gave her a half smile, those dusky pink lips smooth, teeth white and straight, canines a little longer than the rest. His beard was gone—it used to be full and well-groomed, but now it was a stubble, which showed off ridiculously high cheekbones. Those honey eyes against the deep tan of his skin held her captive for what could have been a thousand years, and she briefly wondered if she'd be able to see herself reflected in their depths.

In a flash, she was back in the hospital, Lucas's arm banded around her waist as he helped her sit up enough for Sophia to pour that disgusting potion into her mouth. She hadn't seen him again since, but that scent of his, spicy notes both sharp and sweet, had stayed with her. Each time she'd thought about it, she remembered the exact moment when the healing potion had brought back the color the void had taken away.

It was at that exact moment, after she'd taken the potion, that the wriggly, oily feeling had begun. And it had been with her since.

The spell broke when Victoria caught her hand. She laughed as she spun Julia, whose body felt like gum. The song changed to a salsa this time, and Julia couldn't catch her breath. She stopped in the middle of the dance floor, swallowing hard, looking for him in the crowd. He was gone, and briefly, she wondered if she'd seen him at all.

"I need water," she shouted over the music, and Victoria moved back to grab Thomas.

Julia tried to calm her shallow breath, heart racing. Trembling, she stumbled forward as Helena came out of one of the bathrooms just off the dining area. She looked ruffled, her cheeks rosy.

"Are you okay?" she asked, coming close to take Julia by the forearms, concern on her face now.

Julia swallowed hard. The back of her throat was sticky.

"I have to get out of here," she panted, unable to stop the walls from closing in. The music had gotten too loud, the lights too bright. Amy appeared and came to Julia's other side, her brows tight.

"What's wrong?"

"She just needs fresh air," Helena said quickly, touching Amy's arm briefly. "I'll go with her."

A brief look passed between Amy and Helena, and the former said something, but Julia walked away before the words could even hit her ear. She hurried toward the employee entrance, pulled it open, and stumbled down the long corridor. She couldn't see, but she could hear her breath loudly in her own ears. Helena was right there, holding her up as she threw herself into the heavy back door and burst out into the night.

She gasped as the cold air hit her lungs.

Helena held back her hair when Julia dry-heaved, though nothing came up, thank God. There was nothing there to expel but the heat. Oh, the heat; it rose and spread through her entire body, and her skin moved and bubbled, like it was going to fall off.

"Water," she gasped.

Helena, a panicked look on her face, waved her hand and a glass appeared there. Julia almost keeled over right then. She'd seen magic, but it would never not be weird. Helena held the glass forward, but Julia could only stand there staring at it like it would grow fangs and bite her.

"It's just a glass of water," Helena said, but Julia couldn't take it. Her body simply refused to move.

"I have to go home." It came out as a gasp, weak and desperate. Helena made the glass disappear, and Julia took an involuntary step back.

"Julia . . ."

"Please, I just want to go home," Julia begged, tears springing to her eyes. Her limbs trembled, and fear made her body rigid, neck tight. She pressed herself against the side of the building, her hands behind her on the rough wall.

"What's going on, Jules?" Helena asked urgently, but Julia shook her head, her eyes and mouth shut tightly. She was going to lose it right here in a parking lot, doing something she didn't want to do.

Magic.

It had been there for so long, just under the surface. Ever since they'd discovered that their mom had done magic too, that she'd placed a spell on everyone to forget about magic after Sophia's innocent wish.

"I need to get out of here, Helena," Julia said, opening her eyes. "I have to go now. You have to take me home right now."

Helena's brows were tight with worry, but she summoned her phone.

"I'll get us a car."

"No, you don't get it."

The door burst open, and then Sophia and Grey were there.

"What's going on?" Sophia asked, looking frantic.

"My God, please," Julia cried, her hands burning, her eyes and her stomach and throat on fire. She looked to Grey, her shame forgotten when it came to him. "Take me home now."

Grey seemed to understand it immediately, and he caught her when she launched herself at him, and soon, she felt weightless. She'd never done this before—porting. Not that it was her doing it. More like Grey carrying her through it.

It felt like she could have been looking or standing in any direction and none at all. It was dark and cold, pressure all around her as she reappeared only moments later in the doorway to her place. Her ankles wobbled in her heels, and her hands raised to catch herself before she fell, but the accent table in the entryway slammed into the wall and broke in half with the force of it.

Julia screamed and Grey cried out her name. Julia ran away from him, blindly. She was going to hurt him. She would use this stupid power on him and hurt her sister's boyfriend. How much would Sophia hate her then?

"Julia?"

Sophia's voice came from far away when she found herself in the living room, forgetting that she'd moved at all.

"No, you have to stay away." A guttural noise came out of her as Grey was in front of her just moments later, taking her face into his hands.

Her name was nothing but an echo in her ears. Every groan of the house, even the little bits of skin that sloughed off her body, she heard.

"What the hell is happening to me?" she sobbed. But it happened again, and she didn't know what direction it went, but glass exploded all around her. She screamed and heard Sophia's voice. Grey shouted and Julia was on the floor. The air left her and she gasped from the pain in her back and stomach. Breathing wouldn't happen, and she thought that was it. She was going to finally die. There was only noise around her, and everything was dark. Someone was on top of her, talking to her, but she couldn't understand words, couldn't recognize the voice. Then the whirring stopped and everything was gone.

o o o

When she next woke up, all the lights in the house were on, burning brightly above her. Julia closed her eyes against the offensive glare, confused why she was lying on the floor.

"Julia?" Sophia's voice was strained, and Julia found her from where she lay on the floor. Sophia had tears running down her face as she sat against the wall. Beside her, Grey's expression was tight. His hair was down. It was long, almost as long as Julia's. Pretty and shiny.

What a weirdly inappropriate thought at a time like this.

Confusion overtook her when she saw Grey's hands. They were red, and he was dirty. There was glass everywhere. Julia sat up abruptly, her head swimming as everything came back. But it wasn't only Grey and Sophia in the room. By the archway that led to the kitchen and front door stood Helena, Lucas right behind her, looking at her with an inscrutable expression. She didn't have to ask how or when he'd gotten there.

Julia's eyes found Grey's hands, then his dark eyes. And finally, the cut on Sophia's shoulder.

"What did I do?" she asked with dry lips.

"Don't get up," Grey said, coming to hover over her, but Julia tried to sit up anyway.

"Magic," Helena said.

Julia looked at everyone in horrified silence. There was no glass anywhere, and she imagined one of them had cleaned everything up. Tears streaming down her face, she looked at Sophia's shoulder. No visible wound existed, also a gift of magic, but Julia would never get over the fact that she'd hurt her sister. She crawled forward and hugged Sophia tightly. Sophia hugged her back, and it should have made her feel better, but it didn't. It just made her feel guiltier that the person she hurt was consoling her instead.

She was pathetic.

"I'm so sorry," she whimpered into Sophia's hair. "I don't know what's wrong with me."

"I know." Sophia pulled back to meet Julia's gaze, and her eyes were wet too.

Julia looked at the healing wound on Sophia's shoulder, which was stained red with blood. She shut it down, the place where her emotions came from. It wasn't wise to allow herself to feel too much.

"That seems to be the problem in the first place," Lucas said from the doorway, not making a move to come further into the room. Julia found his tall frame, his eyes, but she looked away quickly. It was like staring into the sun.

"I don't know what you mean," she said hoarsely. "And why are you here?"

"I asked him to come," Grey said from where he sat on the arm of the sofa.

"Why?"

"Because your magic seems to be tied to your emotions," Lucas said. "Upon preliminary assessment."

Magic.

It was like a bad word.

"I don't think the magic thing is for me," she said stupidly.

"Jules, pretending it isn't there won't make it go away," Sophia said quietly.

She'd known about the magic; she wasn't stupid. But maybe she'd thought that not thinking about it would make it disappear. Nothing about magic interested her in the least. Seemed like a destructive force more than anything else.

Except that period of time when she'd been sick. Now, she knew that it had been a figment of her imagination, but before she'd been given the cure, her life had been different. The world had breathed there, stretched, and time made no sense. Her mom, alive and well, and she was every bit the parent Julia had always craved. One she'd missed deeply.

Roselyn, their oldest sister, was also alive there, and they were all happy, free from all the trauma.

They went to their favorite restaurant, Sutton Place, every Sunday for brunch. Just the girls, including Roselyn's little girls. Their mother, Silvana, older and more beautiful than ever, with her long curls and deep golden complexion. Sophia still had her club, Amy, her clothing design. Julia had never married Harold in that place, and she was happy, helping their mother in the family business they'd created. Body care, medicinal potions, and beauty products infused with magic from the music of the plants, her mother's specialty. Julia had done magic freely, without fear, and with the dexterity of someone who'd grown up practicing.

And Conrad was nowhere to be seen. Gone from their lives, as it should have been.

Then she'd woken up and she was back here where she always felt like an elephant lived in her chest.

"I know what it feels like," Helena said, coming closer. Lucas stayed where he'd been standing, watching silently. "It messes with you, thinking you're going to die. It's not exactly easy to let go."

"And everything else," Sophia added gently. "It's a lot, Julia."

Julia didn't move a muscle, afraid she'd break into pieces if she even dared.

"I'm trying," she whispered, desperate for these people to understand her. That they knew she wasn't *trying* to self-destruct; she just didn't know how to move on.

"I can help you, if you want," Lucas said and she looked back up at him, unable to help herself from admiring his beauty. He had an air about him that emanated calm, even as Julia's nervous system went numb. Maybe it was shock.

"You used to be a therapist, right?" she asked, knowing fully well it was the truth. The girls talked about him enough, since he, Grey, and Helena were best friends.

"Yes," he said with a single nod.

"I have a therapist." Something in her wanted him, them, to know that she was doing everything she could.

"I don't have a traditional practice anymore," he informed her with a shadow of a smile. "I take a different approach to helping my clients."

"What kind of approach?"

"A magical kind, mostly." He said it carefully, as if waiting for her to immediately tell him to go to hell. But she wouldn't be saying that, because if anyone needed help, it was her. She could do nothing but agree to it. She had absolutely nothing to lose.

4

After Grey and Lucas left, Sophia and Helena stayed behind and called Amy and Victoria to join them. The two arrived not too long after, and Julia'd had to explain why she'd rushed out like that. Telling them was like reliving the entire thing.

In truth, she wanted to be alone, but the girls wouldn't allow it, so Julia settled on the windowsill with her joint. She was starting to get tired, but talking to her girls was of the utmost importance now that she had so many things to think about. Like working with Lucas.

Sophia had disappeared into the kitchen to make a snack, Amy with her, and Victoria and Helena were finding something to wear in Julia's drawers.

Before he left, Grey gave her a small vial with a calming potion. Something to take the edge off, he'd said. The dark bottle sat on the windowsill, by her feet, and Julia hadn't smoked the joint yet either. Somehow, the jitters had died, but she knew they would come eventually. They always did. It was like she had a barrel inside, and it filled over time, exploded, and then started over again. Magic filled it quicker than most other things.

"Maybe if you look at it as anxiety medication, it'll be easier to swallow," Sophia said, coming back from the kitchen with a bowl of yogurt and fruit slices. She handed one to Julia, who wasn't hungry, but would eat it anyway, if only to keep the girls off her back about not eating.

Julia picked up the little vial. It was tiny, delicate. The last time she'd taken a potion, it had been the cure for the void, and since then, any talks of potions sent her into a spiral of what-ifs.

"I'm numb right now," she told Sophia and Amy, who'd appeared from the kitchen with more bowls.

"Makes sense," Amy said as she sat on the armchair. Victoria and Helena came back from the bedroom, dressed in some of Julia's silk pajamas. She'd preferred the silk in the past, but recently, she'd only been able to handle the feel of sweats on her skin. The silk was too soft sometimes, an issue she'd never had before.

They all sat around the marble coffee table, eating and chatting about nothing. The money tree that usually sat on the center of the table was sitting by Sophia now, and Sophia kept throwing looks at it.

"Something amiss?" Helena asked, and Sophia looked up at her.

"Nothing. It's happy," she said with a wan smile.

Julia had kept up with the watering plan Sophia had stipulated when she'd moved in with Grey, and the plant was doing well enough. Sophia had a special kind of magic where she could hear music from the plants. Many times, Julia had wished she could too. She'd be so much closer to her mom, whose magic was also closely related to plants and music. So many things that Julia both wanted to understand and stay the fuck away from.

A flash of anxiety had her reaching for the vial of potion, which was next to her half-full bowl. It wasn't unpleasant, only slightly sweet, and Julia felt its calming effects immediately. Her body felt heavy in the most pleasant way now, and as Sophia and Victoria started chatting about Victoria's wedding in a few months, she sat back and just allowed herself to relax. It wasn't easy; Julia's default was stress on a good day. She lay back on the couch and closed her eyes.

No one was being weird about what she'd done with magic earlier, or how Sophia's shoulder was still a little red, though it was mostly healed now.

Allowing her mind to drift, she thought about the first inklings of magic she'd had. Not when she was a kid, but now as an adult. After she'd taken the cure to the void, it was as if the veil that existed between her and magic had been lifted. And with what had happened with Sophia and her wishing power, it was easy to be afraid of magic in general. Everyone had stopped saying the words 'I wish' out loud since they found out how dangerous it could be, just in case. And now Julia.

She opened her eyes and reached for her phone. Lucas had saved his number into it, and she kept going back and staring at it, as if it could tell her the answers to a test she hadn't known she was taking. Weird that it was him, after all this time. She'd gone into a panic attack by simply seeing him, as if he'd been the one to cause her ailments. Why he stuck out in her memories, she'd never know. He was just friends with people she knew; it shouldn't feel unsettling like this.

But then again, she always felt discombobulated these days.

"I'll work with Lucas," she announced, and four pairs of eyes focused on her with varying degrees of pride. It both didn't surprise her and bugged the hell out of her. She wasn't that unreasonable and hard to work with, was she?

Yeah, she was.

"That's great." Sophia smiled. "He's good at what he does."

"And what exactly is it that he does?" Julia asked her with a raised brow.

"Energy readings," Helena said. "Just being in someone's presence can tell him a lot about a person, and his background in mental health only aids it. Then he uses the information he gets from you and finds the best way to help you heal."

Julia had heard of energy work in the past, but she'd always thought it was nothing but bullshit. But then again, she'd thought magic was bullshit all her life and ended up having it anyway.

"And he really is good," Helena added. "I've worked with him plenty."

"For what?" Amy asked.

"Oh, a lot," Helena said with something close to a laugh. She'd removed her makeup already, so her face was gleaming and clear, as was Victoria's. "I met him in college, and he was already doing energy work then."

Julia turned on her side to look at Helena.

"Was he any good back then?" Julia asked.

"Yeah, but he's only gotten better. He was going to school for psychology because he wanted to use that knowledge in tandem with his magic." Helena sat with her legs crossed yogi style. "He's very thorough."

"How did you find him?" Amy asked, laying on her stomach next to Victoria.

"I was dating Grey at the time, and he and Lucas were rooming together on campus," Helena said. "I was struggling at home."

Sophia ran her hand soothingly over Helena's arm.

"You don't have to talk about any of that," Sophia said softly.

"I know," Helena murmured, but she was smiling a little. Julia had heard about the difficult home life, with highly religious parents who didn't accept that Helena didn't want to follow in their footsteps.

"What did he do that helped you?" Julia asked and Helena grinned wistfully.

"He convinced me to change my degree, which was the best thing I could have done," Helena said. "I was convinced I needed to study something in tech to make all the bucks."

"I cannot see you behind a computer writing code," Victoria said.

"I know, and neither could Lucas. He was the one to advocate for choosing what I wanted to do, which was studying music and singing. It's history from there."

Julia turned to her back, staring at the ceiling. Lucas had, quite literally, changed Helena's entire trajectory. She couldn't imagine Helena not singing and making music.

"I just don't know if I want to do magic," Julia admitted. Look at what she'd done to Sophia's shoulder. Yes, it had healed quickly, but what if Julia had done something worse than a cut?

"I think it'd be hard for me too," Amy said, without putting down her phone, where she was scrolling on one of her favorite clothing sites. Amy, as far as everyone knew, didn't have any magical powers at all. She didn't really talk about it much, but Julia suspected it was a hard pill to swallow that both her and Sophia had magic, but Amy did not.

"I bet you'd handle it much better than I have," Julia said. Not that she'd *handled* anything.

"Hard to tell," Amy said with a lopsided grimace.

The silence was heavy, tired, and they all chose to go to bed soon after. Amy chose to sleep on the couch, leaving Victoria and Helena to the spare bedroom, and Julia and Sophia in the master. She was keeping herself awake, she knew, by scrolling social media. Sleeping usually came with dreams, and hers were pretty disturbing these days.

"I know what you're doing," Sophia muttered sleepily. Julia turned to look at her sister, whose eyes remained closed.

"Does it bother you how close Helena and Grey are?" After Kate and Harold, Julia couldn't fathom having a relationship where her boyfriend was best friends with his ex. It was like a different dimension she couldn't reach or wanted to be a part of.

Sophia's eyes opened and she turned on her side to face Julia.

"It doesn't," she said. "Helena's a good friend to all of us."

"She is and I love her," Julia said quickly, wanting for Sophia to understand.

"I know where you're coming from," Sophia whispered, "and it's okay to find it confusing or weird."

"Kate was my best friend for a long time." Julia suspected she was grieving losing Kate more than her being with Harold now. It was the hiding and lying she couldn't understand or forgive.

"What they did was wrong no matter how you look at it."

"Yeah." She knew. Sometimes she forgot, though. It was easy to blame herself, to wonder what she could've done differently to prevent it.

"Grey and Helena," Sophia said, "and Lucas, for that matter, are different. They're like siblings to each other. The fact that Helena's seen Grey naked doesn't bother me since it was so long ago. Besides, have you seen Grey?"

"Ew," Julia said, but laughed a little anyway. She did not want to see Grey naked at all. Lucas, on the other hand…

The thought came to her suddenly, like one of those intrusive thoughts she had from time to time.

"You good?" Sophia asked.

No, she was crazy, but she said yes anyway and turned back to her phone as Sophia settled in and closed her eyes again. Closing all the apps on her phone, she found Lucas's number again, and with much more gumption than she actually had, she opened the texting app and typed a quick message. He wouldn't see it, of course—it was late as hell—but if she didn't do it now, she might not come morning.

Julia: Hi, Lucas. It's Julia. Thank you for coming over tonight and offering your help. I was hoping we could chat about your methods and how it can help me. Hope to talk soon.

Three dots immediately appeared at the bottom of the screen, indicating that he was typing.

Lucas: Anytime, Julia. I'd like to chat in person, if that works for you.

Julia: Yes. My schedule's wide open these days, so name a time and place.

Lucas: Why don't you come over tomorrow at six? I have clients all day, or I'd see you earlier.

Julia: 6 works.

His address followed, and after a simple 'good night', she turned, closed her eyes, and fell into an uneasy sleep.

5

Julia dressed carefully the following day.

Each time this man had met her, she'd been a goddamn mess, so she had an urge to look put-together for once. He certainly always did with his button-ups and suspenders and slacks. And that scent.

Wondering what cologne he used, she drove swiftly down the highway.

The high-waisted pants she'd chosen were comfortable and fit her well, and she'd tucked a black collared shirt with puffy, transparent sleeves into them. Her heeled shoes lay beside her on the seat, as she preferred not driving with them on. Lucas was very tall, at least six feet, but she wanted to be able to meet him in the eye. Even with the heels, that would be a feat.

The nerves didn't come until she was parked in front of his house a half an hour later. He lived outside the city, in a cute neighborhood with rows of Victorian homes with small front yards and intricate façades. So different than the homes she'd lived in, where things were a little less colorful. Forcing herself to take deep breaths, she tried to quell her panic as she looked up at his cute little house. It surprised her, though she didn't know why it should. She barely knew the man in the first place, but somehow, she'd expected something more modern than the narrow Victorian with what looked like two levels of dark red brick and black wood details. Arched windows indicated he had lights on inside, as it was starting to get dark, especially with the ominous clouds hanging above.

And was that stained glass? Julia had always liked stained glass, though she never had the guts to put it in her own house, but that was mostly because Harold preferred what he called a clean, sophisticated look. Something about that bothered her, but she'd never been able to put her finger on *why*.

The small front lawn spread on one side of the stone path up to the little entryway, with its arches and pillars, and an ornate front door, which also had stained glass on it.

It was so . . . *charming*. Who would've thought?

Even the street, with late spring closing into summer, had lush trees with pink blossoms all down the sidewalk and median. There was little traffic, and it was quiet and peaceful.

The vise around her stomach tightened as she gathered the courage to go up and meet with him.

"Come on, you can do this," she said into the silent car. A part of her wanted to run from there, go back to her perch in the window at Sophia's house, and forget the world existed. But a wiser voice reminded her that hadn't been working anyway. Even if it frustrated her to be this woman who couldn't take care of herself anymore, she had to do this.

Swallowing, she tucked an errant strand of hair behind her ear, put on the shoes, and opened the car door. Her heels were the only sound in her ears as she walked up and opened the short iron gate separating his house from the street. A half wall of the same brick as the house enclosed the little yard, which gave it an air of mystery and whimsy, and there were a couple of hedges, flowering bushes, and an evergreen tree. A trickle of sweat ran down her back, even though it wasn't particularly warm.

The walkway felt like a whole mile.

As she headed up toward the door, she noticed that the green lawn wasn't grass, but impossibly green clovers. She didn't think she'd ever seen anything like that before. Julia was so used to seeing heavily manicured green grass and open spaces that the little clovers made her want to stop and examine them.

They're just clovers, Julia, get it together.

But then again, the house she had shared with Harold had so much land she didn't even know half of it. Maybe stopping to appreciate the wild little garden would be good for her. Smell the roses or whatever. It's not like she'd had much time to do that before. Besides, the house she'd shared with Harold didn't have interesting things like a clover lawn. It was lovely in its own right, just not a place Julia ever wanted to go back to, after Harold and Kate did what they did.

Bastards, both of them.

Could have gone to a hotel, but no. They *had* to fuck in Julia's bed.

Thoughts of her ex-husband put her in a bad mood faster than anything else could, so she set it aside as she reached the small porch. It was only a little covered square, bare but for one potted plant on the side. Grey also had lots of plants, and she wondered if Lucas was the same.

Witches seemed to really like their plants, didn't they? Her mom certainly had, which was fair since her magic had been related to plants and the music they emitted.

A deep breath later, her hand connected with the colorful glass of the double doors, and she heard him moving inside right before it opened.

Lucas Dolores wasn't a man anyone could easily ignore. He stood with one hand on the doorknob, the other halfway in the pocket of his dark slacks. His shirt was a blue so dark it was almost black, and he had black suspenders on. The sleeves of his shirt were rolled up to his elbows. Her mouth went dry.

Something about rolled up sleeves did things to a woman, and when it was a man like Lucas… well, she could hardly resist the appreciative warmth that spread in her belly. The tattoos on his forearms made her wonder if he had more and where. The one that peeked over the collar of his shirt told a story she could've died reading.

She blinked as he said, "I'm glad you're here."

Oof, the accent. He just had to have one of those too, so lush and warm, his diction indicative of the six languages he could apparently speak. Who had time to learn that many languages? Good god.

"I always keep my appointments," she told him, her voice more firm than she'd intended. She refused to look away from his face. The color of his eyes was intriguing to her. In certain lights they were the color of whiskey, the most expensive kind. In others, they were pure honey. Distinct and mystical, and holding secrets she wanted to explore.

"Come on in," he said with a smirk, stepping aside.

Apprehensive as all hell, she stepped inside the house and took a shivering breath.

"You can leave your shoes here." He pointed at the little mat beside the door, and she froze, looking at the mat, then up at him. Yes, it tracked that she'd have to leave her weapon of choice by the door instead of being able to wear them and look him in the eye. Not that she was anyway; he was too tall. Or she was too short. Either way, she took them off and left them by the door next to a pair of red running shoes. She was immediately distracted by the house, her shoes forgotten, though she walked on the balls of her feet without realizing it.

If the outside was charming, the inside was positively magical. There was a little room to her left, where he had an office that was so neat she could barely believe her eyes. Through a short, narrow hallway, a living room opened. The walls were ornate, half wood, half wallpaper that had been obviously updated, as it was both modern and gothic all at once. The wooden panels were dark and warm, the wallpaper a burnished sort of red, deep and sexy. She couldn't think of a time she'd seen so much color in one place, other than Amy's apartment, which was an explosion of color and interesting patterns.

She followed the hallway, Lucas forgotten behind her, and went through the most ornate archway she'd ever seen. It had leaves and vines carved into it. She ran a finger over the shiny, smooth wood, so delicate it looked like lace.

Her mouth agape, she went into the living room, which was in the same color scheme. The light was low there, even with the windows open. On the walls, there was art that both intrigued her and made her deeply uncomfortable. There were antique-looking diagrams of butterfly life cycles, a snake skeleton in a frame, and on a narrow console table, what looked like the skin of a large snake.

Chaos, but in the most organized and unsettling way.

And right there, among all the other little knickknacks and stacks of strange-looking books, was a statuette of the Virgin Mary, lovely brown skin gleaming, her eyes dark and sad. Her clothes were colorful, and he had her on an altar of sorts, along with a little wooden bowl filled with flower petals and other little trinkets she was dying to look at more closely. What she wouldn't do to snoop around unbridled.

She turned away from the effigy, something about it making her insides hurt so acutely and confusingly. What about that depiction of a religious figure made her feel like this? She'd never been religious, and she knew her mother wasn't either. Aside from her magic. And Julia's father… well, he was the kind to pretend to be devoted, but never really did much to show for that. The only donations Conrad Montgomery had ever done came with tax breaks that just made him richer.

The sofa was emerald velvet, sitting in front of an ornate fireplace, and a chandelier above with crystals that sent colorful rays into the room.

"You like what you see?"

Julia turned to find him standing by the archway to the living room with his hands in his pockets.

"Your house is unexpected," she blurted, feeling the heat rise to her face.

What a good first impression, Julia. Great job.

"Is that a compliment, or should I be worried?" he asked, that brow cocked once more.

"It's very nice," she said and took a steadying breath. She was good at those breaths. They even worked sometimes.

"You haven't even seen the kitchen yet." His eyes were bright and excited, and suddenly, she wanted nothing more than to see that damn kitchen. He took off, and she instinctively followed, through another ornate archway. The design was similar to the first one, but it had different carvings—birds, butterflies, and leaves, where the first one was only vines and flowers.

When they reached the kitchen, she gasped out loud.

It was narrow but long, and it ended with a glass door at the end, where she could see a round dining table and spiral staircase. She fucking *loved* spiral staircases.

The cabinets in the kitchen were painted dark teal with gold accents, and the countertop was tawny. It was clean, not a speck of dust, but he did have quite a bit of clutter. A second glass door led to a patio with a hammock and an outdoor couch and table.

"I don't think I've ever seen a more dramatic kitchen in my life," she murmured, nodding appreciatively.

He shrugged with a grin. "What can I say? I have a soft spot for dramatics."

Mmmmmm, the canines… Shivers ran up and down her spine.

"Do you need anything before we begin?" he asked. "Tea or coffee?"

"A drink?" Her own tone annoyed her, the eagerness. She sounded like an alcoholic.

"Maybe not for our first time," he said, and something about his choice of words made her pause. Had she been walking, she would have tripped on air.

"Fair enough," she said, forcing her shoulders to relax. "Maybe a glass of water."

He opened a cabinet, his eyes leaving her only briefly, and pulled out a glass. She heard the faucet turn on, but could only stare at the way he moved. He was so calm, like he didn't have a hurry in the world.

Someone with a body like that, with forearms like that (*Sweet, Sweet Lord*) had to be an active man, but Lucas could have been walking on a cloud for all she knew.

She took the water when he handed it to her and drank.

"What can I expect today?" she asked when she'd handed him back the glass.

"I'm just going to read you today."

"And how does reading me work, exactly?" A shiver of nerves caught in her stomach. "Is it magical?"

"In a way."

Exasperation rising, she crossed her arms.

"Could you tell me what that means, please?" she asked with a tone that had his brows rising cynically. "I don't know anything about what you do, and you being cryptic isn't helping."

"How do you want me to answer you, Julia?"

"Clearly," she snapped, and his expression changed.

"Julia," he said calmly, and it irked her how he said her name. Like he was savoring it. "You're here because you need my help, not the other way around. I will demand respect."

It was like he'd slapped her. Ashamed, her first instinct was to rush back to the front of the house, grab her shoes, and get the hell out of there.

But no. He was the only person who could help her right now. Not true, she could probably get help from Sophia and Grey, but she wasn't as keen to do that when she'd already hurt Sophia and destroyed her house.

"I apologize," she bit out. It was like acid on her tongue.

He grinned, the last thing she'd expected, and said, "I accept your apology."

"Are you always like this?" She'd imagined he'd be like every other hot man in the world—moody and mysterious and cringey. Not this cheerful weirdo.

"I have no idea what you mean." But he certainly looked like he did, and it infuriated her more that he was still smiling. "I work with energy fields."

Her chest tingled.

"It's going to be uncomfortable at first," he said, "but if you stick with it, it can only help."

"I didn't think any of that was real."

"You've seen magic."

Point made.

"So what do you get from me?" she asked, breathless.

For a few moments, Lucas observed her quietly, and Julia immediately regretted asking.

"Nothing," he said.

Her mouth opened, but she couldn't even ask.

"What does that even mean?" Was she dead?

"I only do reads when I've obtained explicit consent from the subject."

Julia snorted, mostly out of habit, because her heart felt ready to explode and her eyes were hot.

Lucas crossed his arms across his hard chest, his brows tight with annoyance. "If you won't take any of this seriously, maybe you can find someone else to help you."

Panic lanced through her.

"I didn't mean to do that." Her eyes were hot and teary, her throat on fire from holding back hysterical laughter. What the hell was wrong with her? "I just have a really hard time with these things."

"These things?"

"Magic."

She looked away, beyond the glass doors to the patio. The sitting area looked cozy with its hanging lights and vines climbing all over the pergola.

Lucas let out a soft sigh, but there was no mirth in his eyes. In that moment, Julia realized that she could trust he wouldn't make fun of her for being ignorant about any of this.

"I understand," he said gently, and in his kind eyes, she found a little solace. This heaviness she'd been carrying had lingered since she'd taken the cure. Often, she'd wondered if she was still sick, or if it was just the mental toll it took on her.

"Sorry," she said, snapping herself out of her train of thought.

"Do you want to tell me more about it?"

Her throat felt like glue had gotten in it. "I guess it makes sense I have to talk to you too."

His brows rose in confusion.

"I have a therapist," she reminded him.

A small smile came to his full lips, and she wasn't necessarily shocked by the way it made her feel to have the approval.

"I suggest you keep seeing them. What we're going to do here is supplemental and not meant to replace traditional therapy."

"Succinct disclaimer."

"Only way to do it."

When he moved toward the living room, she followed him. The low lights gave the room an air of coziness, especially with the dark clouds, and they sat on the couch. That was when she saw the cat beds in the corner.

"You have pets," she said, and he smiled proudly.

"I do. Opal and Midnight are probably sleeping in my bed at the moment."

Something about that made her want to smile.

"How old are they?"

"Four months. From the same litter."

How often had she wanted to get a pet and decided she didn't have enough time? She wanted to meet his.

"We had a cat growing up. Her name was Sunshine." Why was she telling him this? Sunshine had disappeared when Roselyn died only months after their mom.

"That's lovely."

Lovely. Sad. Could be both, right? She tucked her foot under her, as he had, and sucked in a breath.

"I don't want to do magic."

He held her gaze steadily.

"You want my opinion on that? Professionally, of course."

She grimaced. "Boy, do I?"

"The suppression of magic leads to its volatility. In my experience, at least."

"Is it an opinion if it's your experience?"

"I'm not here to argue semantics," he deadpanned. "Pretending your powers aren't there won't make them disappear."

"But I can refrain from using them," she argued. She needed it to be true. "I went almost twenty years without using any and nothing horrible happened."

"That's because you didn't remember. And you probably did do some magic without realizing it. The spell your mom cast only made you forget; it put a damper on your powers."

She pressed her lips together. She'd almost forgotten how close he was to her mess. Of course she'd thought about having done magic without realizing it, but what she thought about that, she'd keep to herself. She'd bury it so deeply, so swiftly, she would forget about it in seconds flat.

After what Sophia had done... could Julia have made wishes the same way?

"I still need you to help me stop them," she said.

"I can't stop you from doing magic."

"No, I just need to not have it blow up on me."

He nodded slowly, as if remembering the mess he'd walked into the other night.

"What you need is training in *how* to use your magic."

Julia had to take another long breath.

"So it doesn't matter how much I don't want to use it? I have to anyway."

"It matters how much you want to use it, but like I said before, suppressing it isn't working."

"And to be able to stop using it, I have to use it?"

"Something like that."

"That doesn't make any sense." She tugged at her hair.

"You have to have control of your magic and then make the choice to not use it for it to not get out of control," he explained in a patient tone that grated on her nerves.

"Seems like a stupid system," she muttered, starting to regret this whole thing.

"The things we keep in the dark rule our lives," he said, and she was caught in his eyes again. "Refusing to use your magic is only going to keep making it stronger until you can no longer control it. Your intention matters."

A pang went through her like lightning. Her mother's words in his mouth were definitely not what she'd expected when she came here today. To Julia, intention didn't matter if the end result was that you hurt someone.

"I don't even know if I can," she said.

"Use magic? You did the other night."

"I didn't mean to do that." Neither had she meant to hurt her sister in the process.

"I know, which is why for us to work together, you have to be open to at least practicing." A glint in his eye told her he wasn't going to give up, that there was no other way she could do this with him.

"Driving hard bargains, I see." She shifted so her knee was on the sofa. "I can appreciate that."

"Can't make it too easy."

"Of course not." She smirked, but when his face went serious, her stomach dropped.

"Now," he murmured, his voice deeper as he extended his hand toward her. She paused, looking at his long, tattooed fingers. He had dozens of tiny black dots drawn into the skin of his hands, up to his wrists. She took his hand and shook it, gripping firmly, and when she would have let go, he held on tightly. Her heart skipped a beat at the warmth she found there, and her skin crawled with a cold shiver.

"I need your verbal consent," he whispered, and a part of her understood what he meant, while another hornier one felt it much lower. His eyes were pure honey now, yellow like a cat's, and she nodded slowly.

"Yes," she breathed.

Instantly, her vision went hazy, and she saw him as if through water. Her softly-spoken word ricocheted around her, and so did his when he spoke again.

"Just breathe."

Her body followed his command eagerly, and every muscle truly relaxed for the first time in months.

"Feel my hand holding yours."

Oh, she felt it.

His skin was soft as velvet, and his touch lingered even when he let go. She blinked, her vision clearing so suddenly even the dim lighting bothered her until her eyes readjusted.

"Breathe," he repeated. "Readings can obscure some of your senses."

Shaking, Julia's eyes found his face again.

"What just happened?"

His expression was inscrutable. "Your energy is a little hard to read, which I expected."

"What does that mean?"

"It means you've been struggling and it will take some time for you to trust me enough to let me read you." He held her gaze. She wanted to look away with how intense it was. "And you need to stop looking at the news and social media."

She froze.

What the actual fuck?

"The energy doesn't lie," he said.

Shaking, feeling like she was being x-rayed, Julia found her feet, but her arms flared out when she stumbled. Lucas was on his feet in a flash, hands holding on to her shoulders to steady her. Her head swam, and she sat when Lucas gently pushed her toward the couch.

"I'm sorry, I should have warned you," he said.

Her head cleared slowly as he bent over her, his hand holding her wrist.

"I think this is the weirdest thing that's ever happened to me," she told him.

His smirk came back, but it wasn't unkind. Unnerved that he'd seen so much in such a short amount of time, she wanted nothing more than to go home. Or do it again.

"For the sake of the work we'll do together, and your sanity, social media has to go."

He repeated himself like she was a child that needed admonishing. Her brows furrowed. "I don't see the issue." Her stomach soured with annoyance, her head clearing marginally. "I don't think it's your place to tell me what to do outside of our sessions."

His expression didn't change, but he held out his hand. She looked down at it.

"You want to hold my hand?"

He obviously fought back a grin. "Keys. Can't let you drive like this."

"I'm fine," she ground out.

"We both know that's bullshit." He kept his hand right there, until she rolled her eyes, took her keys out of her purse, and put them in the center of his palm. "Can't have you driving home after I've exhausted you like this."

Oh?

That tingling of pleasure flooded through her, yet he looked undisturbed. Her mind could have made the whole thing up.

"Come on," he added as he offered her his arm. "I'll drive you home."

She wasn't sure what possessed her, but she refused to take the offered arm, walking behind him almost blindly, her breath becoming more labored as they made their way to the front of the house. But when she'd put on her shoes, she did take his arm. She couldn't very well eat it in front of this smug man. Especially when he looked like that and moved so gracefully.

He opened the passenger door, and she slid into the seat.

"Get rest tonight," he said. "Plenty of water, too."

He got behind the wheel, where no man had ever been. She'd bought it after her divorce and was the only person to have ever been in it. For some reason, that felt like a monumental thing.

"I don't know if this is going to work for me," she admitted as they pulled away from the road, just as it started raining.

"What do you mean?"

"Were you listening when I said I want nothing to do with magic?"

"And were you listening when I explained what happens when you repress your powers?"

"How could I forget?" She annoyed herself with her sarcasm.

"Then your argument doesn't make sense, does it? You agreed."

Huffing out a breath, sounding like a child, she looked out the window at the passing streets.

"You're really annoying," she grumbled.

"I hear that a lot."

"Might want to take notes and change some behaviors then."

He laughed softly and her skin itched. All of it. Her whole body. What the hell was going on with her? She was so twirly in the presence of this virtual stranger, she hardly recognized herself.

"My sisters would agree with you," he said.

"I think I like your sisters already."

He laughed again, but the conversation didn't really progress from there. Mostly because she didn't want to ask the questions she really wanted answered. How many sisters did he have? Was he the only boy? What was his family like? Did they live close? What was their birth order?

Julia clenched her teeth, eyes focused outside, so she wasn't tempted to stare at him as he drove her car like it was the most natural thing in the world.

6

Days later, Julia had convinced herself she'd made a mistake working with him. It was a terrible idea. Whatever he'd done to her left her shaken and second-guessing everything she thought she knew. Mariana would tell her she was being avoidant, but what else was she supposed to do when he could read her like that? And he couldn't even read her that well anyway.

Julia stood still as the seamstress took her measurements. She and the girls were at Sara Marshall, an exclusive bridal boutique in town, owned by a friend of Amy's from school. Sara herself was supervising the measurements and talking about designs.

Amy was by the big tablet with a stylus in her hand. Kind of cool to see her baby sister show her expertise in clothing design like that. Victoria and Sophia were getting measured as well, confirming details about their dresses as they went. They'd all gone much sexier than Julia, that was for sure. The wedding was an all-white affair, everyone wearing their favorite silhouette. Julia had chosen a classic a-line, tea-length dress with quarter sleeves. Classic, familiar, relaxed. Sophia and Amy had gone all out, on the other hand, choosing sleeker silhouettes to accent their curvier bodies. While Julia would have loved to do something like that, she didn't boast the same body type as her sisters. She didn't dislike her figure, except right now she felt like she was all bones.

As the plump woman finished taking Julia's measurements, Helena appeared with a cheerful chime of the doors.

"I'm so sorry I'm late! The boys kept me too long," she said, her cheeks blushed a pretty pink.

"Unlike Grey to do that when he knew we were waiting for you," Sophia said.

"It wasn't his fault. Lucas needed help with something."
Julia's ears perked up.

"What kind of help?" Julia asked, though she knew she was at risk of sounding too interested.

"He was making a brew and couldn't figure out how to make it work the way he needed. Some ingredient or whatever."

"Oh." So not about Julia being difficult.

Helena regarded her quietly for a moment. "Did something happen?"

Julia's heart dropped. "No." *He just read me to filth, really. Nothing much.*

"I know a lie when I hear it." Helena's eyes narrowed.

"I'm not lying."

"Hiding, more like it."

Julia took a deep breath and counted backwards from ten. Her patience was always wearing thin these days, which wasn't good when she had magical powers she couldn't control.

"He read my energy, or whatever he does, and it was weird."

"Weird how?"

"It made me dizzy and he said things that worried me."

Helena nodded knowingly. "It can do that."

"He said he couldn't read my energy all the way. Is that bad?"

"Let me guess," Helena said, "he said he expected it and that seeing him would help."

"Exactly. How did you know? Did he tell you?" Julia eyed her friend suspiciously, but Helena shook her head.

"He doesn't talk about his clients with us. I know because it's typical for energy to get stuck when the subject's gone through hard times."

Lord knew Julia had.

"He said he can fix it, but I don't know if I want to do this anymore," she said.

Helena blinked slowly and cocked her hip. With a fortifying breath, Julia continued.

"I don't want this magical power, but Lucas said I have to learn to use it so I can stop using it. It's all very stupid."

Helena had a knowing smile on her pink lips. "It's not. Repression's what makes your powers surge the way they do." She looked to make sure no one was listening. "To have a choice to not use them—"

"I have to learn to control it first, I know. That's what Lucas said." How fucking annoying.

Helena laughed softly.

"He can be a pain in the ass, but he means well."

"Yeah, well, I hope that's true, because I will strangle him."

"Believe me, I've been there."

Sara approached them with the tablet.

"So these are the designs we have so far," she said. "Is this still what you want?"

Julia looked at her dress. Simple, elegant… boring. Especially compared to the design of Helena's dress, which Sara showed them next. It was a long gown, made almost entirely of the lace Victoria had selected, but for the built-in bodysuit. The décolletage went almost to the belly button. It was sexy and had simple, clean lines, and the bride loved it just as much as the woman who'd wear it. Then there was Sophia's mermaid silhouette, and Amy's dramatic double slit and wide skirt. And not to mention that Victoria's gown would have a cape made entirely of lace, like a bridal riding hood. It was gorgeous.

"It is," Julia said. She looked away from the designs, though she didn't miss Helena's knowing smile. Thankfully, her friend said nothing, because Julia wasn't sure she could handle it. She was set in her ways. And besides, her dress wasn't bad. It was a classic silhouette, and she knew she'd wear it well.

Or maybe she was lying to herself.

She tried… she really tried to not think of Kate and Harold, how Kate had told her that Harold cheating had been her own fault because she was a frigid bitch. Apparently his words.

But was it really her fault that Harold had never given her an orgasm? Her girls would say hell no, that Harold was just bad in bed, but Julia couldn't remember ever having a good time with sex. Not that it had been bad, but it had never been more than pleasant. It felt good until it didn't. Usually because there was too much going through her head.

Perhaps there was something inherently wrong with her.

"You can change your mind," Sophia said quietly, moments later.

"I don't have to change my mind. I'm sticking with what I know."

"It's pretty," Amy said with a smile. "And accessories will also come into play, so there's that."

Julia knew what they were doing, and somehow, it made her feel even worse.

Thankfully, they left soon after, and Julia headed home as her phone pinged with notifications, no doubt bringing her more news about her father. She checked as soon as she was parked in the dark garage. Same old, really, but it still bugged her enough that she rushed into the house and changed into her pajamas. Back on the windowsill, she held the unlit joint between her fingers, wishing she knew how to deal with her anxiety another way. And still, she lit it anyway and puffed out a cloud of smoke as a text came through. A picture of Lucas's kittens and nothing else. One was white, the other completely black, both with blue eyes.

Julia: Are you trying to make me think you're cute?

Lucas: Did it work?

Julia: I think the cats are cute.

Lucas: Damn.

She smiled before she realized what she was doing.

Lucas: How've you felt?

Julia: I don't know why you ask, since I have a feeling you already know.

Lucas: I don't know, which is why I'm asking.

Fair enough.

Julia: I'm fine. Still reeling about the other day.

Lucas: Do you have any questions about anything?

Julia: I honestly don't even know where to start.

It was a while before he responded, and she was taking a long drag of her joint when he did.

Lucas: There's energy stuck in your body.

Julia: Anyone ever tell you how tactful you are?

He sent a laughing emoji.

Lucas: Do you need me to be more tactful?

Julia: Wouldn't kill you.

Lucas: Lo siento, corazón.

The term of endearment had her brows shooting up before they contracted. She wasn't fluent in Spanish, but she knew the words for 'I'm sorry, darling.' Technically, he had called her 'heart,' but the direct translation was ridiculous as hell. Spanish really was a lovely language.

Julia: I don't speak Spanish.

Lucas: That's not what your sister told me.

Julia: Talk about me a lot?

Lucas: Not really. Essential information to get to know you better. Makes my job easier.

Julia typed a message, but it felt incomplete, as she couldn't find appropriate words, so she dialed him instead.

"You could ask me instead of harassing Sophia," she said as soon as he picked up.

"Somehow the number of languages you speak didn't come up when you came over." A meow on the other end made her wonder what part of the house he was in. Could he be in the kitchen, giving the kittens food, or maybe in his sitting room in front of an unlit fireplace?

"I speak little Spanish, and most of it's business lingo," she told him, defiance in her voice.

"Business lingo's hard."

"I heard you speak plenty of languages."

"Six, most of them romance. Once you speak a couple, the rest come easy."

"Speak for yourself."

He chuckled, and it did something to her. Warmed her.

"So about this energy," she said. "How do you know I'm *stuck?*"

"I can sense it."

"No shit."

Another laugh, this one louder.

"I can sense where energy can get stuck in the body," he explained. "It's common for that to happen. The body feels everything the brain chooses to grab onto, and it can cause blockages."

Was that why her back hurt so much?

"How do *I* know if it's energy or a physical problem?"

"You start treating it, and if exercises or physical therapy don't work, chances are it's energetic."

She hadn't been doing any exercising at all lately, and she had a feeling it would take time to find out if that's what it was.

"That's where I come in," he said softly.

The joint forgotten, she looked out at the darkening sky. "Do you have any ideas on how you're going to help me?"

"I have an idea, if you want to hear it."

"You really want my answer to that, or . . ." She let her voice trail off, sure she'd regret being so flippant later.

He sighed. "Fine. Meet me at Nowhere tomorrow."

She frowned at the phone in her hand.

"You're asking me to go clubbing?"

"I am." He sounded so proud of himself.

"How is that supposed to help?"

"Trust me."

She held the phone away from her ear, as if she could see his face.

"Movement might be the best thing for you," he said.

"Movement?"

"Dancing," he clarified, and she was sure she'd heard him wrong.

"I'm sorry, *what?*"

"Unorthodox methods," he said simply, as if that explained it.

"What kind of magic is that?"

"A very special kind."

"And I assume you're just going to leave me with that cryptic comment and not explain anything?"

"Actually, no."

Suspicious, she waited for his explanation.

"It's important to know what you're getting into, since it can lead to emotional releases as well." His voice softened as he spoke, and she found herself riveted, hanging on to every word.

"I'm well-versed on emotional releases."

"I can imagine you are. You've had a tough couple of years. Don't take that for granted, Julia."

She liked the way he said her name. The way every syllable sounded more… seasoned. Julia ran a cool hand over the back of her neck.

"And dancing will help with the magic."

"I believe it can lead to that, yes."

She didn't miss his choice of words.

Fuck it, she thought. Nothing to lose and all that jazz.

"I guess I'll meet you at the club then."

"Good." She heard the smile in his voice. "Nine. Wear comfortable shoes."

"If that means flats, I hope you know I'd rather walk around Seattle barefoot."

He laughed deeply, almost snorted, and it was adorable, and her face did something that felt unfamiliar. As soon as she realized that she was smiling at his adorable laugh, she lost it. What the hell was this man doing to her? Had that been part of his reading, making her feel like this? Could he plant feelings on her?

"Whatever you like is perfect. Far be it for me to take your heels from you."

"I might die of embarrassment tomorrow."

"Why would you be embarrassed about anything?"

"People are always watching." Julia thought of the articles and social media.

There was a moment of silence on the other end of the line, and nervous, she waited for him to speak before she put her foot in her mouth any more.

"You can have fun, you know. There's nothing dirty about it," he said softly.

"Yeah," she said through clenched teeth.

"Okay, then I'll see you tomorrow night."

They wished each other good night, and Julia sat at the window for way too long that evening. But for the first time in a while, she actually got hungry, so she made herself a simple dinner of pasta, and even had a quarter of a glass of wine before it made her feel icky. Tomorrow night was going to be interesting.

7

The following evening, Lucas waited for her outside the club, and he looked… well, delectable. Julia quickly looked down at her blue high-waisted pants and black blouse because she wasn't sure what it was about this man that made her feel underdressed. Not that this was her best outfit, but she loved the form-fitting silhouettes of both the top and the bottom. But even with his black dress shirt unbuttoned at the throat and the sleeves rolled up, he upstaged her. There wasn't a wrinkle on the damn shirt. And the tattoos… They peeked from his collar and sleeves, down his arms, on the part of his chest she could see.

"Lucas," she greeted, feeling awkward as she stood in front of him. She smoothed her hair, which she'd pulled back into a ponytail, held back by a satin bow.

"Julia." He grinned, her name a melody on his lips. "Thanks for meeting me."

He offered her his arm, and she switched her purse to her other hand to take his elbow, a weight settling in her stomach. She barely remembered greeting anyone as they walked inside and into the rhythmic noise of the club. The last time she'd been here, she'd left with a panic attack. Now she was here with the man who'd triggered it.

From the backroom, Sophia appeared through the door, her hair shiny and smooth down her back. She looked cute in dark jeans and a loose button-down shirt in a color Julia couldn't make out from this far. She only had two buttons done, the shirt falling off her shoulder in a haphazard way that suited her well.

When Grey came out of the backroom next, his expression completely shuttered, Julia could have laughed. Sophia's glow had nothing to do with makeup and everything to do with whatever she'd done in the back office with Grey just now. Sophia grinned at her as she came closer and they hugged.

"You look so pretty," Sophia said, and Julia immediately looked down at herself, wondering what she'd done wrong.

"So do you. Where did the shirt come from?"

Sophia blushed to the roots of her hair as Grey came behind her and reached for the back of her neck.

Julia could have died right then and there.

"I had to change," Sophia muttered as Grey pressed a kiss to her temple.

Lucas moved forward and gave Sophia a kiss on the cheek and a pat on his friend's back. When they were engaged in conversation, Julia said, "You two are just nasty."

"I know. It's great!" Sophia couldn't stop smiling. "You and Lucas here together?"

"Oh, that's nothing," Julia said promptly, lest Sophia get any ideas. Julia couldn't have Sophia thinking there was something between her and Lucas.

"He brought you here." Sophia's brows rose slightly.

"Is that weird?"

"No." Her sister lifted a shoulder and accepted a kiss from Grey.

"Drink?" he asked, and when she nodded, he turned to Julia. "Would you like a drink?" His deep voice was like the earth itself, so warm.

"Thank you, but no," Julia told him and he gave her one of those adorably crooked smiles, his little golden nose hoop twinkling before he went to the bar, a faint blush on his cheeks and neck.

In the past, she'd worried about Sophia, especially with her last relationship. But now, her sister was thriving.

Julia couldn't remember the last time she'd been that happy, so consumed with someone that she couldn't help but disappear into a shadowy corner and do unspeakable things to each other. She could certainly say it had never happened with Harold. He was far too controlling. Even getting him to say that he loved her was a battle at the start of their relationship. Red flag number one. And the kicker, he'd already brought up marriage. It'd been confusing and exhausting. But when he'd asked her father for her hand in marriage, she'd said yes, despite all the signs that pointed toward that being a really bad idea.

Grey came back with their drinks, and distracted with him, Sophia turned away from Julia.

"Everything okay?" Lucas asked.

"Not sure, to be honest." Julia turned away from where Grey was bending down to kiss Sophia. She'd had enough cuteness for one day. For a week. Maybe a whole year.

Lucas waited, looking curious.

"I almost didn't come tonight," she confessed. She'd even taken off her clothes and got into her pajamas once.

"So what made you show up?" he asked.

"I hate disappointing people." She pressed her lips together as soon as the words were out. She was far too honest around Lucas Dolores. Time to rein that shit in. "I still don't get how you did it."

"You don't have to understand it for it to be real."

She frowned. "Sounds far too simplistic to me."

"Did I say anything that wasn't true?"

"That's not the point."

"And what's the point?" he challenged, moving even closer.

She shifted her weight, but didn't step back, gripping her purse like a lifeline. She'd meet his challenge if it killed her.

"A little tact wouldn't kill you," she said, repeating the words from the other night, looking into those pools of honey, his scent choosing that exact moment to fill her entire head. An unexpected flash of desire thundered through her body, pooled low in her belly, when his gaze slid to her mouth, then back up to meet her eyes.

"How do you want me to have tact?" His voice was low, just for her. "Should I lie to you?"

Lies? No. Definitely not. She cleared her throat.

"Why did you want me to come here?"

"I already told you that last night."

"Yes, but why bring me here specifically? Do you bring all your clients clubbing?"

His brows rose. "I don't, and I don't see you as a client."

She blinked.

He continued, "Look, you're my friend's sister, and you need help. I know how to help. But I'm not your therapist, and I won't take money from you."

Baffled, she stared with her mouth halfway open and couldn't respond.

"Healing whatever energy's locked in that body of yours is the key to controlling your power."

That body of hers? What the hell did that mean?

"You're already ruminating on the words I chose instead of what you need to do," he teased.

"My therapist says my issue's ruminating."

"As a former therapist, I can affirm it doesn't help to ruminate."

"Yeah, well, you're not my therapist." She was being a dumb jerk on purpose, but she liked the way it made his eyes shine for a moment. Whether in annoyance or challenge, she couldn't tell.

"Thoroughly aware," he murmured, briefly looking at her mouth again.

Julia tried very hard not to let it show how much it confused her. Was something happening, or was she crazy?

His lips were dusky pink and full in a way no cosmetic procedure could replicate. Envious, she looked away from them. He smelled so good, she wanted to bury her face in his neck where the ending lines of a tattoo teased her.

A lesson was going on the dance floor, the club getting more crowded by the minute, and Julia's fingers and toes tingled. Even those on the dance floor who obviously didn't know how to dance to Latin music were having the time of their lives, but each time she put herself in their place, every one of her organs quivered.

"I still don't understand how it's supposed to help me." Her voice was weak, breathless as she fought her panic.

He'd already explained it more than once; she knew what his words would be. But he still explained it again, his voice turning soft, and she couldn't look away from him, as if everything around them was suddenly gone and it was just them in the dark club. Music played as a background to their conversation. Like a movie.

She was going to have to be committed.

"I know what you're saying," she told him. "I get it."

"But you're still resisting."

"Yes, I am. This is all very weird."

He leaned his head. "What's weird about it?"

"The idea of energy getting stuck in your body."

"Everything we do is either conscious or unconscious—the brain is ruled by the latter."

"I've been told I have a choice," she said. "That I feel like this because I choose not to move on." Amy had said that a time or two.

He frowned. "That's bullshit. You don't know what you don't know."

"But the choice still exists out there, even if I don't know about it," she argued, because it was easier to do so than accept that maybe she'd been taught wrong and had been living this life without purpose.

"Sure, but if no one's there to hear it, does the tree make a noise when it falls?"

Hypnotized by his voice, there was no one else in the world but them.

"How do you arrive at such conclusions?" she asked. She felt like she did when she went on a cruise years ago. The minute she'd walked onto the boat, she'd felt the way it made her unsteady. Her stomach felt insubstantial, but her heart raced. Panic always felt like this, foreign, like she was floating out of her body and watching herself go through the motions.

"I read a lot," he murmured, but she'd forgotten her question. Someone knocked into her, making her stumble forward so she was closer to Lucas. Suddenly, like everything exploded out of a vacuum, the sound was back. Groups of people walked around them, ordering at the bar, being shown to their tables, and her vision blurred at the edges.

"Does magic help you?" she asked, but only to distract herself.

"Sometimes."

"And dancing."

He nodded, watching her closely. She felt like a zombie.

"I don't think I could dance to this." She was a liar. Of course she could. She knew how to salsa perfectly well.

But right then, the wave of panic washed over her and she looked around the club, the dancers, the music, the chatter, and the drinking, and the food. It was too much. She couldn't take a breath. And then his hands were there on her shoulders, holding her in place when she wanted to melt into the shadowy corners of the club.

"Look at me." His voice was to her mind what a lighthouse was to boats. The moment she looked at him again, the noise fell away and it was just him and his warm hands, their weight comforting on her shoulders. "Breathe, Julia."

She obeyed automatically. Under a trance, she breathed slowly to the count he softly uttered.

"You don't have to do anything you don't want to do," he murmured, and as soon as his words were out, the panic subsided. Not entirely, but a lot.

"What did you just do?"

"I just used a little bit of magic to avoid a panic attack. Is that okay?"

"A little late to ask for consent."

He pressed his lips into a line. "I'm sorry."

"It's fine." She felt the absence of his hands acutely as they dropped to his sides. "Thank you."

He looked serious when he said, "You're welcome. A drink?"

She nodded because she needed something to take the edge off, not because she particularly wanted it. Lucas gestured to the bartender when they'd gotten to the glossy bar, and the woman smiled at him sultrily.

"Usual?" she asked him, leaning over the counter. He only gave her one of those devastating grins and a nod.

Julia found herself looking at the woman. Pretty, tall (surprise, surprise), with short dark hair that was shaggy and stylish. Why did it bother her? He could flirt with anyone he wanted. As far as she knew, he was single, and maybe the bartender was too. Maybe they'd go home together…

Hands shaking she took the drink from Flirty McFlirty and gulped half of it in one go.

"More?" he asked, bringing his glass to his lips. She was staring, but it was interesting how his larynx moved as he swallowed. She did ask for another drink, and she swore the bartender's smile was a little colder.

Lucas leaned into the bar, and her attention snapped back to his.

"I think I went about this all wrong," he said, placing his glass on the bar.

"What do you mean?"

Flirty came back with Julia's drink.

"Crowds are hard for you, obviously."

How did she explain that it wasn't the crowd exactly? It was the crowd *and* the noise, plus the lights…

"Let's start over," he said.

"Start over how?"

"Maybe we start with something to relax you into dancing."

"Depends on what you mean by relaxing." She narrowed her eyes at him.

He mimed crossing himself. "Jesús, get your mind out of the gutter, woman."

She snorted a surprise laugh. "Get over yourself."

"I'm wounded." His hand rested on his chest.

"Good. Have to knock you down a peg or two."

Her cheeks pulled at a grin, but she fought back against it.

"Tell you what," he said, bending down to come a little closer to her ear as the entire club exploded into a sing-along. Shivers along her spine, she leaned in to listen. "I'll come over tomorrow after my last client. Is that okay with you?"

"And do what?" She narrowed her eyes at him.

"I don't know." His smile sparkled in his eyes. "I'll just have to show you tomorrow."

He took her home after that, as she had taken a ride-share to Nowhere. Parking on the driveway, he got out when she did, and walked her up to the door. He left her standing just inside the house with a soft good night.

When Julia agreed to have him come over tomorrow, she could have easily convinced herself that she did because she was curious. Now, she wasn't so sure anymore.

8

Sometimes, people made dumb choices, like agreeing to do magic on purpose. Julia was people.

Restless, she paced up and down the hallway as she waited for Lucas. She'd been overthinking since his text came through last night, barely able to sleep. Okay, the lack of sleep was already her thing, but still.

When the doorbell rang, Julia stopped in her tracks and went to open the door. She found Lucas standing on the stoop with his hands in his pockets. His white button-down was crisp, the sleeves rolled up to his elbows, in perfect contrast with his navy blue pants and shiny gray shoes. Her eyes were drawn to his mouth briefly, but she forced herself to stop it right there.

This was going to be a very long night if she couldn't be cool.

"I always feel really underdressed around you," she blurted and almost slammed the door in his face with frustration at her own stupidity. She didn't though, and instead pulled at the long sleeves of her soft ochre blouse. She wasn't frumpy, just not as fancy as he was.

"You look great," he said.

She almost believed him.

"Thank you," she said. Purse on her shoulder, she followed him to his car. It smelled of rain, and the wind was a little chilly. When he opened the door for her, she wasn't surprised or wary of it, and her eyes followed his movements as he got behind the wheel.

"Where are you taking me?" she asked, all her senses consumed by him.

He looked at her briefly, putting the car in reverse and sliding onto the road.

"I thought we could go pick up some potion ingredients together," he said. She froze, her eyes glued to his profile.

"Like, at the supermarket?"

He chuckled. "No, it's a little herb shop. A couple, actually."

Julia swallowed tightly. "So, what kinds of potions do you need things for?" She didn't really want to know, but she didn't know what else to say.

"I'm running out of porting potion, so I'll make a batch during the full moon."

He said that so naturally, like it was normal. Like he was telling her there was a chance of rain tonight. It left a slimy film in the back of her throat.

"You say it like that." She side-eyed him.

"Like what?"

"I don't know." Julia shrugged. "You talk about it so casually."

At a red light, he tilted his head as he looked at her.

"I'm not entirely sure I understand."

"When you speak of magic, you're so matter-of-fact. Meanwhile, I feel like I've entered a parallel universe."

He smiled as the light turned green. "I've been doing magic my whole life."

It struck her how her life could've been like that if her mom hadn't died. Julia could have been a different person if that had been the case, and she didn't really know how she should feel about it. If she wanted that reality or not.

"So, if a friend calls and asks you out during a full moon, what do you say?"

"If they're a witch, they're not going to call," he said.

"Do you only have witch friends?"

"No, and if someone asks, I just say that I'm busy."

"And that works?"

"More often than not, unless it's one of my sisters asking. Then they'd insist until I told them."

"Are your sisters…?"

"Actually, none of them are. My oldest practices, but she doesn't have any active powers."

"I thought you didn't either."

His brows rose and he threw her a sidelong glance. "What makes you say that?"

"I thought that your powers were non-active ones."

"According to whom?"

Her shoulder twitched upward. "I don't know." She based it on what she knew about the kind of magic she'd seen on TV shows, but she wasn't going to admit to that now.

"It's active because it's usable," he explained, his tone neutral. "I was born with this ability to read energies, but none of my sisters developed anything."

Like Amy.

"Sorry, I don't mean to interrogate you," she said with a shake of her head.

"You can ask anything you want. This is an opportunity to get to know each other."

"Why?"

He gave her another brief glance as he maneuvered the car onto a side road, and her face and neck heated at the intensity in his eyes.

"Because when I spend time with those seeking my help, I tend to find the right methods quicker."

Sound argument, sure, but she'd worn pants two days in a row to see this man. It was already a little much.

"I know how it makes you feel," he continued.

She doubted that.

He parked on the side of the road, which was kind of a miracle that he found an empty space in the first place. It was a single lane road, and they'd parked right across from a little shop hidden between two taller buildings. The front was one big square window and a matching door with peeling teal paint. A tall street light illuminated the front, where a hanging sign had a simple crescent moon with stars painted on it.

"I didn't know this was here." Why would she? She wasn't often going to herb shops for potion ingredients.

"It's a good one. We often trade with the owner."

Trading potions, Grey's specialty, and now Sophia's, Julia supposed.

"Ready to go in?" he asked with a grin, getting out of the car.

She had to have fallen asleep and was dreaming, she thought as she followed him.

The door jingled cheerfully when he opened it. A set of steps led to a small store with several round tables out front. There were crystals hanging off spindly, metal structures on the tables, similar to the ones hanging off every window and doorway in her own house. Charms for protection, she guessed, though she had to wonder if they were like Grey's at all. His, she remembered, had exploded to allow her and Sophia to get away when someone had tried to attack them two years ago.

The lights were warm and low, and Julia took small steps, her heels clacking on the worn, wooden floorboards. The walls inside were also blue, though they weren't peeling like the outside, and on the shelves sat many other items for sale. Crystals, more jewels, tiny bottles with bright liquids in them. Julia ran a finger over a large purple crystal, enjoying its sparkle in the low light.

The shop smelled strongly of a scent she couldn't place but wanted to remember.

"This is cool," she mumbled, distracted by a rack with flowing fabrics in a corner.

"It's one of my favorites," he said, his hand pressing between her shoulder blades for a brief moment. Her skin tingled when he pulled away.

"Welcome to Stardust," a blonde woman said. She was tucked behind the counter to their right, in front of shelves that held what looked like a billion jars of herbs and various states.

The woman's hair was long, wavy, and a little frizzy. She had on a colorful, flowing dress and a dreamy half-smile on her pretty face.

"Mr. Dolores," the woman, whose name tag read Rowan, said.

"Good to see you, Rowan. I have a package from Miss Luna on hold," Lucas said after he'd approached the counter.

Rowan disappeared through a beaded curtain on the side.

"Who's Miss Luna?"

Lucas looked down at her.

"The owner," he told her. "She has quality ingredients, especially her compounded jars."

"And what are compounded jars?"

"Imagine you're making a sandwich," he said. "You don't make a fresh loaf of bread every time you make a sandwich. Compounded jars are the bread."

She hummed.

"And we're picking up bread today."

"Exactly."

She narrowed her eyes. "And tell me again how picking up bread is supposed to calm me down."

"Are you stressed right now?" he asked with a raised brow.

"Not particularly."

That was a lie; she was always stressed out. He turned to her fully, leaning his elbow on the wooden counter.

"Is that the truth?" Lucas asked, his eyes luminous and far too insightful. It reminded Julia a bit of her old cat, Sunshine.

"No." She gritted her teeth.

"Why are you stressed?"

"I'm literally always stressed."

"Sounds exhausting."

"You're so insightful. Has anyone ever told you that?"

"And you're an infinite source of sarcasm. Anyone ever told *you* that?" He stepped closer still. Suddenly, the room was tiny, and all she could see was his chest right in front of her.

"All the time." Her tongue felt too big in her mouth.

Rowan returned with a package, and Julia could swear she heard glass breaking, like she was in a cartoon. The package Rowan handed Lucas was wrapped in brown paper and stuffed into a reusable bag with the same moon and stars as the sign outside.

"Miss Luna says you're good to go," Rowan said, her eyes practically the shape of little hearts as she looked up at Lucas.

"Thank you so much," Lucas said with one of those charming smiles of his. "I will see you next time."

Why did it bother her that Rowan's pretty face was flushed?

They left the store. Rain had started to fall gently, and they rushed to the car. He put the package in the back seat when he was behind the wheel.

"And what was that all about in there?" she asked after clipping on her seatbelt.

He raised his brows in confusion.

"You asked me to come to the store with you." She crossed her arms. "What are you getting at?"

Lucas turned to her. "I took you to the club last night, thinking it was the right move. Clearly, it wasn't."

"And you thought bringing me to a magic shop would be an improvement?"

"I just thought that showing you what the magical community is like would be good for you," he said. Relaxing against the seat, she looked out the window.

"Do you think Rowan does magic?" she asked as he pulled onto the road.

"I don't know Rowan very well," he said.

"You're telling me you can't just tell?"

He shot her a quick grin. "Consent, remember?"

"How could I forget?"

Julia looked out the window, suddenly awkward. Once upon a time, she'd been the queen of small talk. Now, not so much. But to be fair, she'd never been in this situation before. Running around the city, talking about magic, going to magic stores together… It felt so mundane.

"So," she said after a long silence, "who did you get your magic from?"

"My mom."

"Me too."

He nodded and smiled, and she let herself relax a little. They had something in common. That was good. She could establish a conversation like that. It was just about pretending that it was a business thing instead. Take an interest in the person you're talking to, create rapport, seal the deal.

"Does your mom do the same kind of magic as you?"

"No, she didn't. My mom died when I was sixteen," he said, and she had a moment of pure panic.

"Hey, mine too," she said a little too brightly. Something about it struck her as funny, though it wasn't remotely funny, and she had to force herself not to laugh. "But you already knew that."

"I do." His voice was gentle, and so were his eyes when he looked at her at a red light. "I'm sorry for your losses."

With instant warmth behind her eyes, Julia looked out her window and watched the water droplets on the glass.

"I'm sorry for yours," she mumbled. "That must've been very hard."

Speaking from experience.

"It was. I'm grateful I had my sisters and my dad."

"How many sisters do you have?" She twisted to face him fully, though he was now driving and paying attention to the wet road.

"Three, all older."

Her brows jumped up. "You're the baby!"

He grimaced, and even that was attractive. "Yes, and my sisters will not let me forget it."

"Overbearing older sisters," she chuckled. "I can relate."

Lucas parked the car in front of another shop. The building was one of those old warehouses, which was converted into a mall of sorts. The front was clean and industrial-looking, with vines growing on the side.

"I doubt your sisters think you're overbearing," Lucas said as they got out of the car.

"Have you hung out with them recently?" Julia followed him as they crossed the road toward the building.

He opened the glass door for her. "Why do you say that?"

Julia paused before she walked in ahead of him, not caring that it was raining a little heavier now. "Why do you ask?"

"I'm just trying to understand."

"Maybe we leave that for another time," she said and took the lead into the building.

The decor inside the building was minimal in the common areas. A couple of benches and pots with greenery and flowers sat on either side of an iron staircase that led up to a smaller second floor. Once upstairs, they entered a tiny shop with nothing more than a counter and an older East Asian man behind it. His face was deeply wrinkled, back bowed slightly.

Like the last shop, this one also smelled like something she should remember, and it hit her that it had something to do with her mom. She'd always burned herbs and incense. As Julia followed Lucas to the counter, she wondered if her mom had known this person, this shop. Maybe the last one too.

"Mr. Kim," Lucas said to the older man. Julia stayed behind a little, looking around at the gold dragons that decorated the walls.

"Lucas, good to see you," Mr. Kim said as he took Lucas's offered hand. "And with a lady friend."

Julia smiled at the man, wishing she could correct him, knowing it wasn't necessary.

"This is Julia Candela," Lucas said, gesturing at Julia, who then stepped forward so she didn't seem rude.

"Candela." Mr. Kim blinked, then smiled wide, and Julia's heart almost leaped out of her chest with something that felt like anticipation, or hope. "It means fire, right?"

Julia nodded and swallowed, jittery. She wasn't sure what she'd been hoping for—maybe that Mr. Kim had, in fact, known her mother.

"It does," she said.

"Beautiful." Mr. Kim's smile was warm and kind, and his eyes were sharp and clear, like he could see through her words and to her deepest self. But he directed his attention to Lucas then, and Julia felt like she couldn't breathe. The shakiness came back, deep within her, and she held it together by repeating to herself that it was almost over. That she'd be in the car with Lucas soon and he'd take her home. She didn't hear a word they said, just watched as if from far away as they spoke. Mr. Kim disappeared for a moment and came back with a small square package.

"Grey and I will deliver the rest of your potions after the full moon," Lucas said as they shook hands again.

Julia's legs were stiff as they walked down the stairs and back out into the rain.

"Are you alright?" Lucas asked when they were safely in the car on their way back to her house.

"Yeah," she whispered, but said nothing more.

He parked in the driveway, but she didn't move to get out, wishing she could tell him that she wasn't this person. That this anxious, scared, insecure woman was not the Julia he would have met two years ago.

"Julia, look at me," he murmured, and she did. She stared into his clear eyes as he spoke. "None of this is going to be easy. Doing these mundane things is meant to help you relax around me, but that might not extend to others for now."

She nodded, numb now that they were home. All she wanted was her joint and windowsill, but she still didn't move.

"You want to tell me about it?" Lucas said softly.

Trembling slightly, she sat back against the leather seat, but it was a long while before she spoke again. The struggle inside her, whether she would tell him or not, nauseated her. She wanted to trust him—he seemed perfectly trustworthy—but these days trusting was hard, no matter who it was, and she forced the words out.

"I wondered if Mr. Kim knew my mom." She turned to look out the windshield. "I don't know why."

"I think it's natural to want to know those things."

"I hate that I don't." She threw him a look, discomfort making her skin itch. "I wish I knew everything about her."

She wished she could proudly tell people about her heritage without sounding like she was performing a bit.

"It's not too late." Lucas's tone was gentle, and somehow that made it worse. Voice shaking, she thanked him and got out of the car. When she'd keyed the code at the door, she turned back to find him looking up at her still. With a quick wave, she went inside the house, and practically ran to the living room.

Joint in hand, she took her seat on the windowsill, surprised there wasn't an ass print on it. She took a long drag. Letting it out slowly, she opened her social media app. There was something about the way it felt to look up things she should be avoiding. A weird pain that had felt like a need.

Kate's latest photo was the first thing she saw. She was solo, Harold nowhere in sight.

Kate Belvedere was lovely, with a huge smile and straight white teeth that were all the exact same length. She had a delicate little nose, upturned like a doll, and not a freckle in sight. Her blonde hair was always tastefully curled and brushed out to look perfectly wavy, and it rested just on top of narrow shoulders. So classy and simple. She was smiling in the photo, and Julia found herself staring at the picture for a while.

How could she have missed what was going on with Harold and Kate? And for so long. Julia had always been an observant woman, always on top of things.

Not observant enough, a voice said in the back of her head.

They'd been friends since college, and it had been easy to bond with her. Kate was lovely, attentive, and generous. Coming from a rich family, old money, she'd married Stephen (also old money) at twenty-two.

Julia resisted the urge to click through to Kate's page, to see what else she was posting, and instead went into the search function.

Lucas's profile was private, but she stared at the thumbnail of his profile photo for a long time, wondering how someone could be that beautiful in real life. She'd thought he was handsome before, when they'd first met all those months ago, but now he was hard to ignore. He still had a well-groomed beard in the photo, something she hadn't really found attractive before, but he certainly pulled it off.

And after tonight… Just going on a drive with him, chatting like Julia was still a normal woman, made her feel like she was making a friend of this man who'd come to help her. And god knew she needed the help.

She pressed the follow request button. Before she could close the app, a notification popped up that he'd accepted her request and followed her back.

Curious, she opened his feed. It was a nice one, not too overloaded—he didn't seem to post much—but pleasing to the eye regardless. And it revealed a few things she hadn't known about him.

He liked taking pictures of nature—there were many of him on hikes, some with Grey and Helena, others on his own. And a well-tended garden too, which reminded her of her mom.

Other photos showed things like nights out with friends, a saxophone, which made her wonder if he played. More recently, there were a few pictures of his kittens. Opal and Midnight were adorable. Lucas was adorable. Especially the picture of him with both kittens laying on his stomach, snoozing as he lay on a hammock.

Alright, that wasn't adorable, but sexy as all hell. He had a white tank top on, and well-defined arms showed full tattoo sleeves. She couldn't have been prepared for how it made her feel, warm and curious and turned on. He had depictions of the ocean, animals and plants, waves on both arms, but also what looked like tribal designs. Intricate shading brought every piece to life, and she had to wonder how many more tattoos he actually had.

And how was it that in almost every photo, he looked like a model. Or a Latin pop star. How annoying.

Julia wasn't sure she had time to be attracted to this man. She needed his help, and she would keep things professional. Reluctantly, she closed the app, then the window, and headed off to bed.

She thought of him until she fell asleep.

9

The skies had opened when Julia went to see Lucas two days later. She wondered what he planned to do today. After their mild adventure across town, she didn't really know what to expect. Maybe he'd want her to dance, but she wasn't sure how she felt about that. Dance had been fun in its time, but setting it aside to focus on her career had put it so far in the back of her mind that she didn't know if she could find it. And the other night, when they went to the club, she'd freaked out even thinking about moving.

Besides, there was also the problem of how Julia couldn't stop thinking about Lucas's hands, how they'd felt on her shoulders while the entire club disappeared. He'd calmed her panic attack before it even hit.

He was wearing slacks and a t-shirt, both gray, when he opened the door. Her stomach fluttered. Especially when the kittens wound around his legs, looking up at her suspiciously.

"You like monochrome looks," she said, like a complete dumbass. She'd opted for jeans this time, a little tight, but they hugged her ass nicely. Why she needed that, she had no idea.

Okay, that was a lie. If she was going to lust after Lucas, a part of her wanted him to lust after her too. Even if it didn't go anywhere. And it wouldn't because she really *wasn't* interested in him that way at all.

At all.

"I do." He smiled and stepped aside to let her in. Like the other times she'd been here, she took off her shoes and left them at the door as the kittens took off down the hall. He led the way down the narrow hallway through the ornate archways.

It was easy to just follow him, admire the length of his back. The man had an ass on him, that was for sure.

"I thought we could make some tea." He smiled, turning to look at her briefly.

"What kind of tea?"

"Why don't we decide that together?" he said as they walked into his lovely kitchen, the kittens bouncing and meowing around them.

When he opened the door to the small pantry, showing her a shelf of jarred herbs and spices, she froze with her mouth half open. There had to be at least fifty jars with herbs. Labeled. And if that was his handwriting, she was practically salivating already.

She was like that cartoon character trope with heart eyes and her tongue rolling out of her mouth.

"Holy shit, this is impressive." She looked up at his smug expression. "Wouldn't have pegged you for a tea snob."

"I don't know what's snobby about wanting good tea and zero waste."

Fair.

She helped him choose the herbs, which meant he told her what to grab, and she did so obediently. She had no idea what half of these spices were.

"Sometimes bagged isn't that bad," she said, setting down the jars.

"Once you have a proper tea, you'll never want bagged," he said. Squinting, he reached for a knife inside a drawer. "Can I trust you not to stab me?"

She took the knife, holding his dancing gaze. "Behave and I won't have to."

He laughed, turned, and bent over to find a pot. She could have spent hours just observing that view.

Good God. She really needed to get laid. And soon.

"What do you think about lemongrass?" he asked, unaware of her filthy train of thought. Her heart rolled over.

"In general?"

His lip twitched. "For tea."

Yeah, that made a lot more sense. "My mom used to make lemongrass tea."

His luminous eyes found hers. "So did mine." His smile was sad as he put the pot on the stove and turned it on with a twist of a button. "Kind of a staple in DR."

She wouldn't know.

And there it was again, like clockwork. Fucking guilt.

"What are you thinking?" he asked, and something in his gaze told her he knew what was going on inside her.

"I don't even know."

He didn't want to push, she could tell, and gratitude allowed her to relax. When he asked her to slice a lime, she did so, and recalled a time when it was her own mother telling her how to do it. Why hadn't she made this tea since?

Every smell sent her back there, and for a moment, she allowed herself to wade through the memories.

"Let's go get the lemongrass."

She blinked up at him, then the jars on the counter. He pointed at the door.

"From the garden."

She swallowed tightly as she walked past him through the door. The patio was made with lovely reddish stonework. There was the hammock he'd been on in his photo, a couch against the wall, and a small round table. They went around to the other side of the house, where the garden she'd seen on his page was. He had many herbs she couldn't put a name to if she tried, and they were meticulously organized in rows in the small side yard and on raised beds. Cool earth beneath her feet, she followed through the neat little rows and watched him cut long, narrow leaves from a bush, and the nostalgia hit her when the scent did. Inside the house, he washed them in the deep stone sink. Julia could imagine her mom doing the same thing, taking the same steps.

She watched him put the ingredients into the small pot. The sweet scent of the herbs, combined with the lemon and the spices, embedded into her brain, into her skin.

"So, if one were looking to get lemongrass," she started and paused until he was looking at her. "Other than growing it, that is."

"I know someone who could possibly help." He leaned forward to smell the pot, and his scent mingled with the herbs and spices. It was intoxicating.

"I would love some, if that someone would like to help a girl out." Was she… flirting? She was certainly closer to him now, taking a deep whiff of that scent that drove her crazy. He smelled of the herbs, but something else spicier and warmer.

Heat in her face, she took a step back.

Get a hold of yourself, Julia.

Lucas stepped forward, making her heart rate go haywire as he reached for the cabinet next to her head. She could feel the warmth coming from him. He pulled out a small glass container with a wooden lid.

"I take sugar in mine," he murmured. "Do you?"

Her body felt heavy, warm. His intense gaze was like the universe itself. She could get lost there, looking for things she couldn't imagine. Nodding, she watched him move to pull out two mugs from another cabinet.

Heart racing, she watched him stir the golden concoction before he poured it into the cups, the cloud of scents making her woozy.

"I haven't had this since I was a kid," she told him when he'd handed her the mug. "What a shame, right?"

"It was your path."

When he said things like that, it struck her how easy it felt to talk to him. Everyone else wanted her to be better, to move on, but few understood that the pressure only increased her anxiety and made it that much harder.

Lucas saw it differently, allowed things to be what they were without trying to find meaning that may not even be there.

"I'm not complaining about my life," she said. She needed him to understand that she didn't take for granted the privileges afforded to her.

"Complaints are natural and necessary." He turned to her, leaning his narrow hip on the counter, the tea behind him. "Privilege doesn't protect you from struggle."

Yeah, she knew that already. "Is this how you get me to relax?"

He tilted his head. "Whatever I have to do."

Her stomach heated like the tea in her hands.

"There's an entire part of myself I don't even know," she admitted in a rush, because she was already here and what the hell.

"Tell me about it."

"I've always loved the food and the music, but I don't even know if I have family left on the island. I never knew anything about my grandparents, let alone anyone beyond that."

"That doesn't make you any less Dominican, Julia." His voice was so soft, so understanding, and the heat came to her eyes. She was *not* going to cry, though; fuck that.

"It makes me half."

"Who's counting?"

"Me, I'm counting." She pushed away from the counter, where she had found herself drifting toward him, closer and closer. "I can't speak Spanish."

"I've heard you speak Spanish."

"The Spain kind, and pretty much only business lingo. I don't know the Dominican dialect." She paused because it dawned on her what he'd said. "When did you hear me speak Spanish?"

"At the club," he murmured with a wistful little smile, one that spoke of things she did not know. "You were with your sisters, I was there with Grey, and you spoke to someone you knew. Seemed like a business thing."

The memory came to her then. How random. Julia had run into a partner of an international PR firm who'd been in town for business. She'd actually been the one to tell him about Sophia's club, and he'd gone with his associates to enjoy a show.

"It was kind of a business thing." She told him how she knew the guy, whose name she couldn't recall. Not that it mattered. "You didn't tell me you'd heard me speaking Spanish the other day when the language thing came up."

"I didn't think about it."

"Somehow, I doubt that."

He grinned. "You know, I can teach you the bad words if that's what you want."

"Why would I need you to teach me the bad words?"

"Because they're hilarious. Dominicans, and Puerto Ricans for that matter, are very creative with their slang."

"Isn't that what slang is in the first place?"

He nodded appreciatively. "Fair. Come, let's sit."

In the sitting room, they each took an end of the green couch, and Opal perched herself on the arm of the chair to look at her with huge blue eyes with pupils blown wide.

Just then, her phone went off, then it went off again, until it felt like a single really long vibration inside her purse, which lay beside her on the floor.

"Want to get that? Seems important." Lucas nodded toward her purse.

Julia pulled out her phone and unlocked it to find she had twenty-seven messages waiting for her. One from Sophia caught her eye, asking if Julia was okay.

But it wasn't Sophia's message that she tapped on, but a message from an old friend of hers and Harold's. One of those who'd decided Julia's life was far too messy to be seen with her. Trisha had sent her a screenshot of Kate's feed.

Julia would have been lying if she'd said it didn't rock her. She felt the blood drain from her face, and the hollowness that lived in her chest expanded.

"What happened?" Lucas scooted closer, looking concerned.

She turned the phone toward him so he could see for himself.

Kate and Harold were having a baby.

Great.

But it wasn't jealousy that she felt. At least not on its own. She didn't want Harold—she'd rather throw herself off a moving train into a vat of glass shards than to ever go back to him. He was gorgeous. Golden and blonde and tall. The perfect boy-next-door with a big bank account. And he was also an asshole.

"Why does it upset you?" Lucas asked, and when she looked up, she found no mockery on his expression. She was always expecting mockery, she realized, and didn't really know why.

"I'm not in love with him, if that's what you're asking," she told him, her chin rising defiantly, knowing that she sounded defensive because she was at least guilty of letting it bug her that Harold and Kate were happy. That they'd lied and cheated, and now they were building a life like they hadn't hung Julia out to dry.

"That's not what I'm asking." His voice was nothing but a husky murmur.

That steady presence, the way he wasn't interrogating her, simply allowing her to arrive at the right feeling on her own terms.

"Trisha was one of the friends I lost when all that happened with my dad," she told him. "I haven't heard from her in months, and now she sends me this."

"It bothers you that she's acting concerned."

"It's not even that." Julia set down the cup on the coffee table as both the kittens jumped onto her lap, purring loudly.

"Life-long friends turned their backs so quickly when it all happened, and yet they're aware of every single little thing that happens that might or might not have anything to do with me."

"People can't help it, sometimes."

"Least of all those who consider themselves better than others. Talking from experience."

His brows shot up, but she didn't have to explain any of that. It was enough how humbled she'd been when everything happened and she found herself without any of the support long-term friendships were supposed to offer.

"And it bothers me that they're happy." It came out almost like a question. "Specifically them. They went behind my back for years, and so many people around me knew. People I considered friends knew and no one told me. They just talked about it behind my back."

"How do you know that?"

"Because when I left Harold, a friend called me to say how sorry she was to hear about Harold and his infidelity," Julia told him. The friend didn't know she had left him because he was an asshole and assumed it was because Julia finally found out about Kate.

"That's how you found out?" He looked disturbed.

"Can you even believe it?" Despite everything, she relaxed as Opal put her little paws on Julia's chest and meowed up at her. She ran her hands over the downy fur, while Midnight turned himself into a loaf on her lap, purring deeply.

"How did it feel?"

It had taken her breath away. She'd found out right after her father confessed that he'd killed her mom, that everything Julia thought she knew had been a lie. She told Lucas all that, how the world felt like it was sinking, and how much she'd wanted it to swallow her.

"He sounds like a piece of work."

"You have no idea."

Julia rubbed her fingers on her forehead, as a headache suddenly formed behind her brows.

"I always wanted kids," she said, unable to hold back the words because they were the truest truth she owned. "But with Harold, I convinced myself I didn't want them. Is that sad?"

"Far from it. If someone can let you go like that, then what was the point anyway?"

He meant that. She could see it in his fierce expression.

"Do you want kids?" She only asked because she was curious and felt mushy and soft.

"I think so."

He stood and held out his hand.

"Come on."

She took his hand automatically, and once the kittens jumped off her, she watched as he flipped through screens on his phone. Music began playing through what seemed like the entire house.

It was soft but rhythmic.

"Are you going to make me dance?" Her heart was in her mouth all of a sudden.

"Not at all." He smirked. "But you have nervous energy running through you right now, and I want you to walk around the room."

She blinked. "You want me to walk around the room," she repeated dumbly.

"Around the room, beyond the room; my house is yours. Just listen to the music and walk."

Had it been two years ago, she would have told him to go fuck himself and stop wasting her time. Now, she listened to the music and found herself taking a small step forward. Her knees shook—it frustrated her. Huffing out a breath, she turned back to Lucas.

"How is this supposed to do anything?"

"You've asked me that question before, and the answer's the same now as it was those other times," he said, obviously trying to be patient.

Maybe she wanted him to get mad at her. The idea was kind of thrilling.

"I'd like to ask you a question," he said, his arms crossed over his chest, head leaned to the side.

"Fine," she said. She mirrored his pose, and his rising brows told her he knew exactly what she was doing.

"Tell me," he began, "when was the last time you had fun?"

It practically broke her brain. Julia let her arms drop to her side, grasping for a memory somewhere, and for the life of her, she couldn't remember when the last time was when she'd felt carefree and happy. And maybe it was her obvious depression and everything else going on in her body, but it stunned her that she couldn't think of a single moment.

She was a dead butterfly. Wilted and pathetic.

"Kind of sad that I can't automatically answer that." Or at least lie about it.

"But that's why you're here," he said.

"Yes, and why I've been doing therapy, but that also doesn't seem to be helping me much at all," she grumbled. She felt like a child throwing a tantrum.

"Well, you can't really talk to your therapist about half the things that contribute to your feelings."

She wanted to roll her eyes at him, but he'd vocalized the exact thoughts she'd already had herself. And because her thoughts were starting to race, going back to Kate and Harold and their joyous news, Julia let out a long breath and said, "Okay, what do you want me to do?"

"Just close your eyes and take a deep breath," he said. "Listen to the music."

Keeping her head down, she did as he said. She didn't get it, maybe never would, but nerves overtook her, and every step was heavy and shaky all at once. Seeing Harold and Kate on social media wasn't exactly pleasant, but she didn't know why she couldn't look away. It wasn't just that someone had sent it to her; Julia would have seen it anyway. The buzzing started in her feet before racing up her leg. Stumbling, she threw her arms out, and Lucas was right there to stop her from falling, his hand on her arm.

"It's normal for that to happen," he said, and his voice was inside her head. Shivers erupted all over her, and the heat gathered between her legs so swiftly, it left her reeling.

"It's just walking," he murmured when she looked up at him. "Just listening and walking."

Her breath was in her own ears as their eyes met and she forced herself to look away. How easy it would be to get lost in his eyes. He discombobulated her, more so when his warm hand didn't leave her arm right away, not until they'd reached the kitchen in her aimless walking and went up and down the narrow path between cabinets and appliances.

Curiosity for the space beyond the kitchen, which was separated by a brilliantly sparkling glass door, didn't entirely make her forget he was there behind her. But she wanted to see it, the round table beyond the double doors, which she opened. This was, by far, the most remarkable house she'd ever seen. The floor in the dining room had a pattern in the very center, tile maybe, in a colorful design that looked like stars in the cosmos. The rest of the floor was dark tile, maybe blue, but she couldn't tell since the lights were so low and it had gotten darker out since they finished the tea.

There were so many little details that gave the house character, as if it were a sentient thing. There was art on the dark-colored walls, photos of different landscapes. She was pretty sure she'd seen a couple of those in his profile the other day and wondered if he was into photography then. One picture caught her eye. It was of what looked like a hundred brightly-colored butterflies on a bush. They could have been moving. The colors were vivid, and she had a hard time looking away.

The dining room wasn't large, and the round table under the chandelier of colorful crystals made it feel .

There were a lot of jewel tones in the house, giving everything an air of mystery and elegance. And the spiral staircase was the most incredible wooden structure she'd ever seen. It matched the archways that had charmed her so when she'd first come here.

"This is the most amazing staircase in the world," she whispered as music continued to play around her, and she swayed before she knew what she was doing, all the while wishing she could go upstairs and see what else he had to offer.

"My uncle carved the railing," he told her, and she turned to him in surprise.

"Did he do the archways too?"

Lucas nodded proudly. "I got this house at a steal." He touched the railing and her eyes glued themselves to the way his fingers ran over the ornate surface. "It was falling apart from neglect after its original owners died."

"How much of a steal?" She narrowed her eyes at him.

He said the number and she whistled, still swaying to the music, which had changed to something even slower.

"Damn, I'm mad that wasn't me finding it." Though she would have never been able to make it look like this. Julia, a few years ago, would have hired someone to give her something she considered tasteful, which usually meant devoid of color. This was so much better.

"I got lucky," he said, coming closer. "Last time I asked you, I put you on the spot." The song had switched again to a soft pop that was popular even in English radio.

"So you want me to dance with you now?"

"Yes." He grinned, and his canines gleamed. Her stomach plunged.

It had to be those smutty novels she picked up from time to time, recommended by Helena, because that went straight between her legs too. He raised his hand, where he still had his phone, and she watched it poof into nothing, shrinking back from the little thrill it gave her.

"I . . ." She cleared her throat. "How does that work for you?"

"My magic is mostly contained to energy, but I take potions to be able to do things like that from time to time."

"You want to use magic to put your phone away?" She was stalling.

"Among other things."

What things? she wanted to ask, but didn't.

"There is no pressure here," he told her. "I just want you to relax."

"You have a joint anywhere? That usually helps."

He laughed softly as she gave him her hand.

Not a joke, but okay.

"Just follow my lead," he murmured, taking her by the waist and pulling her close. His scent enveloped her like a cloud as he swayed side to side. She was just tall enough to reach his chin, and she wished she had her shoes on. Lucas was barefoot too, which was super hot for some reason she could not—*would not*—ruminate on.

When he took a small step back, her leg followed and their bodies stayed close. Dancing didn't scare her; she could pick it up quickly, but being around this man might just end up killing her. He twirled her, and with her heart in her throat, she allowed herself to be led. They danced around the table, avoiding the staircase, and she yelped when he twirled her all the way around unexpectedly. A laugh escaped, a rush of serotonin making her forget where they were and why. It was just the charming room, the sparkling chandelier, and the music. His face transformed with his own laugh, and when he dipped her, her heart leapt to her throat.

"You're trying to kill me." She giggled as he pulled her up and their chests collided, lighter now than she had been in forever, and his mouth was right there in her line of sight. His lips moved, but she'd stopped hearing altogether.

Oh god.

The song changed into something romantic, something about dying of love, and Julia awkwardly stepped on his foot.

"I'm sorry," she mumbled.

"Julia," he whispered, and she looked up. His eyes had to be a magnet, because why was it that every time she looked into them, she couldn't look away? They swayed, and he twirled her again, this time slower, and they came together until no more space existed between them. One of his legs came between hers. His hand on her waist reached to her back, holding her close, so tightly, like she had never been held. His warm breath was on her face.

But he let her go just as his phone went off somewhere, and she realized it was on a window ledge in the far end of the room.

Blowing out a breath, he walked away, his steps quiet, and she took the chance to fan herself. He spoke rapid Spanish when he answered, and she maybe got three words.

He turned, as if he felt her staring and mouthed, 'I'm sorry.'

Uncomfortably turned on, she found her opportunity to leave now that he was busy. Maybe take a cold shower. Or a bath with one of her favorite toys.

"I'm going to head out," she whispered and ran off before he could react. She was a coward, but her legs carried her to the living room where she had left her purse, then the door, where she had to pause to put on her shoes. She would have run, shoes in hand, but she still had a little bit of dignity, so she dealt with the stress of knowing he had most likely followed… and yep, there he was.

"Espérate, Josefina," he said into the phone. "Where are you going?"

"I thought we were done." Her voice was too bright and loud. *Filthy liar.* "I'll just let you get back to your call and I'll see you at our next meeting."

She opened the door, but he stopped her with a hand on her arm.

Her nostrils flared when she turned back to him. A pink tongue darted out and he licked his lip. Yep, she was going to jump him, his call be damned.

"Text me when you get home," he murmured, his eyes glued to her lips, his breathing as irregular as hers felt.

She nodded, hypnotized, and left, her knees shaking the whole way out to her car.

When she got home, she picked it up to find messages from her friends and sisters waiting. She texted them that she was okay, then texted Lucas that she made it home, and immediately opened up the photo sharing app to see the post for herself.

Kate was standing, proudly showing a sonogram and grinning broadly as Harold kissed her flat stomach.

I can't begin to describe how excited I am to share with you that Harold and I are going to be parents! said the caption to the photo. *It feels surreal, but we couldn't be more thrilled to welcome our little one into the world. I can hardly wait to see Harold as a dad. He will be amazing.*

A plethora of ridiculous hashtags followed, but Julia slid her finger on the screen and the post disappeared. Anger boiled her blood. She most likely would have said similar words, if she'd been the one expecting Harold's baby. Her stomach seized at the thought.

She resisted the urge to gag as her phone buzzed in her hand and she saw Harold's name slide in at the top of her screen. She clicked the message.

Harold: Just wanted to check on you after our announcement today.

Of course he would. Motherfucker.

Harold: I know things are hard these days for you, but hang in there.

She threw the phone against the wall. The glass screen shattered. Immediate regret washed over her, and she got up and cleaned before she went to bed.

10

Julia knew, as the next days came and went, that she needed to stay busy so she didn't lose her mind. The messages from old friends kept coming, the comments and the pity. It pissed her off, and it made that uncomfortable, oily thing inside her move.

She hadn't been able to keep herself from looking at social media, to see what else Harold and Kate were posting. It was like the one post had given them permission to talk about the pregnancy incessantly. And Julia could not look away. The first thing she did when she set up her new phone was go back on social media to check.

She was obsessed with the punishment, the anger, and the jealousy.

Lucas texted her that weekend about getting together. He'd been at Nowhere the previous night. Helena had posted pictures on social media about it, and Julia realized that it bothered her to not be included. Everyone else was there, and Julia had instead spent the night torturing herself. But maybe it was for the best when her gut writhed with magic every time she got angry.

When Lucas arrived, she was putting on some socks. He'd specifically asked her to wear comfortable shoes, and when she'd argued against it, told her that she could wear whatever she wanted but to trust him. So she was doing that. Trusting him.

Damn the man and his agreeable nature making her wonder things she should not be wondering about. She opened the door and found him wearing the most casual clothes she'd seen him wear yet. Black jeans and t-shirt, black shoes, and tattoos in full display on his arms.

"Hello." He smiled.

She swallowed, heaviness swirling in her gut.

"Are you okay?" he asked when she didn't move.

"Yeah, of course." Sitting on the little bench by the door, she pulled on her leather lace-up boots, which were shiny and black as her own stretchy slacks.

"Ready?" he asked as she stood again.

"As I'll ever be." When they were in the car, she asked, "Where are you taking me?"

He grinned, his eyes glowing. "You'll see."

She looked at him sideways, suspicion rising. "Wait a damn minute."

But he refused to tell her until they were parked at the front of the one-story building.

"Ax-throwing?" she deadpanned.

He nodded and looked so proud her heart did a three-sixty in her chest.

"I come here when I'm stressed," he said.

"Who said I'm stressed?"

One of his brows shot up.

"That transparent?" she asked.

"I'd be upset too," he said.

Her first instinct was to deflect, but she found herself breathing deeply instead. There was no getting away from hard topics with Lucas.

"I don't know why it bothers me," she confessed. "I don't want to be with Harold."

"I don't think that matters. It's the history."

She paused, telling herself she shouldn't say it. "I lied about stopping my birth control. Isn't that terrible?" Her eyes were glued to his face as what she said registered.

"That you avoided having a baby with him?" He frowned. "I don't see what's wrong with that."

"I lied to my partner about it. Some would say that's reprehensible."

"If you had to lie about taking birth control, I think the issue's much bigger than the lie."

"Has someone ever lied to you like that?" she asked, perhaps because she needed to not be the only one whose entire life had been a lie.

"Yeah." When her brows rose, he added, "Not the same situation, of course, but I thought I was going to spend my life with someone who ended up sleeping with someone else."

Why it shocked her so much, she didn't know. Maybe because he was… well, him. Gorgeous, intelligent, and also kind and understanding. In what world was this man someone who got cheated on?

"It makes you feel crazy," he said. "Wondering what you did wrong, ruminating what you'd do differently to avoid it."

Julia looked out the window, thinking she should start listening to Mariana, because she'd been saying all along that Harold cheating wasn't about her.

"Well, fuck," she said, turning to him.

"Fuck indeed. Let's go throw some axes."

They walked in together, and it didn't escape her that he opened all doors for her when he could manage. Some considered it old fashioned and unnecessary, but she liked it. Inside the place, there was music playing, and there were dozens of people playing and laughing. The sound of axes hitting wooden targets reached her ears, above the music, which was louder than Julia was used to in a public place that wasn't Nowhere. She felt a surge of excitement as she listened to the safety briefing by the young woman attending them. She was cute, a redhead, and she was eyeing Lucas like she'd never seen anyone so beautiful before.

Same, girl. Same.

The girl left, throwing Lucas a look as she rounded the corner to go back to the front desk. Julia could have laughed, but Lucas looked oblivious.

Julia took a step forward, taking hold of an ax and standing in front of the target, a white and blue series of concentric circles ending with a bright orange dot in the center.

Lucas stood to her side as she looked back, checked that no one was behind her, and lifted the ax above her head in the way the young attendant had shown them. Something about it sent thrills through her chest; its weight, maybe. She stepped forward and flicked her wrist, letting go of the ax. Stepping back, she watched as it embedded itself into the wooden target with a satisfying thud.

It was exhilarating.

And even more exciting was Lucas's reaction. His mouth was open as he looked at her ax. Then he threw his head back and laughed heartily.

"What?" she asked, wondering if she'd done it wrong.

"I can't believe you got it to stick."

A little befuddled, she put her hands on her hips. "Is it supposed to be hard?"

His laughter turned into a snort, and he slapped his hand on his knee.

"I couldn't get mine to stick at all at first," he said when he finished laughing. "It took me a few times."

"Are you serious?" He was pulling her leg.

"Like a rattlesnake bite." He brought his hand up, like he was a scout. She laughed and watched him grab his ax and throw it so it landed right next to hers. He turned to her with a grin.

"Not so bad at it now," she said, something sparking inside her, though she couldn't name it.

"I told you I come here when I'm stressed."

"And are you stressed often, or…" They went to get their axes and walked back.

"Sometimes," he said, his smile lopsided. She struggled to take her eyes off him, but turned and threw the ax again, having it land right in the center. When she was stepping away to allow him his turn, there was a sparkle in his eye, and she realized the feeling spreading through her. Competition. It zinged through her, the need to show off, to make him see how capable she could be. Lucas threw his ax and again it landed next to hers.

Feeling a little reckless, she asked, "Care for a wager?" They pulled out the axes from the wooden target and walked back.

"What did you have in mind?" His expression was one of pure interest. So he was competitive too. Good.

"Every legal move possible, whoever's closest to the center gets a point."

His eyes sparkled with the challenge. "Loser buys dinner." He held out his hand. She took it with a smirk. "You're going down, Candela."

"Get ready to be humiliated," she said, narrowing her eyes at him. They were close, so much that she felt his breath on her face. His pupils were blown wide.

"I can hardly wait," he said, sending a rush of warmth through her.

Nope, she hadn't made that up at all. He was flirting with her. Wishing she knew what to say to make him feel the way he made her feel, she stepped back. She lifted the ax, resting its back against her shoulder.

Julia turned toward the target, acutely aware that he was watching her. She lifted the ax above her head, and splitting her stance, let the weapon fly through the air. It landed with a thud almost in the center. She turned to him with a smug smile, gesturing for him to take his turn.

His canines glinted at her as she took his place. As he was facing away from her now, she allowed herself to admire the way his arms flexed as he pulled the ax over his head. When his ax landed straight in the center, he turned with a grin a mile wide.

"Oh, it's on," she said as they walked over to get their axes.

"It wasn't on before?" he teased.

She bumped him with her shoulder, drawing a laugh. Two more rounds, and they were tied. Julia surprised even herself when it happened, since she'd never done this particular activity before.

"Damn, I have my work cut out of me," Lucas said after he threw his ax and it landed on the outermost circle of the target.

Julia narrowed her eyes at him. "You're not being bad on purpose, are you?"

"Why would I do that when I get a free dinner out of winning?"

She crossed her arms and stared as they reached the target to pick up their axes again. It was a workout, walking back and forth, pulling the weapons from the wood.

"What?" he challenged, crossing his arms across his hard expanse of chest. She forced her eyes to stay on the upper half of his face.

"You better not be," she said after a hard swallow, heat rising to her cheeks.

"Or what?" He leaned forward a fraction.

"I might get mad at you."

"Scary." He mimed shivering. She felt the tug of a laugh behind her cheeks. "Be sure to make it hurt."

Her breath caught, and sweat broke down her back when he reached to unembed her ax from the target. She took it from him and walked ahead of him, maybe swaying her hips a little more than normal. Arms screaming from the unusual amount of exercise, she sent her ax flying again before she did something stupid.

Four more rounds later, her arms were trembling from overworking her muscles. When he hit the center of the target again, she let her shoulders slump in defeat.

"I want to force myself to keep going just to erase that smirk off your face," she grumbled as they headed out of the noisy building. The sun was starting to set as they got into his car moments later.

"Hey, you had me sweating there for a minute."

"Don't patronize me, Dolores."

He pressed a hand to his chest and mock-gasped. "I could never."

Fighting a smile, she pulled out her phone, and found the website to her favorite Mexican restaurant in the city.

"A bet is a bet," she said, fighting back a smile. She pulled out her phone and opened a browser. "How do you feel about Mexican?"

"One of my favorites."

She found the website for her favorite Mexican restaurant.

"Preferences, allergies?" she asked.

"None at all. I love everything."

"That's impossible."

"Never tried anything I didn't like." He grinned at her briefly before turning back to the road.

She stared at his profile for a few beats, then turned back to her phone. "You're in for a treat then."

She added her favorite items to the cart; a Oaxaca and carne asada quesadilla, carnitas tacos, a torta, and enchiladas verdes, several types of drinks to share, and even dessert. She was starved.

They stopped to pick up the food, which was ready when they got there, and headed to her house. Instead of sitting at the dining table, they sat on the floor of the living room with all the containers between them.

She learned that he liked spicy foods and handled his spice well. That, and he ate like it was his last meal on earth. He commented on everything he ate, even ranked it, and she found it adorable.

"Is there anything you won't eat, for real?" she asked as she finished swallowing her last bite of a taco.

"None. I like everything." The tips of his fingers slipped between his lips, his pink tongue darting out, and her eyes following the movement.

Internally, she was fanning herself vigorously. Externally, she just took a drink of agua de tamarindo and hoped it didn't show on her face.

"I don't like intestines," she told him.

"That's because you haven't had them cooked right."

"I'll take your word for it."

He grinned. "Thank you for dinner. That was delicious."

"You did win our bet, so I guess it's only fair I treat you to the good stuff."

"I like making wagers with you." He reached for the containers and started putting things away, and she joined him. In the kitchen, she put leftovers in the fridge as he washed his hands. It was a small kitchen, so they were very close, and there was his scent again, and that presence about him that calmed her so much and simultaneously made her skin erupt in goosebumps.

She cleared her throat unnecessarily as he finished drying his hands on the white kitchen towel on the counter.

"How do you feel?" he asked.

Flustered. "Fine. Maybe I should listen to my therapist when she says that exercise helps your mental health."

"It can, as long as you're not trying to punish yourself with it."

"What good is it if I can't punish myself?" Sad part was that she believed that to a certain extent. She used to work out because she had a need to be small. People expected that from a woman in her former position. Now she was small but weak, not solid like before, and come to think of it, she didn't want either of those things. The rigid discipline of her gym experience was miserable back then and seemed like it would be miserable now.

"Maybe yoga," he supplied, and she was left with the distinct impression that he'd read her mind.

"How do you do that?" she asked, perplexed.

"Do what?"

"Don't waste my time, Dolores," she said flatly.

"Wow, you're last-naming me? Must be serious."

"I'm very serious about my time." *Used to be. I have nothing to do now.*

"Maybe what you need is to waste time on purpose."

"I'm already wasting a ton of time these days."

"But you feel guilty about it."

She put her hands on her hips and his eyes went there. Trying not to squirm at the warmth that came to his gaze, she said, "You have to stop reading me like this."

"I'm not reading you at all," he said. "I will always ask before I do that."

"So I'm just that predictable and pathetic?"

"You're everything but."

She opened her mouth, but closed it when no words came to her brain right away.

"I know you don't believe me," he said, "but I'm serious."

"You're only saying that to be nice," she told him, convinced she was right. How would he know how pathetic she actually was?

"I'm not nice."

She rolled her eyes and went back to the living room, reaching into the wooden box on the coffee table. "Do you mind if I…?" She showed him the joint.

"Be my guest."

"I'd offer, but you have to drive." Julia lit the tip of the joint and took a long drag, then held her breath. She opened the window and blew the smoke outside.

Lucas moved forward, his eyes on hers the entire time, and took the joint from her fingers.

"You forget I have magical powers," he murmured and brought the joint to his lips. He didn't look away from her once as he inhaled, blew it out into the night, and handed her the joint back.

Julia didn't move away fast when their fingers brushed, and she didn't look away either. It was like the joint had its effect faster than normal, or it was Lucas and that magnetic thing he had. Music started playing somewhere, but she wasn't sure if it was in her house or in her head. He put his hand forward, and she took it, leaving the joint on the windowsill. Pulling her body toward him, he led her around the room in dance, her foot between his, their bodies swaying together. It was the first time there was no anxiety preceding it. The lights dimmed above them, maybe by magic, she wasn't sure, and the bass of the song created a rhythm so intimate it brought a flush to her face. And still, she couldn't look away from him.

"When was the last time you closed your eyes and saw stars, Julia?"

What the hell kind of poetic shit was that? She tried to step back, but he held her secure to his body, and her heart skipped a beat. In perfect synchrony, they avoided the furniture around them as they moved to the music.

"I don't even know how to answer that," she said.

"When did you last choose yourself?"

She kept moving with him, hypnotized. "When I left Harold."

"He didn't deserve you."

"You didn't know me back—"

"He didn't deserve you," he repeated, making her snap her mouth shut.

Soft and gooey on the inside, she put her face to his shoulder, dancing on the balls of her feet.

"When I was sick, I had this lucid dream." She wasn't sure why she was telling him this. She hadn't told anyone about it. "My mom and sister were alive. Roselyn had kids, and I never married Harold. I felt peace there, as if those things never happened to me. My dad wasn't in it. I didn't see him or think of him more than a couple of times, just wondering what kind of life he had. Then I woke up and you were there."

Julia looked up at his face and found compassion in his eyes.

"Yours was the first face I saw, and I remember thinking that maybe you came to…"

His expression shuttered for a moment, as if he was remembering something painful.

"If the void had progressed more…" he started, but trailed off. She knew what he was going to say, though. She'd heard about it from Sophia; that Grey and Lucas had once had to be the bridge between life and death for hundreds of witches until they found the cure.

"You know why I distance myself from Sophia?"

Lucas nodded with a slight grimace. "You feel guilty."

"I do."

"Why?"

"Because my dad killed Grey's," she told him. Lucas had to understand that her self-loathing wasn't unfounded. It didn't matter that her mom and Will, Grey's dad, had been in love with one another since they were kids. The fact was that her father had convinced himself that her mom had been cheating and killed her. Just like that.

Mariana called it projection, since Julia's father had been sleeping with other women for the entire duration of his marriage to her mother.

It was so bizarre.

"Grey doesn't hate you, Julia."

"He should."

"Why? You didn't do anything. You were a kid." He stopped moving and searched for her eyes with his, his neck bent forward so she felt his breath on her skin. "Those are not your sins."

It would be nice if she remembered that when she was alone and trying her damndest to self-destruct. But at that moment, she didn't want to think about that. She wanted to close the rest of the distance between their lips. They were so close, his lips so plump and pink she wanted to bite one. Wrap her hands around his neck and push him to the sofa, have her wicked way with him. She could blame it on the fact that she was high, until she remembered that he was too, and she didn't know how much. It was like a bucket of tepid water had been poured on her head.

Consent? Needed. She didn't want another thing weighing on her conscience.

Full of heavy regret, she stepped back from him, missing the way his hands felt on her body, and turned back to her window and her joint.

"Sometimes I wish you had been the angel of death," she told him after a long silence. He came to stand beside her by the window and plucked the joint from her hand.

He took a long, deep drag and let it out slowly. "I'm glad I didn't have to be," he said, his voice deeper now.

After he left, his words continued to echo around her.

11

One week later, Julia sat in Mariana's office, which was warm and cozy despite the rainy and moody weather outside. She hadn't seen Lucas since the last time at her house. He'd been traveling, apparently—something about his sister needing help. She hadn't pried, though she'd wanted to.

And as soon as he was gone, the nightmares returned with a swift vengeance. Each time she closed her eyes, she was back in the attic. This time, the blood reached her waist, and she always ended up burning the entire house, just to wake up relieved that it wasn't true. She was holding on to the house. To all of it.

"Tell me about them," Mariana said softly, her pen and notepad in her hands. She had a dress on today, flowing blue with a flower print.

"It's the usual. I don't want to talk about them." She was bored of that same old story. So her subconscious was trying to tell her something; well, until it spoke more clearly she was inclined to not listen. Why was it always the same image? And now the power thing. Okay, so she had magical powers she was learning to use. She couldn't really tell Mariana about that. She would think Julia had lost her mind.

Julia sighed, exhaustion making her shoulders droop.

"What's going through your mind?"

"I've become interested in a man," she told Mariana, then pressed her lips together. She hadn't meant to say anything, but what the hell. "He's good-looking, and kind, and I don't know how to handle myself around him."

"What do you mean by handle yourself?" Mariana made a note.

"He throws me off." She thought about that last time she'd seen him, how tempted she'd been to kiss him. But she'd been a coward and stepped away and then punished herself for days looking at Kate's profile. The woman was posting multiple times a day about her amazing experience with pregnancy, and Julia was watching every post like her life depended on it.

"Can you tell me more about why it feels that way?" Mariana asked.

"He does this thing where he quiets my mind before I can even realize what he's doing. It's like…"

"Like what?"

Julia looked up at Mariana.

"Magic." Julia's voice was almost inaudible, and she peered at Mariana, watching for a reaction. But Mariana nodded, as if it made all the sense in the world, and Julia allowed herself to breathe normally. "And it's bad to see him like that. He's…" He's supposed to be helping me with my magical power, and it's working because the damn thing hasn't surfaced since I started seeing him. And worst of all, he seems to be attracted to me too, unless I'm making that up. Wouldn't be surprising.

But of course, she couldn't say that to Mariana either. Instead, she said, "It's best to keep my distance from him."

"Why?"

"Because…" Julia shrugged defensively. "Harold and Kate are moving on and I was spiraling until…"

Mariana waited, then said, when Julia didn't continue, "Until the new man came along."

"Yes, and what does that mean about me?"

"It means you're willing to open up to someone after everything you've been through," Mariana said, her tone gentle. "I think that's really wonderful."

"You say that, but if you knew him, you'd see it."

"See what?"

"That there's too much I need to work on still before I can even think about being with someone else."

Mariana smiled a little. "I think you're being very hard on yourself."

"That's nothing new," Julia muttered.

"All I'm saying is you can have fun in the process of healing. If being around this man makes you feel good, why not let it happen?"

"That's all it takes, feeling good?"

"Sometimes, yes."

Julia thought about it for a moment. They'd just have to see about that. Not that it was even a sure thing that Lucas would want more with Julia. He, more than anyone else, save Mariana, knew exactly how fucked up she was.

"And besides," Mariana said as they were ending the session, having spoken about it more, "sometimes being intimately close to another human can help us regulate. As long as their energy matches yours."

"Is that what the kids call it now?"

Mariana laughed, and with a promise to see each other soon, Julia left. She'd just pulled into the garage when she got the call from Stephen about the building. Immediately, she dialed Sophia.

"Is Victoria around you right now?" Julia asked as soon as Sophia answered. Victoria came to the phone, so Julia told them the good news. "We got the building."

Squeals came from the other end. Julia held the phone away from her ear, laughing at the sounds of happiness from her sister and friend.

"We have to celebrate," Victoria yelled. "Tonight, we'll toast with champagne and eat amazing food together. What do you say, Jules?"

Julia didn't even think about it. Of course she was going to celebrate with them. This was huge, everything they'd wanted, and she was very much a part of it. So, she was going to get dressed, and she was going to go out tonight.

Later, when she'd showered and done her makeup, just a simple cat-eye and nude lips, she pulled on a black bodysuit that was a little lower on the neckline than was normal for her. Dark blue slacks molded to her body, and she pulled on a pinstripe blazer, as the club could be chilly. Her hair was pulled back into a sleek bun at the base of her neck, and she opted for delicate gold jewelry and a black clutch and heels.

She called a rideshare and arrived at Nowhere right before the show was to start. Walking through the front doors for a change, she searched for Sophia among the crowd. The theme tonight was apparently opulence, because everything was sparkling with what looked like thousands of strung diamonds; on the walls, on doorways, and as tall curtains all over the stage. A celebration indeed.

Julia grinned, feeling the electric excitement of the club as everyone waited for Helena to come out. It was always a treat to watch her sing, the way she bewitched everyone. Julia found Sophia and Victoria in one of the big tables across from the stage. One of the best seats in the house, which was nice. What was the point of having this place, these singers and musicians, if not to enjoy it every once in a while too?

Julia greeted everyone, including Thomas and Grey.

"Congratulations on the acquisition," Grey said with a crooked smile.

She couldn't help the grin that stretched over her face, and she chatted with him and Thomas about the building and how exciting it was. Between Grey and Victoria, Sophia gestured happily every time she talked. It allowed Julia to relax further, knowing that everyone was happy and here to have a good time.

"Have we ordered any food?" she shouted above the music.

"No, we're waiting for Lucas," Victoria said, then looked up. "Oh there he is."

Julia's stomach rolled, and she twisted in her seat to watch Lucas walk toward them with a smile on his face. He looked as good as ever, those golden eyes glowing in the low lights of the club. He wore black and gray checkered pants and a button-up in a deep blue, and took the seat right next to her. At that moment, Amy came from the back and took a seat on the other side of Lucas, her eyes already on the stage as the lights went even lower.

"How was Puerto Rico?" she asked. It surprised her how glad she was to see him, and found herself looking forward to whatever happened tonight.

"Hot." The way he said that, how his eyes dipped to follow the deep vee of her top, made her flush all over. She was reminded of Mariana's words that morning.

Before she could say anything at all, the show started as Evan, the guitarist, took the stage to announce Helena. The excitement was palpable now, even for Julia, who could feel Lucas's presence beside her like a furnace. Before she knew it, two dancers were flying over the stage in their intricate outfits. Crystals and vines swung around them as they moved their bodies to the sultry song overhead. When those two were done, a solo dancer came out. Next to her, Amy looked riveted, eyes locked on the stage. Julia imagined she tried to see any failings of the costumes she'd provided for the show. If Julia knew anything about Amy, no wardrobe malfunctions would come to pass.

As the dancer finished her routine, no issues in sight, the stage went completely dark and Helena's voice rang through the club.

People whooped and cheered as she began without a backing track, her powerful voice soft at first, in a pretty, rounded place in her range. Not that Julia knew much about singing, but she'd heard Sophia and Grey geek out about it enough that she sort of got it.

Helena walked out from the back of the stage to the spotlight placed for her in the center of it, surrounded by crystal curtains as she moved her body to the rhythm of the song. Her voice was smooth and never faltered or hesitated. It was like listening to a recording. Helena's dress was a bright red, cinched at the waist and opening at her hips, reaching toward the floor. Her hair was tied back into an elegant chignon, curls around her gorgeous face. Her red lips opened into a final note, something Julia would struggle to sound human with if she ever tried. Cheers and screams erupted from the crowd as the music swiftly turned into a different tune. The crystal curtains retracted toward the sides as two dancers came out and pulled at the skirt of Helena's dress, which turned into a catsuit in the same shade of red. It looked to be made of almost entirely red crystals, and it molded itself to Helena's fit figure. She was barefoot, dancing with her two dancers, her microphone in hand. When she brought the mic to her mouth, she could have just been standing there. Her breathing was perfectly calm for her singing, nothing seemed hard. Even Julia was panting by the end of it and she wasn't even moving.

"She's amazing, isn't she?" Lucas leaned close to her ear, and Julia turned to look into his luminous eyes. He was right there, and a flash of light from the stage lit up his face for a moment, showing her the expression on his face. Eyes half-lidded, lips parted…

"Incredible." She let her eyes slide to his lips, then back up to his eyes. His pupils widened.

Feeling bold, Julia.

She turned back to the stage, watching her friend but hearing almost nothing now that all her attention was trapped by a certain man who smelled like absolute sin. As the music swelled and trailed off, the crowd went wild, and when people started to stand, Julia did too. Beside her, Lucas was on his feet as well, his arm brushing hers. She told herself it was a terrible idea, but Julia still leaned into him a little more. Helena spoke into the mic and started talking to the audience, as she often did. People absolutely loved her sense of humor and immeasurable talent.

"Excuse me," someone said, and Lucas stepped behind her as he got out of the server's way. She almost felt his shadow press up against her, but Lucas wouldn't do that unless he knew that she wanted it. Julia fought the urge to fan herself. There was something very hot about that.

Soon, back in their seats, a server showed up with several platters of the new foods in the provisional menu. It was an incredible spread: mofongo with shrimp, rice and gandules, tostones, stewed chicken, and fried sweet plantains. Julia's mouth watered, her stomach rumbling.

She ate and chatted with everyone as the band started playing, and a dancer came out as Helena exited the stage.

"You were right," she said to Sophia over the music, which had turned lively. "This is all incredible. People are going to demand this be permanent."

"I've had a lot of good feedback." Sophia grinned. "What do you think, Lucas? Is the mofongo to your standards?"

"I'm very impressed," he said with a huge smile, eyes sparkling.

There was no one more appealing than Lucas Dolores, Julia concluded, but her attention was pulled away from him to Sophia. Her sister was frowning as one of her managers said something in her ear.

"What's going on?" Julia asked as Sophia got on her feet, her expression thunderous.

"I'll be right back," she said and disappeared through the front doors.

Julia watched Victoria excuse herself too. Now she was curious.

"I'm going to see," she said to no one in particular. She didn't stop to see if anyone even heard her. Julia went to the doors and heard the arguing before she walked through the threshold.

"What the hell?" she muttered, and when her eyes focused on the commotion, she froze. Her brain refused to think, whirling like it was on one of those spinning tires in playgrounds. It didn't make any sense at all. Harold and Kate were in the lobby, Harold's face red. Sophia stood in front of him with her fists clenched.

"Oh my God," Kate squealed, as if it was insane that Julia would be at Nowhere. The question was why the fuck were Kate and Harold there? "You look amazing."

Julia couldn't even open her mouth to respond. Any moment, her nervous system would catch up and react, but for now, she stood there absolutely numb as Kate came forward slightly, before Harold grabbed her arm and made her stop. She was glowing, her blonde hair buttery and perfect around her.

Harold's face split into an ugly grin, his sharp blue eyes like lasers on Julia.

"How are you?" Kate asked, and Julia remembered she was there. Lord, what was happening to her?

"You need to leave," Victoria growled.

"What's going on?" Julia whispered and Victoria turned to her, but her eyes looked beyond Julia.

"Mami."

Julia turned to see Lucas right behind her. Mami? What was happening?

"Who's this?" Kate's bright eyes were on Lucas. And so were Harold's.

Julia stepped back and collided with Lucas softly. His hand automatically caught her waist and her breath shivered out of her, and deep inside, she relished in the way Harold's eyes flashed with anger.

"That's none of your damn business," Victoria snapped, walking forward to stand in front of Kate. "If you don't leave right now, I'll call the cops."

Harold's lips practically disappeared, his jaw tight. Julia knew that look well.

"This is rich, Sophia," he snapped, "refusing me entry into your club."

Julia went to move, violence rushing through her veins, but Lucas held her back firmly.

"This is a private business," Julia snarled, and she didn't even hear whatever Harold said before security stepped forward and forced him outside. She wanted to follow him and Kate, give them a piece of her mind. But she was back inside the club instead, Lucas leading her toward the employee entrance. She could hear her breath in her ears.

"What the hell?" she demanded as soon as they were in the long hallway. It was bright but empty, and she continued toward the back door, adrenaline rushing through her. Cool air hit her face. It'd started to rain again.

Lucas came after her moments later, the door slamming behind him. He glanced down at her, looking innocent.

"What was that?" she snapped.

"What was what?"

"A penis contest?" She was shaking all over. "I didn't think you could stoop that low."

"What the hell are you talking about, Julia?" He was frowning down at her, his features dark and tight.

"You and Harold out there sizing each other up."

She could see his features well, from the couple of lights in the parking lot. His expression softened a little.

"I came after you right after you left, and when I saw Kate, I didn't really think."

"You didn't have to do that." She couldn't bring herself to thank him, though she'd used him too. Goddamnit.

"I know I didn't," he said. "All I know is that Kate affects you."

He had a point, but fuck him for bringing it up anyway.

"I'm not talking about my ex-husband and his mistress-turned-mother-of-his-child with you."

"I didn't ask you to. You're the one ranting." His voice rose a little. It was the first time she'd gotten him truly annoyed with her.

Oh. Why did it feel like that? Thrilling.

"And you don't have to come save me as if I'm incapable of handling myself." Her heart was racing. She could feel it in her throat as she watched the color rise to his cheeks, darkening them slightly.

"I never said you can't handle yourself."

"But you still had to come up calling me Mami and for what? To make Harold jealous or something?" To confuse her more than she already was?

"I already told you that I intended to come between you and your ex-best-friend. I didn't even register Harold right away."

Harold definitely registered Lucas immediately.

She crossed her arms and looked up at him. He looked perfectly sincere, and she didn't even know why she was so upset in the first place. She was glad he'd come when he had. The last thing she wanted was to see Harold or Kate, let alone having to talk to them. What they were doing at Nowhere, she didn't know, but she was infinitely glad Sophia and Victoria had obviously banned him.

Swallowing her pride, she looked down at their shoes. His were shiny black. "Thanks, I suppose."

He gasped mockingly. "My god, it's like I just watched you expand in real time."

She slapped his arm playfully and rolled her eyes. "Well, shut me up."

Lucas stepped forward, his body blocking the warm light from a streetlamp. Her heartbeat was in her ears now, and she could barely take a full breath, as nerves tightened her stomach.

"I have a method for that," he muttered.

She tried to swallow, but her throat was dry and sticky.

"Are you going to ask me for consent?"

"Yeah," he breathed.

A flutter of nerves made her pause for a split second before she grabbed his collar and pulled his mouth toward hers. His teeth bit her bottom lip sharply, and she sucked in air. The heavy heat that descended on her concentrated between her legs as his hands gripped her waist.

Lucas kissed like his mouth was made exclusively for it. Hungry, deep, like he wanted to consume her whole. He tasted sweet and spicy, and she simply couldn't get enough. A moan escaped her when he pushed her against the brick wall by the door and pressed himself against her. Bright headlights pointed straight at them, and she unglued herself from him as his hand rested on the wall beside her head. The car drove off, but the moment was broken. She reached for the door and stepped away. Lucas didn't make a move to stop her, but she almost wanted him to. Acutely aware of his presence behind her, she rushed back to their table, hearing his footsteps near. Her lips, and other parts, pulsed as she sat and went back to watching the show. Pretending that nothing happened nearly killed her. She knew what Lucas tasted like now, and her eyes looked but saw nothing for the rest of the night.

Julia was aware of Helena joining them for the rest of the night, after her show was over, but she couldn't concentrate long enough to have any clue what anyone was talking about.

On her way home, she got a text from Lucas.

Lucas: Come to Latin Night.

She thought about it all the way home, but before she went to bed, she texted back.

Julia: I'll see you there.

And despite the ecstatic anticipation, the knot in her stomach, she slept deeply that night, and even forgot about her trusty joint.

12

Julia woke up early and left to meet with Amy at her shop. It had been a while since she'd worried, fretted, about what to wear to Latin Night. It was so stupid. Damn Lucas for making her worry about stuff that shouldn't matter at all. She liked her clothes… for the most part.

She waited in her car for Amy to arrive at the boutique. Candela was an exclusive little store Amy had started a couple of years before that started as an online boutique. The brick and mortar store, despite Julia's recommendation not to open it, actually did very well, due to Amy's eye for design. If only Amy used her own designs now, that would be perfect. Julia had no idea what her sister was waiting for.

Amy arrived a half an hour after their appointment, carrying two coffee cups, one of which she gave to Julia. She looked… radiant. Amy's skin glowed like she had a light under it, like Sophia had looked the other day when she'd come out of the backroom with Grey.

Julia narrowed her eyes as they went through the doors, and Amy turned on the lights.

"Did you have sex?" Julia asked far too loudly, and Amy turned to her with wide eyes.

"What makes you ask that?" But there was a sly little smile in there that all but confirmed it to Julia.

"I didn't know you were dating anyone."

"Who says I have to be dating to be having sex?"

Julia sipped the coffee. A little sweet, but it would do.

"Good point," she said.

"Is it bad that I'm having sex?" Amy asked, the picture of innocence.

"So you *are*."

Amy shrugged and said nothing else on the matter. She turned to Julia, her blue eyes bright and clear. Her dark hair was up in a messy thing on top of her head.

"Well, seems like everyone's having it but me," Julia grumbled.

She honestly didn't know how to feel about it anymore. The flirting with Lucas was getting to her. And then he'd gone and kissed her like it was the end of the world and it was the only thing he wanted to do before he went.

God, she was so dramatic.

But she was a woman who hadn't had sex in far too long. And her last sexual escapade had been… fine. Stephen had been good enough and pleasant. That Julia hadn't orgasmed wasn't his fault, and he'd been nice.

Ugh, how sad was that? A man was nice to her after sex and she was giving him props even though he didn't do anything for her. She really did have a lot to work through.

One kiss from Lucas and she forgot why she didn't go to Latin Nights. But, as Mariana said, it wasn't wrong to allow herself to have fun. She had fun with Lucas.

"What are you thinking?" Amy asked as she moved into the space more, turning on bright overhead lights as she went. There were a few dresses on stylish racks against the wall, and some mannequins in different shapes and sizes showcasing some of the best designs Amy carried.

Suddenly insecure, Julia wiped her sweaty palms on her jeans. Amy cocked her head, eyes narrowed.

"Why are you so worried about how you dress all of a sudden?"

"What? I can't buy a dress?" *Defensive.* Amy noticed, too. "I can buy a dress Amy, and for no reason other than I want to."

Amy crossed her arms. "Do you actually think I was born yesterday?"

Julia deadpanned. "Yes, Amy. That's exactly it. You're a brand new baby."

Amy's eyes narrowed slightly. "Are you into someone?"

The question took Julia by surprise and she opened her mouth to deny it. Rolling her eyes, she snapped it shut and sighed.

Amy smirked. "If this is about Lucas, I don't blame you."

"Who said this is about him?"

Amy's stylishly thick brow rose. "You're telling me you haven't looked?"

"Please, have you seen the man?" She pressed her lips together to stop herself from blabbing to Amy about the kiss. "But this is about me, really." Partly true.

"Okay, what were you thinking?"

"I realized that I don't have things that make me feel sexy."

"You looked sexy last night," Amy said.

"Thanks, but I mean really sexy stuff. Something I haven't tried before."

"You have excellent taste, let me start there. But a little more color wouldn't kill you. Maybe a slit here and there. And cleavage. You have great boobs."

Julia automatically brought her hands to her small boobs. She didn't have a lot, but it wasn't nothing. Amy and Sophia were the lucky ones there.

"Do you have anything with a slit?" she asked her sister, not even sure if she wanted a slit. She wasn't that daring. Cleavage here and there was okay, or a nude back, but the slit thing… what if it moved too much and people saw things they shouldn't?

And if she was going to dance, then she needed to be careful. These were all things that raced through her head as Amy pulled out a few pieces for her. All were jewel tones, the perfect marriage of vibrant, sophisticated, and sexy. Her eyes went to a tea-length dress, silk with a slit that would definitely be a little bit too much. The chest plunged in a deep v-neck with spaghetti straps criss-crossing in the back. It was incredible. Not something Julia had in her closet, for sure.

"Amazing," she whispered, touching the soft material.

"Try it on," Amy said, grabbing the emerald green dress and taking it toward the changing rooms. There were only three small rooms, all with tall doors of heavy black wood. Inside one of them, Julia stripped, leaving her own jeans and blouse hanging on brass hooks on the wall. The paint in the dressing room was bright pink, and mirrors surrounded Julia so she could see herself in every angle possible. Her hip bones jutted out a little, but though she lacked muscle tone, she realized she wasn't as skinny as she'd been in the past months. In the past, looking at herself in the mirror meant finding every little flaw and beating her natural curves into submission with vigorous exercise routines and strict diets devoid of carbs. But not anymore; those days were over. She liked that her figure was filling out.

Julia pulled on the dress, and when she looked at her reflection, heat rose from her chest to her neck to her face. The v-shaped cleavage fell right between her breasts, thin straps over her shoulders and crossed at her back, which plunged so low, her current underwear showed at the top a little. And the slit. It was high, close to her hip, and showed her entire leg. Julia fought the urge to tug it shut.

"Amy, I can't possibly wear this," she called, and Amy opened the door and squealed in delight.

"Holy shit."

"Come on, I look ridiculous."

"Are you kidding me?" Amy stood behind Julia. "Look at this color with your skin and hair."

"The slit is so high. I can't go around risking flashing my privates at people."

Amy raised a brow. "Privates? What are you, eight? Call it a pussy."

Julia cringed.

"Oh, grow up." Amy rolled her eyes. "Look at the boobs; perfect amount of cleavage. You look hot."

Julia peeped at her reflection in the full-length mirror. Setting aside her mortification, she could admit that she looked pretty damn good. The silk molded itself to her body shape. It didn't make any sense why she felt like this, like it was wrong to wear something sexy. Julia had never been a prude, but her struggles had turned her into an insecure person, and she hated it.

"It's a lot," she murmured anyway, turning to see how the material flowed over her butt.

"That's the whole point." Amy's blue eyes met hers in the mirror. "Look at yourself. You're beautiful, and you deserve to feel like it."

Julia looked at herself in the dress. Amy was right. It wasn't just about her attraction to Lucas, but how it made her feel to wear something just because she wanted to. She wouldn't keep erasing herself for the comfort of others.

"And," Amy said, gesturing widely, "if you do dress for him, make it so he can't take his eyes off you."

"I can't tell if that's a good idea or not."

"Sex with a hot person?" Amy deadpanned.

Julia sighed impatiently. "You know what I mean. I'm working with him. Isn't that wrong?" But they'd already kissed once, so wasn't that contract void already? And she wasn't paying him anyway. A favor for a friend, he'd called it.

Amy put her hands on Julia's shoulders and turned her around so they were facing each other.

"You're allowed to have fun," she said.

"Fun doesn't have to include sex."

"I'm aware, but if it's on the table, why not?"

Julia closed her eyes for a moment. "He's close to Sophia and Grey. And Helena. And everyone else. Isn't that weird?"

"Why?"

Julia took a fortifying breath. It was like talking to a toddler. "Because of what I just said, Amy."

"This isn't about Lucas, it's about you," Amy said slowly. "About healing and having fun again. And besides, if he's into it, why deny the man the chance?"

Julia thought of Lucas's words the other night, and she swallowed and nodded. Having fun should be a given. So why was Julia so hesitant and anxious to allow herself to let go? She used to have fun once. Right?

God, she really didn't want to pull at that thread.

"Get the dress. It's amazing, and you look incredible," Amy said. "Wear a neutral shadow, a cat eye, and a neutral lip. Just in case." She left, and Julia changed back into her clothes and headed out front.

As Amy was ringing her up, Julia's phone went off, and Sophia's face smiled up at her.

"Sophia, I'm with Amy," Julia said and put the phone on speaker. The two greeted each other.

"I wanted to talk about last night," Sophia said.

Amy made a snarling sound in her throat. "I cannot believe that Harold showed up to Nowhere with his mistress."

"I thought I was hallucinating when I saw them," Julia said. "What the hell was Harold thinking?"

"I don't know, but you should know I've had him on our list since all that shit happened," Sophia said. "This was just the first time they've shown up."

"Sophia, this could be really bad for business." She hadn't even thought about it before now. "Harold is a man of influence."

"Fuck Harold and his goddamned influence," Sophia barked. "He and Kate are banned from Nowhere and any business related to it in perpetuity."

Julia had to hold back a laugh. It wasn't funny, but she felt so loved when her sisters stood up for her. It made her heart roll. Amy put the dress into a black garment bag, which had her logo of a mirror with flames printed in purple. The three of them chatted for a little while longer, but soon, Julia was on her way home. But she couldn't stop thinking about Harold and Kate, and by the time she got home, she was shaky and anxious.

This shit was getting old.

She lit the joint before the window was even open. Phone in her hand, she texted Lucas before she could convince herself it was a bad idea. He'd know what to say to help her calm down. She hoped.

Julia: Hi.

It was such a stupid message, but she didn't know what else to say. His response didn't take too long.

Lucas: Hello.

Even just receiving that simple greeting helped somewhat. She sat on the window, taking another puff.

Lucas: Everything okay?

She bit her lip. Her hands were so shaky, she could barely form a response.

Julia: I think my power's surfacing again.

But she didn't know if it was actually that or if it was just anxiety. The phone rang and she sighed.

"I'm okay," she said as a greeting. "It hasn't happened."

"What triggered it?"

"Sophia banned Harold and Kate from Nowhere."

"As she should."

"But what if he does something against her? Harold's a vindictive ass, and he certainly has the money to keep himself out of trouble."

"Sophia's club is protected by magic."

It shouldn't have shocked her, but it still did. She lit the joint again. Magic.

It was really that easy, huh?

"It is," he mumbled, and her heart jumped.

"You keep doing that."

"Doing what?"

"Reading my mind."

A brief silence, and she felt enthralled. What was it about this man?

"I don't read minds," he said.

Just energy, which was close enough.

She could almost see that smirk she hadn't stopped thinking about. The way his canines were longer than the rest of teeth, making him look like a predator. She shivered, her nipples tight, her mind back on that kiss. For a moment, she felt as if his lips were right there against hers. Julia brought her fingertips to her lips.

"Talk to me," he murmured.

"I still follow them on social media." Maybe she wanted him to realize how pathetic she was. It would make this so much easier to get over; this desire she couldn't stamp down no matter what she did. She was like a yo-yo, she realized. Back and forth, over and over.

"Why?" His tone remained neutral.

"Because I guess I like to punish myself, according to my therapist."

"I'd say so, if you asked me," he said.

"But since I *didn't* ask you—"

"I said nothing. I'm not a therapist, after all."

"Why do I do it to myself?" she asked anyway.

"It's a part of being human."

"To suffer?"

"To get stuck." His words made her put the joint and lighter down between her feet.

"How do I stop caring?" she asked.

"You start by pretending so hard that it comes true eventually."

It drew a little chuckle. "Is it that easy?"

"It would be nice, but no."

If only.

"Not telling you what to do, but maybe it's a good idea to stop following them," he said.

"You're right," she responded automatically.

"Very good."

Her ears filled with the echo of her heart beats. Praise. Hmmm. Julia ran her hand over her feverish neck, all thoughts of her power now gone.

But she had that deep-seated need to mess things up, so she said, "It's not just Kate and Harold, either. Sometimes, I look at mean things people have said about my family online too. I have an alert. How pathetic is that?"

"Pathetic. You say that word a lot."

She was aware.

"We've all been pathetic at some point, but this isn't that," he told her.

"Somehow I can't imagine you being pathetic."

He chuckled. "That opinion might shift if you knew the embarrassing spots I've put myself in."

And now she wanted nothing more than to know what those things were, but she didn't ask.

"Maybe I'll share when I see you at Nowhere," he added.

"You're so sure I'm showing up."

"It's not as scary as it looks."

"Speak for yourself."

"Are you always this argumentative?"

"Always." Not true, but mostly. "Is that a problem?"

"That you're a bossy pain in the ass?"

She barked out a surprised laugh.

"It's not a problem at all," he continued.

"Oh, so you're telling me you don't mind a strong-willed woman? Seems to be a problem for most men out there."

"Oh, believe me, I do not mind one bit." His voice softened, and her face warmed. Other places also warmed, but she was trying really hard not to think about it.

She was going to need a cool shower after this call, that much was evident.

"I'll see you tomorrow night," she said after clearing her throat.

She ran a bath after. It was going to be a long night, but as she went to bed much later, relaxed, she realized what she felt now was anticipation instead of nerves.

13

Nerves flashed through Julia as she pulled the gorgeous green dress over her body. That day, she'd decided to take her time doing things that helped her feel good. A long bath with fragrant salts and oils, careful and thorough hair care, and best of all, her phone on silent. It was the best day she'd had in a while. Amy and Mariana, and everyone else for that matter, were right. It was time she prioritized herself.

As evening approached, she dried and styled her hair in soft waves, as close to her natural texture as she could get it. Looking at her reflection, she smiled, liking what she was seeing. She looked like herself, but something seemed different. A sheen to her skin that had nothing to do with the masque she'd done earlier or the minimal makeup she'd applied.

It was nice.

High, strappy sandals completed the look, along with a spritz of her favorite perfume, something floral, warm, and fresh, and she headed out. She was late, but this was a club. No one said she had to be perfectly on time. Walking in through the back door, she left her small purse in the office and headed toward the floor.

The music was lively, exciting, bright. She walked through tables, crowds of people watching the dance floor. It seemed like every eye was on Lucas as he glided to the rhythm of the music with one of the regulars. Even Julia recognized the woman. Pretty, curvy, and a fantastic dancer.

He was dressed in all black, slacks and a button-up he'd left the first couple of buttons undone on.

He moved like water itself, fluid. It made sense. Him and the music together made sense. The way he rode the waves of melodies, leading his gorgeous partner to do things with her rounded hips that Julia had never done, despite her dance background. Ballroom was great, but it was not like *this*.

Her heart beat so fast, it would have left her body if it could have. In a trance, she moved toward the dance floor, past what seemed like a thousand people. Some were eating, some were singing along, some were drinking. Everyone watched the dancers. There were others around Lucas and his partner, but it was like there was a spotlight on him, showcasing his dancing abilities. He was smiling, saying something to the woman, who laughed.

Something happened. Julia approached a railing, which separated the dining area from the dance floor. She gripped the cool iron tightly when his eyes closed, lost in the music as if it had become a part of him. His partner was practically wrapped around him, her body molded to his.

Julia braced herself against the railing as the churning, boiling feeling inside her only grew as she watched Lucas.

Julia. Was. Jealous.

It hit her so hard, she searched for a seat, but nothing was available, so she stood rooted to the spot and tried not to let it show. It bothered her that he danced with that woman like he'd invited *her* to the club instead of Julia. Lucas only had eyes for his partner, grinned at her, laughed, talked, and twirled her around, just to catch her right after with those long hands.

Yep, she was jealous as *fuck*.

The song ended, and Julia sighed in relief when the woman thanked him with a quick hug and left for her table where she had a group of friends waiting. But immediately after, another person, a man this time, approached him and they took the dance floor like they were meant for it. The fast rhythm of the salsa embedded itself inside her, and it was all she could do not to turn around and go home, so she forced herself to watch him with the shorter, slighter man, as patrons turned to gawk.

Color her confused as all hell.

Julia tried, she really did. Jealousy was unbecoming to everyone—especially her. She didn't pine after a man. And what if he danced with every man or woman or anyone else in that club? That was none of her business.

At all.

It didn't bother her. And it didn't when the song was finished and another woman came up to him.

Wasn't he the belle of the fucking fiesta?

This is why, she berated herself, *you don't get crushes on people, you dumbass.*

But what if she walked up and asked him to dance next? If she got her feet to move through the crowd, strutted toward him, and bewitched him with her scent, the way he did to her.

Two more songs came and went, and she watched him all along, willing herself to move either way—to leave or to go to him. When his eyes found her, warmth radiated from them as they roamed over her body, and his lips parted on a shaky breath. She could see it from here, how it affected him, and her stomach clenched.

Good, she thought. She refused to move from that spot, even as he started moving toward her. But the woman who had been dancing with him last stepped in front of him, grabbing his arm and pulling him into dance with her.

A man appeared next to Julia. Handsome, with brown eyes and skin, and black hair.

"Hi, I'm Enrique," he said with a million-watt smile, holding out his hand. It was rough when she took it, and he smelled incredible.

What kinds of colognes did these Latin men wear? Good Lord.

"Julia," she said, catching sight of Lucas dancing with the woman, but his eyes stared daggers at Enrique's profile. "Would you like to dance?"

Two could play at that game, even if it made her want to die or vomit or both.

"I was about to ask you," Enrique grinned. "I love a confident woman."

Oh, she was not a confident woman, but she was petty, and Lucas's attention was certainly on her now. He'd told her to relax. Cool, she'd relax then.

She allowed Enrique to lead her to the dance floor, and moved to the bachata, even though it felt awkward at first. They soon found their rhythm; Enrique was an excellent dancer, and she ventured to look up at him and laugh when she explained she didn't really dance often.

"You're doing really great." Enrique grinned and turned her around. Every time she turned, or if Enrique pulled her one way or another, she found where Lucas was still with his partner, but his eyes on her. The heat of his gaze lasered through her, made her molten inside. There was sweat trickling down her bare back, for many, many reasons, and one song turned into two with Enrique. He was a wonderful dancer, respectful with his hands roaming nowhere near places that would make her want to punch him in the face. But as the songs changed, despite enjoying herself with him, her heart wasn't in it. Not when the person she'd come here for held another woman close.

"You want to make him really jealous?" Enrique asked, following her gaze. She started to apologize, instantly mortified, but he chuckled. "It's okay. It's obvious you're into each other."

He pulled her further into the dance floor, as the song changed to something a little sultrier. A slower rhythm that sounds like what honey would. She allowed Enrique to pull her closer, unable to look away from his little grin.

"He's watching you," he said. "Well, me, actually."

"Why are you doing this?"

"I don't know." Enrique spun her, then brought her close again. "Your boyfriend is jealous as hell. Maybe I like that. Good for the ego."

"He's . . ." She stopped herself from revealing information that didn't pertain to this stranger. Allowing him to lead her through the rest of the song, she found that she was enjoying herself, so she genuinely laughed when Enrique said something funny. Though, if she was honest with herself at least, it was because Lucas was looking and not because Enrique was particularly funny. And when he spun her twice, three, four times, she leaned into him as the song ended. She held onto him, dizzy, breathless laughter mingling with his as they exited the dance floor.

"Call me if it doesn't work out." Enrique handed her a card, which she took with numb fingers, and then left.

"All done with your friend?"

She turned, card still in hand, to face Lucas, whose face didn't show any turmoil at all, though his eyes flashed.

"Are you?" she retorted, because of course he was going to act like a caveman now that he'd seen her dance with someone else. Even when he started it.

"You were late," he pointed out, even going as far as looking at the heavy watch on his wrist. It was gold and shiny because of course it was.

"I didn't know you were going to take strict attendance."

He sighed deeply as if trying to muster patience.

"No, but if I'm expecting you and you're not here at our agreed time, I reserve the right to dance with whoever I want."

"I didn't say you couldn't." She crossed her arms and looked at him squarely.

"Well, would you like to dance with me now?" He held out his hand. She looked down at his hand, then back at his face. "Please?"

Shivers. Heat. Mouth watering.

Yeah, this was turning her on. Fuck. Something had to be wrong with her.

Julia lifted her hand so he saw the card between her fingers. Now she was just being an asshole.

"I should put this away first," she said, but he reached for the card and pocketed it before she could move.

It was magic, how the moment he pulled her close, her feet moved to their own accord.

"I'd like to be your partner now," he whispered.

"What will all the other people in the club do without their favorite dancer?" she jeered, her mind on the man he'd danced with earlier, wanting and also not wanting to ask for fear of what that meant. Lucas was into her, she wasn't so damaged that she didn't get that, but human sexuality was weird and complicated sometimes.

"I want *you*."

The jealous monster inside her backed away and she melted against him, his scent all she could smell, the hardness of his body against her all she could feel. She didn't get how it felt so natural to be this close, how in sync they were. It was like they'd been dancing this song together all their lives. He didn't let her move away from him at first, their feet intertwined in dance, his knee between her thighs. A twirl, a push, a pull, and she was right back in his arms for a brief moment before being spun away again. The flowing skirt of her dress moved with her like it was an extension of her body, and the slit opened and closed with every step she took. She let it. She didn't care if it came up too high or if someone had something to say about it or her. Not in that moment when all that existed on that dance floor was her and Lucas and the music. There was no one else, and the music swerved around them, between them. She swore there was color, swirling like smoke to the rhythm and cadence of the song. It swelled inside her, and she could almost taste it.

She let out a breath through open lips and found him looking down at her. Blown wide open, his pupils were like a dark sea, and she was glued to him. In her heels she wasn't as short as when they'd danced before, and his leg between hers fit them together like a puzzle. She felt every ridge of his hard body, the bulge pressed against her abdomen that told her that he felt the same way she did.

The song switched, a faster rhythm now, and Julia didn't know how she was doing it, but she'd never danced salsa like this. A smile graced his full lips, and she knew that even if she wanted to, speech wouldn't work right then. They stopped being two people, breathing the same air, their hearts beating to the same rhythm.

And his hands, those soft hands with long fingers, found where the vee at her back ended, and his lips moved. She couldn't quite hear his voice, it was too loud for that, but she swore she could with something other than her ears, and her gaze followed every movement of his mouth.

Words came and left, romantic, sexy words about the dance itself, and her lips dropped open, yearning to sing the same words. Though she couldn't hear his voice, she knew she'd love it anyway. That husky tone he had that sounded just like he smelled, like spiced whiskey and mapacho.

Lucas took her hand and twirled her once, twice, then his hands were at her hips as he twirled her twice more, her dress opening so wide she was sure everyone in that club had seen her entire ass.

Stumbling when she was facing him again, disoriented, her laugh was breathless. He laughed too as the song ended and the DJ said something about a show.

"And you said you couldn't dance to this," he said, his grin brilliant, eyes shining with pure joy.

The black lace panties she'd worn practically melted off her.

Bachata began playing; slow, just a tinkling of piano keys and an echoing voice. She'd thought maybe they were done, that he'd move on and find another partner, but he took her hand and pulled her close again, swaying. When the percussion started, they stayed under the beat, barely taking any steps, their bodies flush.

Heat rushed from the bottoms of her feet as he led her, making her move in ways she didn't know her body could move. Her nipples hardened against his chest, and she swore he knew, because his cheeks darkened. She would melt right there into a puddle on the dance floor. Everyone would know how turned on she was, of course, but Julia couldn't care less. A current of electricity rose from her feet toward him. Pure energy, not her power, something else. It kept coming, exiting her body through her joints as they danced in ways that made her think of other activities. Things that they didn't need any of these fancy clothes for.

Though they weren't the only ones dancing, many eyes were on them, but soon there were enough people that she almost felt cocooned. The crowd kept them closer still, under dim colorful lights. In a turn, one where he didn't loosen his hold on her, his face disappeared into the crook of her neck. His teeth scraped her sensitive skin and she bit her lip to stop herself from moaning. Her stomach was full of fluttering wings as she turned her head, and he paused for a split moment, as if giving her enough time to pull back if she wanted. But she didn't want to. She closed the rest of the distance between them and caught his lips with hers. It was brief, deep, their lips meeting so fully, she tasted every space between. But the song soon ended, and she stepped back before she got suckered into another dance. It was too much; her panties were completely soaked with her arousal.

Wanting someone like she needed her next breath wasn't normal. It couldn't be good.

Desperate. She was desperate.

Turning abruptly, Julia practically ran from the dance floor as the music went into something much louder and livelier. Head down, she tried breathing normally, despite her racing heart, as she reached the employee entrance and went straight toward the dressing rooms at the very back. She didn't feel like herself at all, heels clicking as she rushed down the long corridor. She rounded a corner, where the dressing rooms were at the end of the hall, when the light turned off and a hand caught her arm. The world went into a tailspin until she felt the cool wall at her naked back. A gasp echoed in her ears.

Her own. Chest heaving, throbbing between her legs, she could only stand there as Lucas caressed his way down her arms to grab her hands. There was just enough light from the emergency exit signs that she could make out his features, and his eyes were molten on her. He lifted her hands above her head, pinning her wrists underneath his bigger palm, while his other found her neck.

"Is this okay?" he whispered. Voiceless, she nodded, then moaned when he kissed her. This kiss was perfection, a slide of eager lips and warm tongues, hard breathing and soft moans into each other's mouths.

He tasted how he smelled, like smoke and spice and sex. Teeth scraped her lip, followed by a warm, soothing tongue, the perpetual scruff rough against her soft skin.

The hand holding her wrists fell away.

His hand found the slit of her dress, soft against her thigh, but she took hold of his wrist.

"We shouldn't do this," she whispered, but she didn't mean it.

Still, he took an automatic step back, but she gripped his wrist tighter, unwilling to let him go. It was she who placed his hand on her thigh once again and pulled his lips down for a consuming kiss. Every sane thought she'd ever had made no sense anymore as his fingers found her wet core through her underwear. She reached between them, and the snap of a button was the only sound in the dark hallway, aside from their labored breaths. Her heart was beating so loud, so fast, that anyone in a mile radius would be able to hear.

"Julia," he murmured as her hand sank into his pants and found the hard length of him.

"Is this okay?" she asked, and his mouth opened on a half moan. He nodded.

Her heeled feet left the floor as he lifted her against him, pressing into her body. She held on, her arms around his neck as the graze of his velvety cock had her salivating, his fingers pushing her underwear to the side to expose her.

"Please let me fuck you," he murmured, as music swelled in the distance. She answered by reaching for his cock and aiming it to her wet entrance. He slid inside her with one long stroke that had them both gasping in unison.

Lucas in every day life was close to perfect. Lucas inside her was a religious experience. Unmatched.

His mouth was open, eyes half closed in bliss, and as he moved, he kissed her again. She arched her hips, seeking, desperate for the slide of his cock, the only thing that would satisfy the unbearable ache.

He fucked exactly like he danced; fluid, like he was made of music itself, and her body sang under his touch.

A sheen of sweat on his forehead made her insides melt. She loved how he enjoyed her, how his hushed moans hit her eardrums as his hips moved against hers. Braced against the wall with one forearm, she felt his fingers find her clit, and her muscles squeezed him.

He gasped a string of words in Spanish, a prayer maybe, as he lifted her off the ground. His lips found hers when her legs surrounded his waist.

A quick change of angle, and he hit that coveted spot that sent warmth flooding his cock with her pleasure. She moaned loudly, forgetting where she was. Skin crawling with pleasure, she threw her head back against the wall and closed her eyes in pure bliss.

Stars behind her lids, she cried out, as the movement became harder, the slap of flesh obscene, his cock rubbing against that spot.

"Oh my god." He took her mouth again, bruising, swallowing her cry, spearing into her aching heat.

Her mouth opened as it crescendoed, the music and the breaths and the way he felt inside her, the friction and the rhythm. Struck silent, her orgasm peaked. She barely breathed, riding the wave of pleasure, grinding her hips against him, squeezing him. Her body trembled, and for a moment, her sight blackened.

Julia was distantly aware of her feet finding the floor again. Hazy, woozy, breathless, she kissed him back when his lips came to hers, but he let her go soon after. Confused, she watched him adjust himself into his pants, though he stayed close, crowding her into the corner. To protect her, she realized when it dawned on her that the lights had come on. There were voices speaking in hushed tones. Feverish, she quickly rearranged her clothes, though her panties were still pushed to the side. Her pussy was still clenching.

"My car's out back," he whispered, his eyes half-lidded, skin flushed, just as Amy and Helena appeared around the corner. They were flushed with laughter. Amy stopped and let out a full belly laugh that further confused Julia and sent anxiety coursing through her.

"See? I told you I'd seen Julia!" She slapped Helena's arm playfully and turned to Julia. "Oh my god, you look so hot!"

Helena looked from Lucas to Julia, silent as Amy rushed forward and grabbed Julia by the wrist.

"I told you this dress is amazing. I wish I'd worn something other than black," she babbled. "I keep wearing black to all these things."

"Are you drunk?" Julia asked her. Her voice did not sound like hers, but Amy giggled anyway.

"A little. What were you doing?" Amy pulled her, and Julia couldn't help but follow. She threw a look back at Lucas before she was pulled unceremoniously through the long corridor.

How was she going to get out of this? She wondered as she followed Amy, who was babbling, though Julia couldn't concentrate on anything but trying to walk without stumbling. What Julia wanted was to go back to Lucas and continue that, but now she had a drunk sister she felt just as compelled to stay with. Her body was hot, throbbing.

That was, hands down, the best sex of her life. And it was literally a few minutes in a dark corner. What that man could do with more time and a bed, she couldn't fathom. Julia didn't think her toes would ever uncurl.

Horrified that this was what she'd been missing, and feeling a little bad for herself, she accepted a drink when Amy offered her one. Victoria joined them shortly after, but Sophia was nowhere. Probably had the night off to do whatever it was she and Grey did.

Was sex like this for them too? Not that she wanted to spend a ton of time thinking about her sisters having sex, but *shit*.

"You're looking radiant," Victoria complimented her with a kiss on the cheek.

It's the orgasm I just had, thank you.

Julia was sure they would be able to smell the sex on her. See it on her face, the flush of her skin, but Victoria didn't say anything.

"Drop the skincare routine, sis," Amy said, but she was smirking into the drink the bartender had brought her—some cocktail.

Not so drunk after all, then.

Her panties were still not situated correctly, leaving her feeling exposed and a little excited that no one on the floor actually knew what she, Julia Candela, had just done. Who was this wild woman who had sex in dark hallways?

"Oh, I think I know what that was," Victoria added, obviously struggling not to laugh.

Julia wished she could say she cared, but she hid her face into her drink instead, as Lucas and Helena appeared from the back, their faces emotionless.

With trembling thighs, she sat on a barstool. Amy kept chattering about something Julia couldn't care to even listen to, her mind back in that dark corridor. Lucas sat adjacent to her, his cheeks rosy, and his eyes remained molten as they met hers over his glass of whiskey.

14

Regret rose with the morning sun.

Oh my god, she mouthed inaudibly, the shock of what she'd done rushing over her. In a corridor where anyone could have walked in on them. Where two people actually did, even if they didn't see anything.

Because of him, she could admit. Thank god he'd been listening.

When she thought about it, she didn't know if she should take offense or not. She thought back to the moment she felt him slip out of her and move to redress, when she hadn't even seen the bright overhead lights turn on. Maybe it just wasn't that good for him.

Was she bad in bed?

Julia pulled a pillow over her face, wishing she could scream into it, but Amy lay next to her, as they'd spent the night in Helena's house after they were done at Nowhere. She'd been so tempted to slip away and signal him that she didn't want to end things there, but when Amy ended up drinking too much, they'd gone to Helena's. Julia felt the pressure to stay with her sister.

Step by step, she recalled every moment that led her to having sex in public like a desperate hussy. Seeing Lucas with other partners, dancing with Enrique (Lucas still had the card), then forgetting there were other people around them on the dance floor. His face in her neck, how he touched her. Mortified, she sat up slowly, so as not to wake Amy. What was he thinking now? Probably that she was easy. A man like Lucas Dolores could pull any woman he wanted—evidenced by how popular he was on the dance floor. And it wasn't just dancing that they wanted. Julia had seen the way women, and that one guy he'd danced with, looked at him. Like he was a fucking god.

If those few minutes in the hallway told her anything, it was that he was a fucking god.

"Oh my god," she whispered when it dawned on her. She'd had unprotected sex. Good news, she was on birth control. Necessary to control her heavy periods. Iffy news, she had no idea what Lucas's sexual habits were.

And it was good. So good. She wanted more. No one had ever made her feel like this.

Julia'd been married to Harold for six years; he'd known her better than any other partner she'd ever had, and all she could say was that sex with him was okay. What Kate got from Harold's mediocre sexual prowess, she had no idea.

Sad.

She glanced over at her phone on the nightstand. Did she check? What if he reached out?

Or worse, what if he didn't?

Mortified didn't even begin to describe it.

Giving up on edging herself anymore than she had to, she reached for her phone and found several messages waiting for her. Her eyes looked for his name, though, ignoring everyone else. They were all from this morning.

Lucas: Are you okay?

Lucas: Was that too much? I feel like I crossed a serious line here.

Her chest tingled. She had no idea how to respond. Did she tell him how embarrassed she was? She had to somehow make sure he understood that Julia Candela didn't do stuff like that. He certainly regretted all of it anyway. He had to. There was no way he felt good about it when he said he crossed a line right? He was... her what? Teacher? Lover?

She was spiraling.

She stuck her phone into her small purse, too nervous to respond. First, she had to figure out what to say, then how to word it. That could never happen again. And now she had to find someone else to work with.

"What are you grumbling about?" Amy mumbled from beside her.

She still had her eyes closed and was turned away from Julia, still in the same black dress as last night. Julia also had her silk dress on, which was ruined with wrinkles.

"I have to go." She got out of bed. This wasn't normal for a woman in her thirties to be doing—sleeping over after her friends' apartment after a night of partying and fucking in crazy places.

But was a hallway really all that weird?

The truth was she couldn't recognize herself. Her experiences with sex had never been like that. When her friends were talking about having sex in cars and offices, Julia couldn't imagine anything more uncomfortable and strange. Harold had also never been the adventurous kind of lover, and she'd never wanted that from him anyway. But with Lucas… she'd do it anywhere.

Jesus Christ, she was going to drive herself insane by the time she got home.

"Where?" Amy opened her eyes and looked up at her sleepily.

"Therapy. I need to go home and change."

Amy smirked and closed her eyes again.

"It's Saturday, genius."

Julia chose to ignore how it made her feel to be called out on her lie and grabbed her purse. On the way out, she ordered a car. Helena was nowhere to be seen, which she was grateful for as she snuck out, shoes in hand. In the car, she toyed with texting Lucas back, but she still didn't know what to say, so she put her phone away until she got home. After a long shower and a change of clothes, a cup of coffee between her feet on the windowsill, she finally pulled up the text conversation, and typed a message.

Julia: Last night was obviously a mistake.

It wasn't what she wanted to send. Far from it. She wanted to ask him to come over, to do it again and again until she could barely stand. But she couldn't do it. She couldn't beg for attention any more than she could stop breathing.

Lucas: I owe you an apology.

She frowned down at the message.

Lucas: Maybe we should be having this conversation in person.

Yeah, because if they got together right now they'd talk. Sure.

Julia: I don't think that's a good idea.

Lucas: Then what do we do? Talk about something like this over text?

Of course he was right. Heart jumping, she dialed his number. Not because she wanted to hear his voice at all, they just had to talk like adults.

"Hey," he answered, his voice causing her body to spasm involuntarily.

The pull this man had on her would eventually drive her crazy.

"Why do you think you owe me an apology?" she asked.

"I practically jumped you last night. I acted like an animal."

Her mind went back there immediately, all other thoughts gone. Was this what good sex did to people? It made them dumb. It definitely made *her* dumb. Maybe the mediocre sex with Harold was what made her such a good business woman.

"We both know you did no such thing," she told him, clenching her thighs together.

"I didn't have to follow you back there. I should have stayed in the club. And I shouldn't have been flirting with you every chance I got."

The sex should have confirmed that he'd been flirting, but hearing him say it gave her the courage to ask her next question.

"Do you regret it?"

"I'm supposed to be helping you, not taking advantage of you in dark corridors."

Advantage? What the hell was he on?

"You didn't take advantage of me, Lucas," she whispered. "I wanted it, too." Still did.

Silence.

"Then why are you running?" His voice had taken a husky quality, and there was the throbbing again. Cool.

She wanted to know what he was thinking or feeling. If he could be feeling the same way she did right now, if he had his cock in his hand while he talked to her, and she could slip her fingers into her pajama bottoms…

She shook her head.

"My therapist would say I'm running." Had the lovely, capable Mariana done anything like that? Would she be appalled if Julia told her in their next session?

More silence.

"My life," she added, "doesn't make sense right now. Sometimes running's all I know how to do."

She heard his soft sigh. Getting sick of her shit already. Surprise, surprise.

"I understand," he said, his tone gentle. "But at some point, you have to figure out how to deal."

"I'm aware. I have a therapist, and it's not you."

He chuckled. "Alright, putting me in my place yet again."

I wish you were here right now.

"By the way," he said, "I was tested recently, and I'm negative across the board."

Her stomach quivered.

"Me too."

"And I'm making a delivery to your place right now, in case."

She frowned and jumped off the sill. "Where?"

"I'm not sure what space Sophia has designated as a delivery place."

By magic, of course. As far as she remembered, it was the kitchen, or maybe the dining table, which she could see from where she was now standing.

A little flash of light, and a small package appeared on the table, so she went to look at it. She opened the brown box and found a glass container with a bundle of dried herbs and flowers, and a bag of caramels. Oh, there were butterflies. Lots and lots of wings in her stomach.

"What is this?"

He cleared his throat, like he was nervous. "It's a natural morning-after contraceptive, just in case."

A knot formed in her throat where her pulse had quickened.

"I'm on birth control," she reassured him.

"Okay. They're there if you want them. Just pour hot water on the herbs and steep for thirty minutes. You'll know when it's ready."

Julia picked up the caramels. Salted.

What was this man doing to her?

"How did you know I like salted caramels?"

"I asked Helena."

Her eyes prickled. The bare minimum, she reminded herself. This was just someone being a decent human being, and she was on the verge of crying over it because life had sent her men who'd only taken advantage of her one way or another. But not Lucas. He asked her friends what she liked so he could do something sweet for her, without going over the top like Harold tended to when he felt like he fucked up.

She'd learned it quickly, and it was even more sure now, that Lucas was no Harold.

"Thank you," she whispered with an unsteady voice.

"You're welcome."

They hung up after a short awkward silence, and now Julia didn't know if he would be the person helping her anymore. Things had become complicated. Over sex. Mind-blowing sex, but still.

Not too long after, she poured hot water on the herbs, and they glowed inside the cup for the entire thirty minutes it steeped, staring into it and wondering if she was high. When it stopped glowing, the herbs disintegrated into nothing, and she drank the remaining liquid. It wasn't bad, just a little bitter, and she ate a caramel right after.

Later, as it got dark, she was sitting on her windowsill, without the joint this time, weirdly, scrolling through his social media, and her body chilled. Down almost two years ago, he had a photo with a woman, whom he was kissing on the cheek. Julia stared at the slightly fuzzy photo. Lucas still had a beard in it and was sitting on a ledge somewhere, with mountains behind them as a perfect background.

Queasy, she realized that if she'd been jealous last night, it was nothing to what she felt now. Because what the fuck was Mariana Torres, Julia's therapist of almost a year, doing in one of Lucas's photos? And why the fuck was he kissing her like that? And why the fuck was she smiling with her eyes closed, like she loved it? Loved him.

Julia closed the app, chilled, and reached for the joint then.

"What the fuck?"

15

On Monday morning, Julia sat frozen on Mariana's couch. Her hands rested on her thighs, unnatural and stiff as the therapist took her usual seat. Julia didn't know how to act after spending the weekend obsessing over the woman.

They were both wearing dresses, because of course Julia couldn't not put in an effort after what she knew. Truth was, she was competing with Mariana, who had no idea about Julia and Lucas.

Mariana asked something and Julia answered automatically, not really knowing what she was saying. Her eyes slid to the wall behind the therapist. The art certainly was familiar, but before Lucas's house, she'd thought it was a cultural thing for Mariana. Now Julia was thinking it was about something else entirely. There were no pictures of a wedding or a family on the wall or the little side table.

She'd had to force herself to not reach out to Lucas and ask about the very woman sitting in front of her now. Also, she'd had to force herself not to beg him to come over and fuck her on every available surface, resorting to her vibrator instead. It lived tangled in her blankets now. Julia wasn't someone shy about taking care of her own needs, and before Lucas, her vibrator was the best she'd ever had. Now, that shit wasn't working at all. He'd caused chaos on top of the chaos that was her life. How dare he blow her mind like that and then say he crossed a serious line?

"You look really great," Mariana said, her voice soft and genuine. That tone had always made Julia feel like she was talking to a friend. Maybe it was part of her trauma. Or it could be that Mariana was just that good at her job.

And now Julia wondered so many things about her.

How do you know Lucas? Do you love him? Does he love you?

"Thank you," she said when she realized she'd been staring.

"How was your weekend?"

I had sex with Lucas Dolores. Have you done that too? "I had a dream of my father last night again," she said, a little breathless.

Mariana tilted her head. "Please tell me about it."

"He was alive and not in prison."

"How did it make you feel?" Mariana asked, her face impassive. Julia stared for a little too long before she forced herself to look away.

"Mostly numb, I guess."

"Do you mind if we dig into that?"

Preparing for the onslaught of emotions that would surely come from said digging, Julia lay down on the couch. This office had no business feeling this comfortable, especially now that she knew Mariana and Lucas had been close at some point. They couldn't be related, right?

"If your father was alive right now, what would change in your life?"

Julia closed her eyes and counted backwards to calm her galloping heart.

"He wouldn't be the biggest fucking coward I've ever met, for one." She sat up abruptly, facing Mariana. "But that's not true, right? He killed my mom and Will. Left us without our mother, left Will's son without a father. And then he lied his ass off. He was a coward before he chose to not live with the consequences of his actions."

Mariana made a note on her notepad.

"Can I share a bit of insight?" she asked when she looked up again. Julia nodded, so Mariana continued, "Suicide is a symptom of much deeper issues than most people realize. Maybe death is just a relief."

Julia didn't respond. She knew that, logically. It'd crossed her mind that her father going to jail had been the last straw, not the reason why he'd done it, but it was so much easier to see him that way because then she didn't have to feel compassion.

"I know," she finally said. Mariana brought her so much perspective she'd been missing, had given her tools to help her issues, even if Julia didn't use them. Mariana was so much more capable than Julia.

"How does it make you feel to change your mind about your father's suicide?"

Julia's nose prickled. "Frustrated."

"Why?"

"Because I get it, I suppose. It's easier to demonize him, and for some reason, I'm grieving him even when I hate him. There are so many feelings and none of them make sense together."

Mariana nodded sympathetically. "It's a hard line to walk, allowing yourself to grieve for what you lost while holding him accountable."

Understatement of the century.

"He taught me everything I know." Julia sniffled when her eyes filled. It was so strange, talking to Mariana like this, knowing that she and Lucas were connected somehow. Almost as if the fact that she knew about Mariana and Lucas meant that Mariana knew about Julia and Lucas. A fallacy. "I was really proud to be his second-in-command, the only woman he trusted. That was the first red flag I ignored until I couldn't."

"You only know what you know, Julia." Mariana gave her a sympathetic smile. She sounded exactly like Lucas. "The choices your father made aren't about you. Yes, you learned from him, but you're your own person, and that also has nothing to do with him."

Mariana's words stayed with her as she drove up the highway toward the ferry. Going home wasn't right today. She needed to see Jeanette. Her mother's best friend from childhood was the only person Julia had that she could consider a mother figure. They'd grown up together, along with Will. They had been the siblings none of them had at home, but her mom falling for Will had caused a domino effect that no one could have foreseen. Not even someone as intuitive and clairvoyant like Jeanette.

She got out of the car when she was on the ferry and watched the city get smaller and smaller as she left it behind. Maybe what she needed was to stay away from the city; buy a house somewhere more remote and spend her days learning how to cook and play the guitar. And maybe she'd be able to heal and actually use this magical power in a way that didn't hurt anyone.

Was it possible to miss a place that you've never actually been to? A place that didn't exist, like the lucid dream she'd had while in a coma. What she wouldn't give to go back there and stay.

When the ferry docked, she drove the short distance to Jeanette's, realizing she hadn't even asked if she could come over. However, when she arrived at the cul-de-sac, she saw Jeanette's car on the driveway beside another car Julia had never seen before.

The little porch to the house had two rocking chairs in the front that were old and worn. Julia knew that the other two in the set were at Victoria's house. Plants adorned the railing, trailing up the stairs in a neat row of colorful pots, and a yard that was lush and colorful.

"I made it all the way here," she said into the quiet car, then opened the door to get out.

Jeanette came to the door before Julia could knock, a gentleman behind her. She was wearing a bright purple bonnet and matching robe, and he was in a doctor's coat, a bag hanging by his side. He was built like a tank, tall and strong, his skin dark and smooth.

"I'm sorry, didn't mean to interrupt," Julia said, eyeing the man.

"I was just leaving," the man said in a booming voice. He turned to give Jeanette a kiss on the cheek and left with a friendly smile and a wave for Julia.

"Who was that?" she asked, trying not to smirk.

"That's Paul," Jeanette said as she closed the door, and Julia followed her through the colorful, wonderfully cluttered house to the kitchen.

"And who's Paul?"

Did he spend the night? Do you have a boyfriend we don't know about?

"Paul's my friend," Jeanette said as she went to make coffee, but there was a sparkle in her bright green eyes. She looked so much like Victoria. "But you're not here to talk about me, love."

"Convenient for you," Julia muttered.

"Talk to me," Jeanette said when they were sitting waiting for the coffee to finish brewing.

Julia took a shaky breath. She wasn't going to cry. Nope. Tears welled up anyway.

"I need to stop coming here when I'm falling apart," she said, her voice strained.

"Who else will you go to?" Jeanette held Julia's hand. "What's bothering you?"

"I did something stupid."

Jeanette's brows rose, her full lips pursed in a familiar expression that Julia loved. Her heart stuttered—she could never lie to Jeanette.

"I just had a session with my therapist and it brought up feelings."

"And does that have anything to do with the stupid thing you did?"

Julia shook her head. Then she nodded because both things were true.

"Then why don't you start from the beginning and tell me what you talked to your therapist about?"

As Jeanette prepared the coffees, Julia recounted the dream she'd had with her father in it. Jeanette didn't interrupt her once, her plump figure moving around the kitchen fluidly.

"I have to say, I agree with your therapist," Jeanette said as she sat and handed Julia a mug of hot coffee.

"She's very smart." *And she used to date the man I'm obsessively into at the moment.*

"But you're still bothered by the dream."

Julia sat with her hands wrapped around her mug.

"It's not like I want him to be alive," she said and regretted the words.

"Don't you?" Jeanette's eyes were sharp on her, and Julia had to look away.

"I think it would be easier for me if he was."

Jeanette sipped and nodded. Her dark skin gleamed.

"I wish I could talk to her," Julia whispered, and her voice caught. She didn't have to say who she was referring to.

"Me too," Jeanette sighed.

Julia's heart cracked as she thought about what this must feel like to Jeanette, having lost both of her best friends in such a horrible way.

Julia gripped Jeanette's hand with both of hers.

"Have I ever said how sorry I am for your loss?"

Jeanette gave her a soft smile.

"You have."

Letting go, missing the warmth of those soft hands, Julia took a sip of her coffee.

"I find myself wanting to connect with her somehow. I don't know what there is for me to hold on to."

"You're doing that now, Julia."

By going on non-dates with Lucas and then having sex with him? Hardly.

"Now, about this trouble you got yourself into." Jeanette's eyes were back on her, as if she could read her mind. Lucas did that too; looked at her like he was listening with something other than just ears.

Julia took a long breath and held it, then in a rush, she said, "I had sex with Lucas."

Jeanette's expression didn't change much.

"That's very interesting."

It wasn't *that* interesting.

"Did you already know?"

"How could I?" Jeanette shrugged, but Julia didn't believe that at all.

"You're clairvoyant," she pointed out.

"I can see things, but I never take it at face value. The future's fickle and can change on a whim."

Julia struggled to find words to explain how confusing that was.

"Yes, but I've never done a thing like that," Julia told her. She *had* slept with Stephen, but she couldn't really say that was wild at all.

"Like what?"

"We had sex in a public place," Julia said through tight teeth, and immediately felt the heat rise to her face. "I can't believe I'm telling you this."

"Oh, so you have sex. Big deal. You're not the first and won't be the last."

Julia scraped her nails over her arm, scratching an itch that wasn't there.

"That's not the problem."

"What is, then?"

"Lucas just makes me feel not like myself."

"Why?" Jeanette narrowed her eyes, then asked, "And why is that a bad thing?"

Julia opened her mouth to respond, but words failed her again.

"Did you have consent?" Jeanette asked.

"Yes."

"Did you give it?"

"Yes." *Explicitly.*

"Then why is it bad?" Jeanette asked quietly.

"I went to him because I needed help with my magic, not to fuck him in crowded clubs. And he clearly thinks it was a mistake."

"Did he say it was a mistake?"

"He said he'd crossed a line."

"And do you think he crossed a line?"

"I think we both did. We're supposed to be working together to control my magic. But now I went and had sex with him and it's going to ruin everything." And the dancing had kind of worked. Or maybe it was the sex. It was hard to tell now. "What must he be thinking?"

"That he got laid by a beautiful woman he's into."

Julia's face heated more. She had to look like a tomato by now.

"I'm assuming you had a good time."

"I regret saying anything," Julia mumbled, and Jeanette laughed.

"Honey, you've been expected to be the responsible sister. The one who takes care of everyone and everything." Julia couldn't look away from Jeanette as she spoke. "You're the reasonable one everyone reaches out to, and you carry everyone's shit on your back as if it's yours. It was about time you did something just for yourself."

Coffee forgotten, Julia sat back and let out a long breath, her shoulders suddenly relaxed. She really had been that person for everyone, still strived to do that even though she could barely take care of her own shit.

"If you're going to discover yourself, then you have to connect with all the parts that you've silenced for so long," Jeanette continued, the voice of reason. "You're young, beautiful, smart, accomplished."

"The daughter of a murderer."

"Which has nothing to do with you."

Julia let the fight leave her body, and she felt tired. "You sound like Mariana."

"We've already agreed she's a smart woman."

Who'd dated Lucas. Or something. Julia was going to drive herself nuts thinking about this. Why did she have to go snooping? Like she needed another thing to torture herself with.

"How can I even consider anything with Lucas?" she asked. "I'm so messed up right now. I'm not myself."

"Honey," Jeanette said, "what you need is to find the fun in the fuck."

Julia felt her whole face twitch.

"The fun in the what now?"

"Sometimes, everything fucking sucks, and you have to find the humor in the fuck."

Julia chuckled and Jeanette's deep laugh joined hers. Before she left, Julia hugged this woman she loved so much. Her wisdom, and her laughter, and the way she hugged Julia like she was her own child. The fun in fuck. Well, she wouldn't forget about that any time soon.

16

Julia wished she could say that she stayed chill after that, but that would have been a filthy lie.

She'd been thinking about Lucas for days, everything else forgotten. Her vibrator had become her new favorite thing, besides her joint, as she wrote him texts and deleted them before she could convince herself to send them.

And she'd been stalking him on social media. After seeing Mariana on his feed, she'd gone looking for more evidence of what they must have meant to each other. So far, nothing, but Julia had found adorable photos of him when he was younger, the captions reminiscing about times in Puerto Rico. He also had three sisters, all older. The four of them looked very similar, except for the varying skin tones. It was so interesting and beautiful, a lot like Julia and her sisters.

Julia was scrolling through his feed as she waited to be shown the current version of her dress for Victoria's wedding. She sat on a comfortable chair, angled away from her sisters so they didn't see how psychotic she was. Her finger stopped sliding over the screen when one caught her eye. Lucas was with another guy, who was a little bit shorter than him. An absolutely stunning human being, the man had brown eyes and blond hair. Cole, according to the caption, was the antithesis of Lucas's dark complexion and light eyes, and he looked at Lucas with a half grin that made Julia curious as hell. This wasn't the man she'd seen Lucas dance with at the club, she didn't think. Cole was tagged, so she followed the link to his page, but it was private. Going back to the post, she opened the comments, and found that Cole had commented at the very top.

Thank you, love of my life.

There were a few other comments, most of them saying how sweet the post was, and she went back to the caption.

Today is this amazing human's birthday. Cole, you're one of the best people I know, and I'm lucky to have crossed paths with you in this lifetime. I love you. Feliz cumpleaños!

Her brain went haywire. Seeing him dance with that man at the club the other night had been surprising because it was unexpected. She didn't care about his past relationships, no matter who that was with, but they hadn't discussed past relationships much. He knew about Harold, of course, and she knew about the woman who'd broken his heart.

Could that have been Mariana?

Her mind raced with questions, speculation, the need to know.

"Whatchu doing?" Amy said, coming to sit on the arm of Julia's chair. Startled, Julia almost threw her phone across the room. Amy's mouth opened in gleeful surprise. "Now I'm *really* curious."

"It's nothing." Julia placed her hand on her pounding heart.

"Please, that guilty face screams of stalking." Amy smirked.

"Sometimes I want to smack that expression off your face."

"I'm infinitely grateful for your restraint."

A shop employee came by offering champagne, a good distraction, though Julia wasn't drinking that afternoon.

"So, who we stalking?" Amy asked, and Victoria, who had just come out of the dressing room in a robe, stopped in her tracks.

"Are we stalking someone?"

Mother of God.

"Please tell me it's not Kate or Harold," Sophia said from across the room, where she was doing something on her phone.

"You guys really don't expect much from me," Julia mumbled.

Amy got called away to the back, thankfully, so that was one down. Victoria, on the other hand, had crossed her arms, mirroring Helena, who narrowed her eyes.

"I think I know what this is about."

Julia threw her a pleading look. Helena knew what she'd almost walked into the other night, if Lucas hadn't already confirmed it to her. She was not a stupid woman. Helena, thankfully, caught her desperation and distracted Victoria. Sophia was still busy on her phone.

Besides, how did she bring something like this up? Her therapist happened to have dated Lucas. Or something. There was no caption in the photo, and the tag didn't lead to a profile, just an empty page, so there was no way to know unless she asked. And asking him directly meant she had to admit to Lucas that she'd been snooping. She'd rather die.

It occurred to her that she could ask Helena, but she was best friends with Lucas. She might say something.

And now Cole.

Love of his life.

Julia looked at her reflection in the floor to ceiling mirror in front of her and found lines between her brows. Jeanette's words came back then, telling her truths she wasn't sure she'd ever be prepared to hear. She had been the one to care for everyone, but she'd had to. Who else would have cared for her sisters after the death of their mother? Conrad certainly wasn't going to in the way they'd needed. She didn't understand how that could mean that doing what she'd done with Lucas was okay.

In public, Julia.

But all the admonishment did was send a thrill through her core. Jeanette was right. She could have fun, be a little reckless even. Find the fun in the fuck.

Amy came out with her half-finished dress on. It already looked great, though it needed a few adjustments. When it was Julia's turn to slip on the dress she'd had made, she saw it. How different she looked from everyone else. She looked like she was going to a cocktail party, as opposed to being a bridesmaid at one of her best friends' wedding.

"Everything alright?" Sara asked, looking up at her from where she knelt on Julia's side, pins on her wrist cushion.

"I'm not sure about this silhouette anymore," Julia said in a rush before she could change her mind. Her stomach was in knots. "It's not the job you're doing, at all," she reassured Sara.

"Then what is it?" Amy asked.

"I think I should change my design." She looked at Sara, who had stood. It was impulsive, and maybe Sara would say no, but she had to try. Even if her throat constricted, thinking that Sara and Amy would get mad at her.

"I've been waiting for you to say that," Amy said, approaching them.

"She has," Sara said with a smile that indicated she was far from offended.

"You have?" She didn't know if to feel relieved or insulted.

"This look is good," Amy said, "but you could look so much sexier. I took the liberty to design a couple others if you want to look at them."

Sara brought up the designs on her tablet. Both designs were a much sleeker silhouette, long and fitted to the body, with a little flare starting at the knee. But the one that caught Julia's eye was the second. It had a scoop neckline that would definitely allow for just enough cleavage.

Victoria, Helena, and Sophia came to stand behind her to look at the design too.

"That's really pretty," Victoria said. "I approve."

"The lace overlay isn't working for it, though," Sara said. "It'll change the way it sits on the body."

"Here," Amy said, picking up the digital pencil and the tablet. "We remove this layer of lace and add a sweetheart peekaboo neckline here with the lace. Spaghetti straps instead of caps. Maybe a little detail of lace on the waist."

Everyone agreed as Amy quickly sketched the changes onto the tablet. Julia looked at it, then at herself in the demure little dress she'd chosen, and knew it was the right thing to do.

She deserved to feel sexy too.

Victoria patted a beaming Amy on the shoulder with a smile.

After the measurements were updated, the five of them picked up food and went back to Julia's.

As it got dark out, Julia sat with a glass of red wine on her windowsill. The girls lay on the furniture and floor, doing a range of activities, from painting toenails, to scrolling on phones, to reading.

Julia did none of those things, however, because all she could think of was Lucas. And Cole. Love of his life. Mariana and Lucas, and Lucas and his sisters, Lucas and his cats. Lucas, Lucas, Lucas.

The way his eyes darkened with desire in that hallway. How she'd lost herself, lost track of time.

"What are you thinking about?" Helena said softly, coming to stand by the window, her glass in her hand. "Or do I ask who?"

The tablet Amy had been reading on lowered and she was now looking at Julia.

"Is there a who?" Victoria asked.

"Oh my god, who is it?" said Sophia.

"You're all very nosy," Julia growled, looking out at the small clouds floating by the moon.

"And you're avoiding the question," Victoria said. Amy was smirking, but Helena was just looking at her with her head leaned to the side.

"If you already know, why are you asking?" Julia said to Helena, whose blue eyes sparkled.

"He asked about you." She smiled into her wine.

"Wait." Sophia got to her feet, then pulled her jeans up, wiggling her legs. "What are we talking about? Why don't I know?"

"I don't know either," Victoria said.

"Please tell me this isn't about Harold," Amy muttered.

"My god, no," Julia snapped. Ew. But everyone's attention was on her now. "Would you guys stop doing that? I'm fine."

"Are you?" Sophia asked. "We haven't really talked about the news."

"Guys, it's not about that," Helena said.

"Am I annoyed that they're moving on just like that, as if they don't have a debt of karma to pay?" Julia huffed. "Of course I am. But I wish them the best.

"Bullshit," Amy said, tablet back on her face.

"Fine, I'd like for them to have every small inconvenience possible for the rest of their days," Julia told them.

"Paper cuts every time they touch a book," Sophia said.

"Stepping on tiny building blocks every time they're barefoot." Helena drank the rest of their wine as the others laughed.

"And every TV show they love gets canceled after one season," Victoria added through the cackles.

"Tell them who this is about," Helena said, and everyone watched Julia closely.

Julia rolled her eyes. She took a long breath, her heart pounding. "You're the worst." Looking at Sophia and Victoria, she said, "I had sex with Lucas."

Sophia's mouth fell open in a silent gasp, but Victoria only laughed.

"Oh, I had an idea when I saw him follow you to the back the other night."

Julia stared at Victoria.

"Oh, god." It was worse than she had imagined. Heat suffused her face and neck. She wanted to spontaneously combust just to get out of talking about it.

"And you didn't tell me anything?" Sophia shouted.

"We walked in on them," Helena said.

"You saw her having sex?" Sophia screamed. Clearly, she'd drunk enough—Sophia got very loud when she was drunk.

"They didn't see me having sex!" Could she just jump out the window? Preferable to this.

"What did you see?" Victoria asked Helena and Amy.

Amy was the one who spoke. "Nothing, they'd just finished when we found them."

Actually, *they* hadn't finished, Julia had. But she wasn't saying that to them.

"Lord help me," Julia groaned.

"What, you think I don't know what a post-orgasm face looks like?" Amy deadpanned, then looked at the rest. "She was all rosy-cheeked, chest heaving."

"He was so pissed." Helena laughed. "I had to talk him down from hexing Amy on the spot for taking Julia away."

"I was drunk or I wouldn't have been such an annoying cock-block."

Victoria snorted, and everyone joined her laughing, including Julia. The whole thing was fucking ridiculous.

"Oh my god, how was it?" Sophia asked.

"Honestly?" Julia paused, allowing herself a nice deep breath. "No words."

Sophia and Victoria squealed.

"In a hallway, huh?" Amy grinned, wiggling her brows.

Julia buried her face in her hands. "I've never done anything like that before."

"And how did it feel?" Helena asked.

"You promise you won't talk to your bestie about this?" Julia asked her with a brow raised.

"What happens at Julia's..." Helena crossed her finger over her heart.

"It was weird and amazing," she told them. "We've been spending all this time together because he wanted me to relax enough that he could read me, and one thing led to another. And the dancing..." Julia groaned.

"He's a pretty good dancer," Sophia said. "He's teaching me."

Julia felt her face twitch in surprise. "Oh?"

"I mean, he was," Sophia explained. "We had to pause because Grey and I have been traveling so much."

Lucas certainly had never told her any such thing. Not that Julia was jealous of Sophia, that would be ridiculous. Sophia was madly in love with Grey and vice versa. But she would have thought he'd tell her something like that. Was he holding back?

"And what seems to be the problem?" Victoria said.

"There isn't one, other than how fucked in the head I am," Julia told them. "He brought me morning-after herbs and everything. And caramels." She looked at Helena, who grinned.

"And why are you here instead of with him?" Amy asked.

"He told me he regrets it," Julia said, humiliated, but Helena frowned.

"That's not what he said to me."

Julia met her gaze, startled, her heart fluttering in a hopeful beating of wings she wanted to squash immediately.

"What did he say?" Sophia asked.

Helena didn't look away from Julia.

"I think you should talk to him," she said quietly. "It's not my place to intervene."

"Yet you told him about the caramels," Julia retorted.

"Yes, but the rest is his business with you."

A pin could have made a symphony in that room, it was so quiet.

"He brought you the morning after pill," Amy muttered. "Herbs. Whatever. He's considerate."

"It's just like him, honestly," Helena said.

"Grey would do that too," Sophia said. "What is it with these super considerate men all of a sudden?"

"Emotional maturity," Victoria supplied. "It makes everything better. It's like entering another dimension. The conversations are deeper and funnier, and the sex gets even better somehow."

"Yeah, not wrong," Amy said.

"Are you seeing anyone with whom you're having such sex?" Sophia inquired with a narrowed-eye look. Amy clicked the button on her tablet and brought it up to cover her face.

"This is not about me," she said in a neutral tone.

"Are you going to call him?" Helena asked, throwing Julia a sleepy look.

Julia sighed, looking out the window. Rain began falling gently. "I don't know."

She trusted that Helena was right, that she had to talk to Lucas instead of assuming she knew what he meant. All he'd said was that he'd crossed a line, and she immediately made it about her and thought he simply didn't want her. What happened at the club was evidence of the exact opposite. He did want her. And she wanted him right back.

Her phone rang and her heart jumped, but disappointment, followed by annoyance, spread through her hotly.

Fucking. Harold.

Why she chose to answer, she would never know, but she clicked the green button and accepted the call.

"Yes, may I help you?" Julia made her voice sound like she was a customer service representative, except less friendly. The other four only looked at her with various degrees of curiosity and annoyance. Julia rolled her eyes and put the phone on speaker.

"Julia, so good to hear your voice," Harold drawled. "After the other night at your sister's club, I've meant to reach out. You looked so taken aback. I felt so bad."

"I wish I felt bad about you not being let in, but here we are," she retorted, keeping her voice as pleasant as she could.

Harold laughed. He was trying to sound relaxed and unbothered, but the laugh was more of a bark.

"Kate's a fan of Helena's," he said. "I thought it would be nice to take her to the club, but I see you can't let go of the past long enough to let her enjoy a show."

Amy's face was a mask of rage where she still lay on the sofa.

"But also, your boyfriend didn't seem happy to see me, so maybe it was a good thing we left."

Left. What a nice way of putting that.

Julia snorted with laughter. "Oh, don't worry. He didn't really notice you."

A brief silence.

"Is that all you wanted to say?" Julia was proud that her voice was absolutely emotionless, and that she didn't feel egged on as she would have only a few weeks earlier. Harold knew how to get to her, and even if it pissed her off later, now, she wasn't showing him how much he could affect her with his hateful words.

"I just want you to be happy, Julia," he said. "Just like me and Kate. You can be happy again. Even with that guy. He seems… nice."

The pause wasn't lost on her, and Julia had to bite her tongue. She knew exactly what Harold was trying to communicate without saying the words. Some people were very good at talking down to others without a single negatively-perceived word.

"Tread very carefully, Harold." Julia lowered her voice to show him that he wasn't going to play with her either. She wouldn't allow him to bother her with his petty shit, but Harold had always been very clear of what he thought about people who didn't look like him. It had been an innocuous comment here and there, then the politics, and finally Julia had realized how little respect he'd had for an entire half of her heritage.

He sighed. "Look, I'm not really calling about any of that. I actually do have something to offer you."

Ah, yes, as she'd expected. This happened every so often. She kind of welcomed it now. It was just a little game they played.

"Wait, don't tell me," she said. "I want to guess this is about the house."

"You're so smart," he bit out, his irritation starting to show. Short fuse. "I know you've said you're not interested, but I do have a better offer for you."

"I mean, the answer's still the same."

"You and I both know you're never going to use that house, Julia. You're keeping it to spite me."

"Yeah," she admitted, and Victoria dissolved into silent laughter across from her. "I absolutely am."

"You vindictive bitch," Harold spat.

"Ooh, there you are," she said with a big smile. Yes, she was taunting him, but she didn't care. Harold could go jump into a vat of broken glass for all she cared. "I knew the real you would show up sooner or later."

"I'm not playing games with you, Julia."

"And neither am I. That's my house, and I'd rather peel off my own skin than let you live there with Kate, after what you both did. Thanks for asking so nicely, though."

She hung up and blocked him, as she should have done a long time ago. Why she'd insisted on keeping the line of communication open, she had no idea, honestly. Harold used to have a power over her she had never understood. A woman who knew herself and went for what she wanted, around Harold, Julia tended to forget who she was and always did as he asked, down to the fragrances she wore.

Now, the sound of his voice reminded her that every decision she'd made had been for the better. Moving on felt nice.

"Good choice," Amy said, bringing the tablet in front of her face.

"You're not scared of him?" Sophia asked quietly and Julia sent her a reassuring look. No, she didn't think Harold could hurt her directly, but she understood where the concern came from. Her sisters weren't soon to forget what had happened to their mother when she'd tried to leave her abusive marriage.

"I'm protected in this house," Julia reminded her, pointing at the charm hanging off the side of the window.

"And outside of it?" Amy asked. Her face was still pink, but she didn't look like she wanted to go after Harold anymore.

"I got it," Helena said. "I'll have a charm you can wear on your person, just in case."

Julia smiled at her and pulled up her text thread with Lucas, adrenaline rushing through her now that it was all done.

Julia: Hey.

She sent it, then groaned at how dumb it sounded. God. Was she really about to booty-call Lucas?

Yes. Fun. She could have fun. She put the phone down, but kept throwing looks at the screen as Victoria and Sophia looked at the dress photos from earlier. The phone chimed.

Lucas: I'd started thinking you weren't going to talk to me again.

Relief coursed through her, and she looked up to make sure no one was paying attention to her. Amy was still reading, and Helena settled herself on the floor, her legs up on the armchair. Soft music played from one of the phones.

Julia: I've been meaning to thank you for the herbs and the caramels. Much better than the morning-after pill.

Lucas: I've heard as much.

Julia: You can't relate to that much, can you?

Lucas: Not at all.

Pause because she didn't know what to say.

Lucas: So what are you doing?

Her heart was on her throat now.

Julia: The girls came over after dress fittings.

Lucas: Hope it's been fun.

Julia: It has.

She typed, deleted, and typed again.

Julia: You?

Lucas: Not much.

A picture followed the text. His torso in a t-shirt, his two kittens on him, and a book in his other hand. Damn the man; he knew she couldn't resist the kittens!

Julia: Adorable.

Lucas: I know, but I do like hearing it.

She snorted and got a brief look from Amy.

Julia: Full of yourself much?

Lucas: You said it.

Julia: About the kittens.

Lucas: Fine. I prefer being called sexy anyway.

She rolled her eyes, but a smile peeked through.

Julia: Yeah, well, I won't be the one saying that.

Lucas: And if I do it?

Julia: Call yourself sexy? Doesn't that defeat the purpose?

Lucas: Oh, you're funny when you're not being mean.

Julia: How could you say such a thing? I'm the most amenable, easiest-going person on the planet.

He sent a laughing emoji. So simple and so normal, and yet, she was charmed as hell.

Lucas: A brat is what you are.

She gasped gently, and something like—was it pleasure?—bolted through her.

"Are you sexting right now?" Sophia inquired with a grimace.

"Of course not." Julia went back to her phone. What the hell did she say?

She was so bad at this, it was sad.

Julia: Yeah, well, I don't really know how to turn that off.

Lucas: I can help with that.

It was titillating. Julia let her head fall back against the wall behind her. Heating up like she was having a hot flash. She pictured him right here, kissing her neck, removing every piece of clothing, and fucking her on the windowsill.

Setting her phone down, she took a cleansing breath so she didn't burst into flames like a demon at a cathedral.

But as she got ready for bed later, Sophia having chosen to sleep with her, second-guessing led to full-blown doubt that the conversation even meant what she thought it did. She was delusional. Had to be. This thing with Lucas wasn't going to work out. She was too fucked up. He'd only agreed to help her with magic, and she hadn't done any magic at all.

"You're overthinking," Sophia murmured from beside her when Julia had punched the pillow for the third time since she lay down. All the fight left Julia's body, and she found her way to her back, staring up at the dark ceiling.

"Yeah, well…"

Sophia turned to her side, so Julia did the same, hand under her cheek. A lot like they used to do as girls when they left their rooms to sleep together because they were scared or missed their mom. Amy was usually between them, back then.

"Come on, Jules." Sophia sounded tired, but her eyes were alert in the dim light of the lamp they still had on.

"It's hard not letting my mind go to the worst places."

Understanding softened Sophia's gaze, and Julia allowed herself the vulnerability she couldn't seem to keep at bay these days.

"And it's not just Harold calling, though that didn't help matters."

"You have to stop letting him hurt you."

"I know. I keep waiting for that to go away."

"It takes time." Sophia closed her eyes, and Julia thought maybe that was the end of it. Preparing to settle in and spend the night trying not to wake Sophia, Julia rolled to her back again. But Sophia added, "Holding yourself back from what you want isn't helping in the long run."

Was she being objective, or was she just holding herself to impossible standards she'd never hold anyone else to?

"Call him," Sophia sighed, turning on to her other side. "Life is so short. Go have fun. Laugh, and eat good food, and dance, and have amazing sex."

Look at our mom.

Silvana Candela was so lovely and smart, talented and filled with the best of intentions. She'd had the hardest life, her mother gone when she was young, a father who didn't want to be a father, and later a husband who'd ended up killing her.

Julia sat up, the decision made before her feet hit the floor. Sophia threw her a sleepy smile, slipping her earbuds into her ears. In the bathroom, Julia cleaned up a little. She'd even done her skincare and her skin was gleaming. Thankfully, her hair looked nice, a little wavier than normal today. Julia went to the closet, took off the simple t-shirt and shorts she'd put on to go to bed. The lingerie waited for her in a drawer, and she pulled it on quickly, followed by a simple, rust colored t-shirt dress she only wore on the hottest days for running errands. There was no need for fancy with Lucas. Trembling fingers brushed strands of hair from her face, and she went back in the room and reached for her phone on the bedside table.

Julia: Please tell me you're up.

It was probably no more than thirty seconds, but it felt like a whole eternity as she stared at the text thread. Three dots appeared, and her stomach heated with nerves.

Lucas: Yes.

Julia: I've never done anything like this before.

Lucas: Like what?

Julia: Don't make me say it. This is awfully mortifying.

Lucas: I can't read your mind, Julia.

Julia: Oh, now you can't.

She could almost hear him laughing at her, and somehow, her nerves calmed at the notion.

Julia: I don't do stuff like what happened at the club.

Lucas: Me neither.

Julia: I find that very hard to believe.

Lucas: Why?

Julia: Look at you.

Lucas: Could say the same thing.

It was a line. Just a line. He didn't mean it. Still, she ate it up, as desire rose in her at the same time she convinced herself to just get on with it.

Julia: I want you. Tonight. Do you want me?

Lucas: Fuck yes.

Relief made her shiver as she walked toward the front of the house.

Julia: Then come get me.

It was all quiet, mostly dark, and she made her way across the house. As she rounded a corner, through the archways, there he was, having ported the moment she asked him to come. Breathless, she padded barefoot toward him, unhurried despite her nerves. Rain pelted the windows lightly as they made their way to each other, and when they were close enough, he lifted her against him, and everything turned watery and upside down as he ported them.

17

Lucas's mouth was on hers before her feet hit the wooden floor. She had no idea where they were in his house. It was mostly dark, warm light filtering from somewhere else, some other room, and her back found a wall.

This was what it would be like between them—dark hallways and walls. She couldn't care less how it happened as long as it did.

He pulled back and found her eyes with his.

"Luz verde, mami," he whispered, then kissed her again. He wanted the green light, as if she wasn't already glowing like a street-light for him.

"Yes," she said into his mouth.

"You have no idea," he whispered, his breathing harsh, "las cosas que quiero hacer contigo."

In answer, she arched her hips forward, reaching for him as his hands found the hem of her dress and lifted. Her arms above her head, he pulled the dress off and threw it to the side.

It would be burned in her memory for the rest of her days, the expression that took over his face when he saw the scraps of lace that did nothing to cover the most intimate parts of her. The clouding of his eyes, and the way a soft moan escaped his lovely pink lips.

"My god," he whispered and bit his lip. Before she could react, he knelt in front of her.

A gasp ripped out of her, seeing him like that, looking up at her with hazy eyes filled with lust. She could have died in pure bliss, him at her feet, pleading without words.

Long fingers hooked on the edge of her panties, pulling them aside, and she smiled, even as anticipation sparked through her. It was as if he'd wanted to do it over again, start it like this because of what it was like the first time. Like he wanted to do it more completely. He slid a finger along the hot wetness and over her swollen clit. Her mouth opened on a silent moan.

"You don't have to be quiet here," he said, his eyes never leaving the glistening flesh. "Tell me what you want, baby."

Yes. This, she could do.

"Taste it," she whispered. He looked up at her one last time before his mouth disappeared into her pussy. Bracing herself against the wall, she lifted a knee, hooking it over his shoulder as his tongue found her swollen and wet. Julia let her eyes close, her head fully back against the wall, lost to the jolts of pleasure spreading through her limbs.

"Look at me," she murmured, and he did as his tongue flickered. His finger slipped inside her, gently probing. "Oh, god."

"Lucas is fine," he said, and she would have laughed, but his lips clamped on her again without so much as a breath. A moan was ripped out of her, lost to the sensations. The pleasure built and built until she came swiftly. His head in her hands, holding him right there where she wanted him, she squealed as waves of pleasure rocked her, tipping her hips toward his mouth. As she trembled, thinking she'd lose her legs, he came to his feet. She tasted herself when he kissed her again, and she wrapped her legs around his waist when he lifted her.

"I want to taste you." She'd die at the chance.

"Later." Hands on her ass, she felt him moving, even as he continued to kiss her. Soon they were in his bedroom, and Julia saw nothing, felt nothing but him and the bed when he laid her on it. His lips trailed down her body again, over her navel, and past it to where she was still pulsing and trembling. A kiss through her panties and her back arched clean off the bed.

The scrap of material was off in a flash, his mouth back there, and her sigh was one of those that happened when you made it home at the end of a long day. Like everything was right in the world. So, for the first time in a long time, Julia allowed herself to relax. His hair was soft in between her fingers when she touched him as he did whatever this was—a roll and slide of his tongue on her heated flesh that had her climbing again faster than she should have been able to. She begged, cried out, moaned as he held her down and positively inhaled her. It seemed as if he had ten tongues, and when she came this time, she sobbed his name as she rode his face.

As the spasms subsided, Lucas's teeth sunk on the inside of her thigh before he slid up her body, kissing her heated flesh with soft lips. She shivered when he hovered above her, his warm eyes on her.

"Me tienes loco," he whispered, his eyes roaming her body like he had never seen anything sexier. No one had *looked* at her in a long time. Seen her. Worshiped her.

"Take off your clothes," she begged him in a whisper, pushing up until she was on her knees in front of him and pulling his shirt over his head. The tattoos were everywhere, covering his entire torso, shoulders, neck, arms, and probably his back. It was the absolute sexiest thing she'd ever seen. His pants came off, and her bra disappeared, and before he could move, she pushed him back, straddling him.

Emboldened by the look in his eye, that haze of lust she'd craved for days, she kissed her way down his body, finding hard muscles and soft golden skin, and a cock so perfect she almost wept. It was long and thick, the pillowy head dusty pink, shiny and weeping. She hadn't seen it the last time, but thank god for second chances.

When she took him in her mouth, his moan made her clench. It was the single hottest thing she'd ever heard, and it kept coming as she licked him from base to tip, then took him in deep until she felt him in the back of her throat. She looked up at him through her lashes and found him looking at her, his mouth open, his hands in his hair. She would have smiled if she could, but she yelped when he grabbed her and threw her on the bed, his cock leaving her mouth with a pop. Thrilled, her heart racing, her skin glistening with sweat, she opened for him.

"How do you want me to fuck you?" he whispered, his hand reaching toward the bedside table, rummaging inside a small drawer. She reached for his wrist to stop him.

"I'm on birth control," she reminded him.

He nodded, understanding, eager.

"Just like this?" He bit his lip as he rubbed the tip of his cock against her, from entrance to clit, so hard and weeping for her.

"Yes," she whimpered. But he didn't push inside her. He teased over and over, making her quiver, desperate with lust, despite the two orgasms he'd already given her. His hand came around her throat, his mouth devouring hers before his forehead rested against hers.

She could have come right then, just from that look alone. His eyes looked like they were glowing in the dimness of the room.

She. Was. Feral.

"Do you have any idea what you do to me?" he muttered roughly, the tip of his cock right at her entrance, teasing her mercilessly. She lifted her hips a fraction, and it slipped inside her, just a little. Whimpering, she closed her eyes, but opened them when he pulled back, sliding out of her.

Growling, she reached up and her hand went against *his* throat. His glowing eyes widened, and when she pushed, he folded. With him reclined on the pillows now, she climbed on top of him, and reaching for him with her free hand, she positioned him at her entrance before she sunk onto him with a trembling sigh.

Pausing to savor it, she brought her lips to his, and he held her face as they kissed. It was perfect. He was perfect, and so was she in that moment, when all that existed in the world was the two of them.

Hips undulating, she took him deeper, then deeper still as his hands found her breasts. She wouldn't take it easy on him, but at first, it was slow, until the pleasure began to build and she went faster and faster. His hands were on her hips, guiding her, and he rose against her, matching the rhythm she'd set.

"Yes," he whispered before she kissed him. "Just like that."

The first squeeze surprised even her, and she gasped, her head out in the ether somewhere. Every one of her senses was compromised now. She couldn't form a coherent thought if she tried, so she didn't as her body shook uncontrollably, warmth gushing out of her and onto his cock.

She wouldn't have felt an earthquake. Before she was done shaking, the world turned upside down, and she was on her back now. He knelt in front of her, her leg up on his shoulder, his cock deep inside her still.

"Is this okay?" he asked, breathing hard, and all she could do was nod. Surely, her voice wouldn't work the way it was intended. Julia was reduced to unintelligible noises, and her body jerked when the slide became a slam. Close to pain, just at the edge, and her muscles contracted involuntarily. Every sound in her quieted, and it was just the sound of his cock driving through her wetness now. She could barely breathe as it crested, sending shivers up and down her body.

"Oh my god," he moaned, hips stuttering against her, so close. So, so close. The warm waves of pleasure made her body gooey, and she wanted him to join her there. Where that was, she had no idea, but she could see color in the near complete darkness of the room.

She loved the sounds he made, how he looked like was losing control, biting hard into his knuckle to stop himself from coming. Watching his eyes roll to the back of his head, his skin flushed and beaded with sweat, sent her toward the edge again, their bodies coming together in dance to a secret song only they could hear. Julia didn't recognize herself, how tears slipped past her closed lids when his fingers found her jaw, held her still for the onslaught of his mouth, to muffle the dirty sounds coming out of her.

He slammed into her again. She sobbed, and he did it again and again and again. Her orgasm built from the bottoms of her feet, all the way through every inch, every cell. She shouted, his hand a vise in her hair, shooting delicious pain through her scalp and down her neck and spine. Clouds floated in front of her eyes, and she swore she blacked out as she clamped around him and dissolved into uncontrollable trembling as wave after wave hit her and made her see stars.

"Jesus," he groaned as she continued to shake, pulsing around him, squeezing. Her head was light, but her body was taut, her skin slick with sweat and pleasure, nipples hard. But the feel of him inside her was, hands down, the best thing she'd ever experienced. She didn't want it to end. Wanted to just slip into a blissful death right here.

"Come," she moaned. "Come inside me."

It did something to his expression, made his eyes widen and his hips snap, the bed squeaking and shaking. He fell against her, groaning, his face buried in her throat as his body jerked against her.

Rigid, he sobbed against her skin. Delirious and warm, so full of him in so many ways, tears sprung to Julia's eyes as he pressed his forehead against hers before he kissed her. His lips were warm and soft. Shaking, she lifted a hand to smooth a lock of hair from his forehead. She had to touch him to make sure this was real, that she hadn't imagined it.

For a while, they just lay together as rain fell softly against the big window behind the bed, still joined.

"Come on," he said softly, taking her hand, and he slipped out of her to lead her to the adjoining bathroom. She could have just stayed in bed and never moved, but after-sex care was a part of it too.

When she finished in the tiny toilet room, he was waiting for her by the double sink with a warm, wet rag. Standing by the counter, he pressed the rag between her thighs, gently cleaning the evidence of what they'd just done to each other.

It hit her how she'd never felt this comfortable naked around Harold. How it always felt like he was judging the way her body was shaped, even when she did everything to fit his standards. But with Lucas, naked as the day they were born, even with that incredible, hard body of his, it wasn't even a thought in her head to feel insecure about what she had to offer.

Because he looked at her like she was beautiful.

Back in the dark bedroom, she started looking for her underwear as he lay back against the pillows.

"Going somewhere?" he asked.

She turned to him from where she had been hooking her bra back on and stopped. Searching, she reached for places inside her that could explain this need to run. To go be alone after something so big just happened to her. But the answer didn't come, and she suddenly felt awkward, as if she'd been caught doing something wrong.

"I just…"

What, Julia?

"Do you want to go home?" he asked with a slight frown.

Absolutely not. The words got stuck, so she shook her head instead, her breath shivering even as her heart was calming down.

His frown disappeared.

"Come here," he murmured, his hand reaching for her. She climbed into the bed, her underwear forgotten, and he pulled her close. Her leg over his, he slid the soft covers over them both and kissed the top of her head. "I like you in my bed."

And as she allowed herself to relax, she realized she liked it too.

"It's never been like that before," she said without thinking and instantly regretted it. How pathetic was that? He'd have to have amazing experiences before her, and all she had to show for her life was Harold. But Lucas didn't ridicule her, and he didn't jeer or laugh or become cocky. When she looked at him he was serene, a satisfied smile ghosting his perfect lips, eyes closed.

"Me neither."

Butterflies. So, so many of them.

The part of her that was always anxious wanted to talk, to distract from the things she'd let him do, but the silence was too perfect. Too comfortable and soft. How was it that he could make her feel like this? Like she was the sexiest woman alive, like she was the only one.

"Are you staring?" he asked, opening his eyes and twisting his head to look at her. His pupils were dilated. She only nodded, smiling like a dolt, and when he smiled back, her heart did a thing. It took her breath away, how it tumbled and rolled.

Was this what dying felt like? Slipping into a different plane of existence in the blink of an eye.

Emotion made her nose prickle, so she kissed him to hide it. Sleep came easily that night, warm and safe under his soft blankets. There were no dreams awaiting her.

18

Awareness returned with a wet spot on her chin. Julia opened one eye to the ridiculously excessive brightness of the bedroom and found Opal purring like a car engine on her chest. A soft meow made her smile and reach for the downy fur.

"Good morning," she whispered. Opal stood and booped Julia's nose with her tiny wet one, then bounded off as the door opened. Lucas held two steaming mugs. He wore those gray sweats again, though he'd left the shirt off—thank the sweet, sweet Lord. In the light of day, she could see all the lines and colors of his tattoos, the tribal shapes of masks, animals, the sea. It was magnificent.

"Good morning," he murmured when he sat on the bed, setting the mugs down before he leaned in to kiss her. She tipped her head up for him, basking in the feel of his lips like it was the most natural thing in the world.

"I only put a little sugar in it," he said as he handed her a mug. "It's Dominican coffee, so it doesn't need much."

She sipped, closing her eyes in pure bliss and wondering what it would be like to have this every day. A gorgeous man who brought her coffee in bed after doing unspeakable, delicious things to her...

"This is crazy good," she said, refusing to let her mind wander too far. She opened her eyes to find him looking at her, his eyes half-lidded. "What?"

"How are you so sexy?"

Julia's face heated, but her cheeks pulled in a smile anyway. How could she resist this incredible man saying these things to her?

His room was so much like him. Rich and colorful. The walls were painted a bright emerald green, with a stark white trim and an intricate chandelier hanging from the vaulted ceiling. Behind her, it wasn't just one window, but almost the entire wall of glass and white wood.

The bed itself was a cloud. She would have to remedy her situation at Sophia's because this… this was a bed.

"Where do you get Dominican coffee around here?"

"I trade with witches on the island," he said.

"What a great deal," she said appreciatively.

"Indeed. Grey and I brew potions. I use a lot of them for my personal work with clients, and witches sometimes find it easier to buy rather than make potions on their own."

"You get your coffee, and they get the magic. Charming." She chuckled. Maybe it was the haze of sex still hanging in the air, but she hadn't been this relaxed in a long time. What felt like electricity hummed underneath the surface of her skin.

"Trading is a good way to do this kind of work," he said.

Which brought her back to how she was paying him for his help with her little problem.

"You never asked me to trade anything." Or was that what the sex was about?

"My God, woman, get your mind off that track." He laughed.

"Would you stop doing that?"

"Doing what?"

Looking smug, he put his cup on the nightstand.

"Reading my mind," she pointed out. It felt like that's what he was doing, whether he claimed it was or not.

"I don't read minds," he said anyway. "You just have this energy. It shouts and it's easy to pick up."

Julia paused, thinking about what he just said.

"You mean you can read me now?"

"Haven't even tried. My methods are just that good."

Julia rolled her eyes, but didn't stop the tug of a smile as she continued to sip her coffee, which was still way too hot.

"But seriously," he said, taking the cup from her hands and putting it next to his on the nightstand. "How are you this sexy?"

"Are you looking for an actual answer?" Her voice was calm, but her heart was certainly not when he was looking at her like that.

"Well . . ." he mumbled as he pulled the covers to join her in the bed. Her body warmed, buzzed, and she was ready for him for whatever he wanted. Shameless, she was shameless.

"I think you're the only person to ever say that to me." She accepted him when he climbed on top of her, and she used her heels to push the waistband of his pants over his ass so she could grab it.

"A travesty," he murmured, then kissed her.

The next hours passed in a haze of lovemaking, and Julia ignored texts, calls, emails, and everything else as she found ways to have orgasms she hadn't been aware existed before.

For a long while, she tried to figure out what it was she felt, and arrived at the notion that he worshiped her body like it was holy.

When she wanted to take a shower, he prepared the bath for her instead, and she sunk into the claw-footed tub only for him to join her shortly after. He washed her hair with shampoo he had made himself (which, what the hell?) and then, to her absolute shock, he used conditioner. If he'd done anything hotter than that since she got here last night, she would eat her words. This was it. The bar was this. So much so that she couldn't stop herself from climbing on him and riding him until they were both shouting, their voices a lewd echo around them.

Hours later, they dragged themselves out of bed, stomachs growling. So much sex and not enough calories would do that.

"I'm not much of a cook," she told him as they arrived in the kitchen.

"You couldn't be perfect," he said, picking her up by the waist and depositing her on the counter, her ass bare against the cold marble. She'd worn one of his old band t-shirts, and he was in his boxer briefs, the expanse of his skin smooth.

"I'm far from perfect." Her arms snaked to surround his neck as he leaned in for a kiss, his hands roaming into the t-shirt.

"You're perfect right now," he mumbled against her lips. Her heart did it again. Reached for him.

She watched him move around the kitchen, gathering ingredients to make an omelet, apparently, as if he didn't just change everything for her. His words, and the way he touched her, and how she believed everything he said and did. It was magic on its own.

He cut up some vegetables as she cracked the eggs into a bowl he grabbed for her. When all the ingredients were in the pan, she pulled him in for another kiss, which she'd intended on being short and sweet, and turned into a full makeout session.

Forgetting that they'd been cooking, his hands were reaching for her wetness when the smoke alarm went off and he had to turn it off with the handle of the spatula.

She snorted laughing as she jumped off the counter and opened the door to let in some fresh air. It was cloudy, but warm and lovely outside.

"Okay, this is not going to happen," he said, throwing away the remnants of their burnt eggs and the empty carton.

"Mexican?" she suggested, and he lifted his hand and his phone appeared on his palm.

It didn't even dawn on her to feel weird about it. Being around Lucas meant being around magic, and maybe she was super sexed up, but it didn't bother her. When he'd ordered the food, he put on music and grabbed her. They waltzed around the kitchen to a merengue, which struck her as so funny she couldn't stop laughing. Snorting, breathless—happy—they sailed through the doors into the dining room.

"This is not how you dance merengue." She giggled, her ab muscles seizing as he dipped her like they were dancing a tango now.

"Who cares?" He was grinning from ear to ear when she was upright again.

Not me, she thought. Kittens bounded between them. They stopped, laughing as Opal and Midnight meowed before they ran up the stairs. Probably to Lucas's bed, their favorite place in the house.

Same. Though, if she thought about it, every corner of that house was her favorite now that she knew Lucas the way she did.

"What are you thinking about right now?" Lucas asked, and the song changed to a sultry ballad. His naked chest was warm underneath her hands, and she pushed him backward gently until the back of his legs hit the dining table.

"How hungry I am," she said as she reached for the growing bulge in his boxer briefs. His eyes turned molten before he fisted her hair and slanted his mouth onto hers. She felt his other hand grip her ass, and she slipped hers into his underwear, pulling the hard length out of the black cotton. Julia sank to her knees, her eyes never leaving his, pulling the underwear all the way off as she went.

Lucas's eyes hooded and his mouth opened on a soft moan when she licked the head, then the underside. And when she slipped almost the entire length of him in her mouth, his eyes closed and his hands ran over his face. She wasn't on her knees for long. After a minute of taking him deep into her throat, he pulled away and lifted her roughly against him. His kiss was hard, teeth scraping against her lips. He turned her around, pressing her against the table.

His mouth came to her ear. "Is this okay?" he panted. She'd barely nodded when he slammed into her. She keened as Lucas set a punishing pace, his hand on her face, pressing her against the cool wood of the table. It was almost painful this time, but she wanted it like that. Hard and fast until they were both shouting. She was a shrill mess as she came, just as the doorbell echoed through the house.

Panting, he went rigid against her, then fell on her. Lucas remained there for a while, their slick skin sliding together. The doorbell sounded again.

"Oh my god, that poor delivery person," she whispered. He huffed a laugh and she snorted. That poor person probably heard things they would have to tell their therapist about.

After they cleaned up, they went out to the back porch with the giant bag of food. They sat on the couch, sharing every dish, taking bites of each other's food like they'd been doing that forever. And they talked about everything.

"So the potions help you have bursts of magic," she said when he tried to explain how it worked when he used summoning magic. She'd watched him call his phone and put it away several times now.

"I have the magic, the potion just makes it more… active."

"I wish I understood, but I won't lie to you, Lucas. I do not."

He laughed. "Think of it like the moon in the sky. We can see parts of it, but a telescope can allow you to see it much closer, see the craters and the texture."

"When you say it like that…" She narrowed her eyes at him, but grinned. "I think I prefer that to what I have."

She wiped her hands on a napkin, settling into the crook of his arm.

"Your power's pretty magnificent."

"You say that, but you also saw what I did."

"And I've explained what that means," he said patiently.

"I know." She didn't have to hear it again. He'd also had to do things he didn't want to do with magic, though his job had been much harder than Julia's could ever be. Assisting people in dying because they had a terminal, magical illness was awful to think about. Julia didn't even want to imagine if she had to do it. She couldn't.

"We will start practicing soon," he said and kissed her temple.

"My power hasn't even surfaced since I told you last."

"That's because you're relaxing."

"Are you calling me uptight?" she asked with narrowed eyes, but he laughed.

"I could never." He kissed her again, this time on the lips, and he tasted a little spicy. He had a way of being that intrigued her. His demeanor was one of calm, like he couldn't be bothered to rush anything. Julia had never been still in her life—it usually drove her crazy to have nothing to do. But sitting here with him, in the warmth of the day, it felt normal. She wondered how anyone could let a man like him slip through their fingers, and thought maybe Mariana wasn't as smart as she'd originally thought.

But the thought came with anxiety. She and Lucas were just having fun. It was all she could handle at the moment. But thinking of Mariana, and Cole for that matter, made the tightness in her stomach worse. Julia sat up, using her cold water as leverage to put space between them. He didn't say anything, but he must have noticed, because he didn't grab her or try to make her lean into him again.

"Something on your mind?" he asked.

"Nothing."

He narrowed his eyes on her. "I think I know you well enough to realize when you're lying."

"I'm not." It sounded like a lie. She wanted to ask him about Mariana, about Cole, about what they were doing here. But she didn't want to sound psychotic, like she was asking him to define a relationship that didn't and couldn't exist.

"You can say anything you want, Julia."

She looked up to the vines crawling onto the wooden pergola instead of him. The sky was pink, purple, and orange, quickly slipping into night, and she had the sudden urge to get up, dress, and ask for him to take her home.

"What's wrong?" He came closer but didn't touch her, and she looked at him then. Concern was written on that beautiful face, and inwardly, she berated herself for ruining the mood with her stupid issues.

"Nothing's wrong," she said, keeping her voice soft. "I'm sorry for ruining the mood."

"You haven't ruined anything."

He believed that; she could see it, too. When had she met a person who didn't jump to conclusions immediately? Not often.

"You'll judge me," she told him, convinced it was the truth.

"I could never." But that was true too.

Two things could be true.

Damn you, Mariana.

"I was scrolling through your feed the other night," she confessed, looking down at the glass on the table because she was embarrassed. It was sweating and the water dripped to the floor.

"That's what it's there for."

She did look at him then, annoyed. "There's no way you're this understanding. Drop the act."

He laughed. "I swear it's not an act. That's what social media's for. I accepted your request to follow because I don't mind if you see anything on there. Wouldn't have otherwise."

She couldn't argue with that sound logic, so she rolled her eyes and took a deep breath.

"I was scrolling and I saw a familiar face."

"Helena and Grey?"

"Among others."

His look turned quizzical. "Sophia?"

"Mariana," she finally told him, and her stomach soured as his brows rose.

"Mariana Torres?"

Oh, there it was. The confirmation. The jealousy she'd refused to let herself feel came back with a vengeance.

"How do you know Mariana?" he asked, but she had an idea that he knew.

"She's my therapist."

Lucas nodded.

"And you were wondering how *I* know her," he mused.

"I only saw it after we'd…" Julia breathed in very deeply. Anxiety was going to kill her. "After what happened at the club."

With a tilt of his head, he contemplated her in silence.

"Mariana was the last person I had a long-term relationship with," he told her.

Did she break your heart? I will destroy her if you ask me to.

"When did it end?" she asked him instead.

"Two years ago."

About the time she left Harold, then.

"Was she the one you referred to the other day?"

He nodded and looked away, and guilt took a hold of her throat.

"I'm sorry for bringing it up."

But he smiled when his eyes found her again. "I will answer any questions you have."

"Was your breakup messy?"

He shrugged. "It was honestly pretty amicable, considering the reason."

A part of Julia, one that felt weird and unfair, wondered if she wanted to keep seeing a therapist who'd cheated on her partner. That same part also wondered if Lucas was over Mariana. But Julia was over Harold, another, more rational, part reminded her.

"How'd you make that work?" Julia couldn't imagine having an amicable split from Harold.

"She told me about it after it happened," he said, as if it were that simple. "We'd been rocky for a while—I wanted to move forward in the relationship and she didn't. I was distracted helping Grey with the sick witches."

"Her cheating wasn't your fault."

He looked at her with a little smile. "I know. I've worked through it."

Yeah, what would *that* be like?

"She's a very good therapist," Lucas said, and when Julia looked startled, added, "We went to school together."

Oh. It hadn't even occurred to her.

"Why did you stop doing therapy?" she asked him.

"Because my interests were always much more complex than school prepared me for." He looked at the darkening sky, his arm behind her on the back of the couch. She wished he'd pull her close again. "I wanted to use my magical talent, but I couldn't ask for consent to read people in a therapy setting in the way I needed. People are skeptical of magic, as you can imagine."

"Boy, can I?"

"I get it, which is why I chose to leave my practice and start this." He gestured to his house. "Anyone who comes to me here knows that what I do isn't the norm for mental health, and I'm not held to the standards of the state."

"So you get to practice the career you chose, combined with the magic you love."

"Exactly."

"Is it fulfilling?" she asked because no one had ever asked her if her career in business was fulfilling to her.

He looked at her again and beamed. "Very much."

It gave her hope that maybe someday she'd be able to find the same fulfillment in a work that she was passionate about. What that was, she wasn't sure—never thought about it—but there was hope at least. She'd liked doing her job before, but there was no way she could go back to the stressful environment that had been her bread and butter in the past.

"Thank you for sharing with me."

He lifted a cynical brow. "Is that all?"

"What else do you want me to ask you?"

"I don't know. Any other questions about my social media feed?"

She slapped his chest playfully and, equipped with more confidence than she should have had, said, "What about Cole?"

Lucas chuckled. "Cole was an on and off relationship I had before Mariana came along."

"On and off?"

He cleared his throat. "How do I put this?"

"With words."

He chuckled, and this time he did pull her close again. She ordered her heart to calm the hell down. He always made her feel breathless.

"I've always been very sure of who I am, and I had support from my parents and my entire family really, except for a few close-minded relatives." She pressed her ear to his chest, to hear his voice vibrating there. "But Cole came from a different background, where he didn't have that kind of support. He didn't know what he wanted, so we went back and forth for a while, and I got sick of being his secret."

"That's fair. It must have been very hard for you."

"It was. I just wanted to show him how great he was."

"Do you ever see or talk to him?"

"Not often, but he calls from time to time. He finally came out a year ago, and his mom was surprisingly nice about it. He lives in New York with his partner now."

She hummed. "I don't think I've ever been with a man who's been with other men."

"Any different?"

If mind-blowing sex was an aspect of being bisexual, then hell yes, but she suspected it was more that he cared for the pleasure of his partners before his own. What a god, honestly.

"Not at all," she answered primly. Wouldn't want him getting a big head.

When he smirked, she smacked his arm playfully and couldn't help her own grin, leaning back into him.

"I've always loved roses," she mused after a while of watching the soft breeze ruffle the bushes. She remembered working in the garden with her mom and Roselyn and enjoying it. The way her mom always talked to the plants and leaned in to listen.

"Which ones are your favorite?" he asked.

"Those big, super fragrant ones."

"Those are the best. I have four bushes in various colors."

Everything she found out about this man made her clench her thighs together so she didn't jump him.

She was out of control. Now that she knew how good sex could be, that was all she could think about. It was honestly getting ridiculous, and they'd only spent one night together. And even speaking about his exes, she didn't feel the rush of self-consciousness. Lucas was magnificent, every aspect of him warm and accepting. Loving. So open.

Getting on her feet, she picked up the empty food containers (apparently, marathon sex made you *really* hungry) and her glass, and headed inside before he said anything else. She was in true danger around this man, and she had to go home before she did something stupid like let herself fall for him.

Already halfway there, to be honest.

Lucas followed her into the kitchen only seconds later, and they washed the glasses and cleaned the kitchen in companionable silence, which only made the tightness around her chest worse. With shaking hands, she found a towel and dried the couple of dishes he washed with his fragrant homemade soap, and set them on the counter so he could put them away. After, she turned and tried to walk away, but he grabbed her arm to stop her.

"What's wrong?"

Refusing to look up at his face, she settled for a spot on his chest. His band t-shirt was old, as was the one she was wearing, which she'd have to give back and didn't want to. She loved it. It was soft and smelled like him. She could bathe in whatever cologne he wore.

"Nothing's wrong," she mumbled.

"Julia." His tone was patient, but it didn't leave any room for her to bullshit her way out of it.

She sighed deep and long, but the words wouldn't come. His eyes were soft on her when she looked up, as she knew deep inside that they would be. Lucas wasn't judging her—he'd never judged her. She swallowed the apology that wanted to bubble up, as if she'd done something wrong, too used to apologizing for things that didn't need it. Embarrassed, she picked at a tiny lint stuck on his shirt, right by the band name, until his hand took hers.

"Look at me, Julia," he said quietly, a gentle finger coaxing her to tip her face up to his. "Would you like to watch a movie with me?"

Julia blinked, confused. Movies hadn't been on her radar in so long, she couldn't even remember the last one she'd seen. Probably some WWII epic with Harold who was obsessed with war movies.

"Maybe I should go home for a while." Her voice lilted at the end, like it was a question. His brow furrowed.

"You want to leave?"

Absolutely not.

"I just thought I should get out of your hair for a bit. Let you rest." She tried to sound nonchalant, but wasn't sure if it was working.

He didn't react, just gazed back at her like he was thinking about her words. "I mean, if you want to. I'll take you whenever you want."

Disappointment made her feel small.

"Do you want to rest?"

What the fuck are you doing, Julia? Jesus Christ.

"I don't know about you, but I slept really well last night."

"And we spent the entire day having sex."

"Are you tired?" he asked with one of those half-lidded looks.

Honestly, she could go again several more times. She was a nymphomaniac for this man. His knowing smile annoyed her, so she slapped his chest and went to step back. But his hand snatched her arm again and he brought her roughly against him.

"You're not going home," he growled, looking at her lips.

"What if I asked you to take me right now?" she challenged because she wouldn't be herself if she didn't at least put up a little fight.

"Then I'd take you home," he said. "As much as I'd like to act like a caveman and tie you to my bed."

Her whole body tingled.

"And if I wanted to tie you instead?"

His brows shot up and his cheeks warmed. "I'd let you."

She fought a smile, but it came anyway. "What movie were you thinking?"

He grinned and ten minutes later, a bowl of popcorn on her lap, she reclined on his lap in the upstairs TV room.

When he got the house, he'd had the whole upstairs redone, and it consisted of his bedroom, the ensuite, and the big walk-in closet. The rest of the floor was a sitting room, combined with a space where he had weird items on shelves, along with a huge black cauldron in the corner. The television was mounted on the wall, a huge flat screen where he played a comedy he liked from the 90s. She was into it, snorting into a glass of soda they were sharing when the protagonist nearly got shot after a terrible misunderstanding. Under her, Lucas laughed too, and she settled all the way back against him, relaxed, happy. As the movie went along, his fingertips started roaming against her skin, and soon, she was straddling him, the TV nothing but background noise. When she'd driven him half crazy with her mouth, he threw her over his shoulder and carried her to the bedroom, where he took his time showing her just how much he wanted her.

19

Over the next few days, Julia went home once, to pick up a bag with clothes. Because Lucas was with her, of course, they'd ended up fucking on the windowsill, and that was one less thing she had to check off her sex bucket list.

Once they were back in his house, since it was easier to do magic there, they sat across from each other in the dining room, with the beautiful design on the tile floor. Julia felt like she was actually out in the cosmos. Lucas had made the table disappear to who knew where, and they sat on the floor, the curtains pulled over windows and the lights off completely. Candles surrounded the entire room, sending warm light into every corner. It felt like a movie, and the wings of his butterflies seemed to move with every dancing shadow.

"Ready?" he said when he'd finished his potion.

"Not even a little."

He held his hands forward, palms up, so she put her hands on them, relishing his warmth.

"Can't we just have sex again?" she said, only half-joking.

He smiled. "Don't worry, I have plans for you later."

She squirmed and leaned forward. Smiling into her eyes, he placed a kiss on her lips, but pulled back way too quickly.

"Breathe," he commanded softly, and she focused on her breath. The sooner she did this, the sooner they could be done and get naked.

"Now," he said, "remember where in your body you feel your magic."

With her stomach churning, she tried to focus, but her heart was beating really fast now.

"Remember to breathe. Nerves are okay," he said.

That was easy for him to say; he already knew how to use magic. But when it really got down to it, it wasn't hard going to the exact place she always felt her magic first. It was a warmth in her gut, something tight. Then, it always moved like it was a living thing, like she had a snake sleeping inside her and it awoke to make its presence known. Her hands trembled even as they warmed. The heat was on her face, right behind her nose, and every time she breathed out, it felt like pure fire.

"Okay, now look at the feather," Lucas said, sounding very, very far away.

She opened her eyes, found the long white feather he'd placed on the floor between them.

"Concentrate on it."

All she could see was the feather, but when she moved her hand to make it fly, a vase that sat on a small table across the room flew into the wall and shattered. Julia screamed, throwing her arms over her head, even though it wasn't even close to her.

"What the fuck?" she yelled. Lucas dissolved into a deep laughter that left him red and with tears in his eyes. She could only watch him, stunned, trying not to laugh too because what she'd just done was bad.

"I broke your vase," Julia said, pushing him a little.

"It was just a cool vase I saw at the home store one day."

"And?"

"It's not a big deal."

Julia stuck her hands under her thighs.

"And if I'd hit you over the head with it?" she asked.

"Then I really wouldn't be laughing."

"Come on, Lucas. Be serious."

He pushed forward onto his hands and knees and kissed her.

"I'm so serious." Another, deeper kiss. "Serio como un ataque al corazón. I don't care about the vase. You used your power on purpose." He took her lips in a kiss so deep, so luscious, she forgot what happened. His hand slid into her bra—she'd left her shirt somewhere in the house, maybe the kitchen—her nipples hardening against the rub of his thumb.

"I could have killed you," she muttered around his lips, her body warm all over with desire now.

"You already do that, no vases needed." He pulled away, and she leaned forward as he did so.

"No," she whined and took hold of his neck to kiss him again.

"Don't try to distract me, woman."

Julia sat back. "If I have to try, I've lost my touch."

His eyes flashed and he directed his gaze downward, where his pants were tented.

She snorted. "Noted."

Grinning, he gestured to the feather. "Let's try it again."

"Shouldn't we clean that mess first?" she asked, but with a wave of his hand, the shattered vase disappeared, and so did her procrastination gimmick.

His raised brow made her roll her eyes, but she still closed them and listened to his soft guidance.

It happened faster now. She was able to find that place where the snake at the base of her spine moved. Her power warmed her and moved all over her body. But this time, it was also *outside* of her, running over her skin and leaving her elated.

"Very good," Lucas said, but his voice was only a soft sigh, as if the sound had been picked up and diluted by the wind.

Julia opened her eyes, and she was in her mother's attic. She froze by the door, where she could see the entirety of the space, wondering how she was here. Had she... ported? It was the only thing that made any sense. One minute she'd been sitting across from Lucas, and now this.

The attic was small, and there were a lot of things crammed in it. Somehow, it didn't feel cramped, though, just cozy. Cool hardwood floor under bare feet, Julia took in the room. Two windows with white curtains, all in different styles, gave the room an air of whimsy. A narrow table held a colorful shell with a long bundle of herbs her mom liked to burn. The house always smelled like it, but Julia wasn't sure what the herbs were. She'd never asked when she'd watch her mom whisper things into the corners of the house, holding the herbs while they burned, smoke swirling. Briefly, she was reminded of the shop Lucas had taken her to. That was why it was so familiar.

"But what if Daddy gets mad?" The young voice came from behind Julia, and she moved out of the way—though it occurred to her that she may not need to—and watched a young version of herself walk into the attic. Little Julia looked around the age of five, maybe six at the most. Skinny and wearing a cute flowing dress like those her mom liked to wear, her hair was long and pulled back into a couple of braids.

And right behind Little Julia, her mom came into the room, holding a little stick of incense in a wooden holder.

Julia froze, and a shivering sound left her. There was the urge to cry, but no tears came to her eyes as she walked forward and stared at her mom. She was so beautiful, with gorgeous dark skin and long curly hair that she'd left loose around her. It reached the small of her back, just like Julia remembered. Hazel eyes sparkling, she set the wooden incense holder down on the table next to the shell and turned to smile at Little Julia.

"Daddy won't get mad at you," her mom said, and hearing that voice, one she'd missed so, so much, Julia closed her eyes and just savored whatever delusion this was.

"I don't like it when he gets mad," Little Julia said, holding on to her mother tightly.

"None of us do."

Little Julia missed the look of pure heartbreak in her mother's expression, but Julia, the one who was grown and had way too much experience with grief, did not.

"Mommy," Little Julia said, going over to where her mom had a small iron cauldron. "When will you teach me to listen to the plants?"

Her mom chuckled. "Always so eager for more, my sweet jewel. All in due time."

"Sophia says she hears them. Did you teach her and not me?" Little Julia asked with a little pout. Sophia, at that time, would've been three.

"I didn't have to teach Sophia," Mom said.

"I want that power too. It's so unfair."

"Sophia can't move things with her mind, and you can."

Little Julia still wasn't having it, already resistant to her magic at a time when wonder should have been the default emotion.

"I broke the window and Daddy got mad."

Her mom bent at the waist to look at Little Julia in the eye.

"Daddy doesn't know you broke the window."

Julia's heart squeezed painfully at those words. How many things had her mom taken responsibility for, to avoid her husband being upset at her daughters?

"Why can't I tell anyone about my magic, Mommy?"

"Because there are a lot of people out there who don't know about magic, and it's best to keep it that way."

"Why?"

"Because magic is a beautiful, dangerous thing."

"If it's dangerous, maybe we shouldn't be doing it then."

Her mom smiled. Julia came closer so she could hear them, because things were hazy, and their voices were getting faint.

"You get to choose," her mom said softly, her voice an echo, "if you want to use magic or not. But first, you have to learn."

Their figures froze, as if someone had pressed a pause button, and the scene around her dissolved swiftly, and now Julia sat under the piano in the parlor. With her, Little Julia and Roselyn. Little Julia was trembling, and she remembered this. It was after she'd broken that window, when she realized how much trouble she would be in if her father found out what she'd done.

Little Julia wasn't crying, just throwing looks toward the archway, the only way into this room from the front of the house.

"He's not home yet," Roselyn said. She was two years older than Julia, and though they all looked alike, it was Roselyn and Julia who looked the most like one another. Her mom used to say that Julia and Roselyn looked like their grandmother the most.

But at that tender age, Roselyn had eyes that were wise, even to adult Julia.

"It's going to be okay," Roselyn said and held Little Julia's hand. Instantly, Little Julia stopped trembling and her tears subsided.

Julia's mouth was open, looking at the scene, trying to understand what happened. According to her mother's journals, Roselyn had the power of empathy, and she could siphon feelings into her own little body.

Julia could have stayed there forever, could have gotten out from underneath the piano and gone to find her mom, but the tiny versions of Sophia, Grey, and Victoria ran across the room toward the back, and Roselyn and Little Julia took off after them. The scene dissolved, and she hoped with all her heart that there would be another as everything went completely black.

Julia's eyes opened and focused on the ornate chandelier above her. Everything was still mostly dark, just the candles burning around her.

She felt normal and it was weird.

"Oh my god, you're awake," Lucas whispered and she found him kneeling next to her on the floor. He was still naked from the waist up, just as she'd left him when she went… Well, she had no idea where she went.

"What happened?" she croaked as she tried to sit. He helped her up and took her in a tight hug. His heart was racing, and he was trembling slightly.

"I couldn't wake you up," he said against her hair.

"For how long?"

"I think maybe two minutes?" He took her face in his hands and peered into her eyes. It was so dark she could barely make out the color of his. "It felt like an eternity."

She'd scared him half to death and she'd wanted to stay back there with her young self and her mom.

Her body felt tired, sluggish and heavy, like she'd run three marathons in a row.

"I had memories of my childhood," she said when she could form words again. "I saw myself as a little girl. And Roselyn. I forgot how much we looked like each other."

Her chest spasmed, her breath coming in short bursts. Lucas held her hands.

"Take deep breaths for me," he instructed gently.

She tried, she really did, but trembled uncontrollably as tears gathered in her eyes.

"Julia," he said, coming closer. "Baby, breathe. Just take a deep breath for me."

Julia did as he asked, though it cost her. She laid down on the floor as the world started spinning and the buzzing started in her ears. Shutting her eyes, she lengthened her breaths until the whirring stopped.

"That's it," Lucas whispered, and she opened her eyes to see that he'd laid down next to her. Letting tears fall, she turned on her side just as he did.

"I saw my mom," she whispered, and told him the details of her dream or delusion or whatever the hell that had been. He listened in complete silence, not even stopping her to clarify anything. When she finished, his eyes were misty, and his hand reached up to wipe at a tear that ran over her nose.

The look of pure concern on his face made her want to cry even more.

"What does it all mean?" she asked before she melted under his touch and spoke words that resonated inside her. That spoke of the way she felt about him at that moment.

"We learn all our unconscious processes when we're too young to remember what caused them," he said, and she could imagine him explaining this in his own practice, or in an office like Mariana had.

"I've never had anything like that happen before. It was like hypnosis." It occurred to her that maybe he'd done it, but he shook his head before she was done asking.

"If we ever used hypnosis for any reason, we'd talk about it extensively beforehand," he said.

That tracked.

"I'm just glad you're okay," he murmured before he kissed her softly. When he pulled back, Julia reached for his chin, touching that face that she'd come to love so much. The thought came to her swiftly, so gentle that she couldn't even fight against the notion of it. She was just left with the way it felt to have her heart now living outside her body. With him. Always.

Julia leaned forward and kissed him again to stop herself from saying something she would surely regret. Her kiss turned deep and hungry for him in a way she hadn't experienced before with him. A yearning, a need, a melancholy that was unexplainable as she reached for the waistband of his pants.

"Mami, espérate," he whispered, pulling away. "Are you sure you don't want to rest after what happened?"

To answer him, she kissed him again, leading his hand to her shorts.

"I want you," she whispered back, arching against his hand as it slipped into her underwear and found her hot and slick for him.

Slowly, they moved together, taking off the little clothes they had, making their way toward the stairs. But they hadn't made it halfway up when she straddled him and rode him until they were both panting and she came so hard she saw stars in his clear pupils. Picking her up when she was trembling, he waved a hand and all the candles extinguished as he took her up to the bedroom and drove her to the edge of madness all over again.

Later, naked and breathing hard, laying on top of the covers, he turned to her with his hand under his cheek. The lights were burning brightly above. No need for sex in the dark with a man who looked like that.

"There's a celebration at my dad's house on Sunday," he said, maybe a little shyly. She knew what was coming and steeled herself. "Would you like to come with me?"

A shivering breath left her as panic gripped her by the throat again. She couldn't escape it, the fear that bounded all over her body, so she didn't answer right away as she tried to calm down her heart.

"It's okay if you don't," he reassured her after watching her silently. "It's been a hard night, so if you want to think about it, I can wait."

She'd forgotten how much he picked up on, even when he wasn't using his magic to peek. He looked a little disappointed, and her heart melted a little. Julia had never been able to bear the disappointment of her loved ones, and this man... She would do anything for him. Forcing herself to breathe and relax, she said, "I've never been to Puerto Rico."

His smile was so wide, it hurt her soul. How could she be an anxious, grumpy gremlin with this adorable man?

But that night, with all the experiences she'd had, the memories she'd somehow accessed, she slept very little, wondering when their bubble was going to burst.

20

When she'd said yes to going to the island with him, Julia now suspected she'd been under the influence. Under the delirium of sex and that desperate heartsickness she didn't want to put a label to.

Lucas was on his way, which meant he'd be there any second, as he was porting them to the island. Of course, why would they take a plane when he was a witch and could travel instantly? His family knew about the magic, and he had places to port to without being seen by other eyes.

Julia must have changed ten times before finally opting for jeans, which fit nicely, and a tailored blouse with short sleeves and a sweetheart neckline. Paired with some heels, she'd look put-together and not the hot mess she felt like.

The nightmares had returned the moment she'd gone home from Lucas's, just when she'd thought she was making progress. But she'd needed to be alone, to allow herself to think clearly, which she could not do when he was around.

This time, she'd dreamt that the blood reached her neck, with a promise to drown her in future nightmares. The worst part was that in her desperation, she'd reached for Lucas on the other side of the bed, just to find it empty. She'd nearly called him, needing that comfort he brought with his mere presence. A few nights with him and her mind was too accustomed. It couldn't end well, this need.

Finished getting ready, having left her hair wavy, she walked toward the front of the house with her shoes in her hands to wait for Lucas. He appeared not too long after, and her heart skipped a beat when she realized they were wearing almost the same shade of blue on their shirts and black pants. As if they'd planned it.

His smile was bright and sexy as all hell when he saw her. The collar of his shirt was left open, the long line of his throat exposed, showing the ends of some of his tattoos. Resisting the urge to press her lips to her favorite spot right underneath his ear, she smiled instead.

"You look so sexy," he said as she approached him, and leaned down to kiss her. Glad that she'd opted for just a little bit of gloss, she clung to him as her body warmed. Suddenly, everything felt okay; like she could go to his father's party and enjoy herself, then come back here and have her wicked way with him.

"We should go before I change my mind," she said as she slipped on her shoes, with his hand around her arm to stabilize her.

"Why would you change your mind?"

She looked up at his handsome face. "I'm meeting your father."

His hands gripped her shoulders comfortingly.

"There's nothing to be worried about. They're going to love you."

There was something left unspoken after his words, but Julia found that her mind didn't want to go wherever that was. Swallowing another knot of anxiety, she stepped close and held on to him. Soon, the world turned dark and watery as they ported. Her heart gave a wild lurch when they reappeared in what looked like an orchard. There were trees of many kinds; mango, coconut, a passion fruit vine creating a canopy over them, and other fruits she didn't know. All she could think of was how happy this would have made her mom, and how much she wished she could bring Lucas around to meet her family. To have him there for dinners and special occasions.

He caught her hand and kissed it before he led them out of the little orchard, which was surrounded by a tall concrete wall that afforded them privacy for magic. The house was ahead, and walking toward it holding hands with him was almost surreal. The house was a soft blue color, two stories, with glass louvered windows and ornate bars on the outside. They followed a small dirt path through an iron gate, her heels sinking into it a little, so she mostly leaned on the balls of her feet. The ornate, iron back door opened to a covered carport, where a white truck was parked.

The front of the house was also enclosed by iron bars. Lucas opened the gate in front of the door and knocked once before he twisted the doorknob. Unaware that she was holding his hand too tightly, she followed him into the house.

Grayer and only slightly more wrinkled, dressed in a white button-down shirt and dark pants, the man before her looked like an older Lucas. He was sitting on a rocking chair with a book in his lap when he raised his whitening head and smiled brightly.

"Hijo!" he called when he saw Lucas. Standing, he came forward and the two hugged.

"Bendición," Lucas murmured, and his father kissed him on the forehead. Julia's heart gave a squeeze. What she wouldn't give to have a father like that, or to have had her mom for long enough to ask for a blessing. To receive that kind of open affection, like it was normal and not something they avoided.

"Dios te bendiga," his father said, and then his eyes found Julia. "Me imagino que esta es la jovencita que lo tiene loco."

She got like three of those words, or at least the gist of it anyway. Julia blushed as she stepped forward, putting on her best face—like she'd been taught. She would treat this like a business meeting; charm them with what she knew and learn what she didn't.

Lucas squeezed her hand. "Dad, this is Julia," he said, smiling. "Julia, my dad, Roman."

"It's wonderful to meet you," she said, holding out her hand, which Roman took warmly.

"A pleasure, Julia," Roman said in heavily accented English, which was just as charming as Lucas's was. "Bienvenida."

"Gracias," she said, and the level of awkwardness was what hell must be like every day.

She took a seat when it was offered, and they talked for a while, before everything got chaotic as everyone started showing up. Lucas's oldest sister, Antonia, showed up first with her two teen sons. She looked a lot like Lucas, but her skin was lighter, and her short hair was straight as a pin on her shoulders. Antonia was friendly but reserved, and Julia found herself fidgeting. Lucas's sisters meant everything to him, and she wanted to make a good impression.

"You're so pretty," Antonia said after greeting her with a kiss on the cheek, which Julia was definitely not used to.

Julia mumbled a thanks, already overwhelmed and wishing she could control her heart rate. But she didn't have time to relax as Lucas's other two sisters, Karla and Josefina, showed up, alongside two uncles from their mother's side, an aunt from his dad's, and about fifteen cousins who may or may not be actual cousins but were close to the family.

Karla was sweet and warm, and she and Josefina greeted Julia with a kiss on the cheek each. However, the chill coming from the youngest of the sisters was not lost on Julia. Where Karla immediately established a conversation with Julia, Josefina just eyed her from head to foot.

"Those are amazing shoes," Karla said. Her black hair was pulled back into a giant bun, and her eyes were a lot like Lucas's.

"Thank you," Julia said with a smile, glad she had something in common with at least one of them. Her smile flickered as Josefina widened her eyes a little, her smile more a grimace than anything else.

"Muy bonitos," Josefina said as some of the cousins came to talk to them.

There was a flurry of introductions, so many names she'd struggle to remember, but she was friendly to everyone, wanting to make sure that Lucas left his home feeling like she'd made an effort. Her Spanish was limited, but she realized that she could understand more than she'd thought as she listened to everyone talking to each other.

If she paid close attention, she could respond to questions directed at her, even though it took her a little long to figure out the right words.

Josefina kept her distance, and it made Julia want to fawn hard. She didn't have the need to be liked by everyone she met, but the chill from Josefina unnerved her. Julia knew that chill well—she'd dished it out often in boardrooms.

Later in the afternoon, having eaten delicious mofongo, made by Antonia, Julia laughed as Roman talked about the shenanigans he got into when he was younger. It was loud in a way that was both a little much and comforting. There were people dancing, others singing loudly and off-key, and when Lucas pulled her onto his lap, she smiled down at him and settled back against him. And she tried to ignore how Josefina was throwing her covert dirty looks.

It was pathetic. Had she really learned nothing in the year of therapy?

Lucas's laugh rumbled through her, and she looked back to meet his warm gaze as he laughed at whatever joke she hadn't heard. He took her hand, kissed her fingers, and said something in rapid Spanish she didn't even catch half of.

Julia hadn't had this kind of fun in… well, ever. A Latin party was something else; chill, without the pomp and the showing off. None of the parties she'd ever been to in her high society circles had ever felt fun like this. No one sat around a domino table and yelled at each other when they thought someone was cheating.

Her father had always taught her that a party was a great opportunity to talk to important people in a less formal setting. It was always about the business.

But not here as she sat on Lucas's lap as if they'd been doing it forever, as his uncles shamelessly flirted with her, and the oldest of the two, Rogelio, told her she should run off with him instead.

She even danced with him as another game of dominoes started, then with Lucas's dad after he blew out the candles, and finally with Lucas.

There was no shame in him as he led her around the tight space, dancing among his loved ones with her and mouthing the words of songs while his eyes were on hers. As if he were singing to her, not just singing for the sake of it. It made her glow, and it hit her then how she didn't want to live in a world in which she wasn't doing this every weekend with him. She wanted to come here and visit his dad, learn more about their family, their culture.

She even forgot to worry about this feeling that grew in her every time Lucas looked at her with those honey eyes and touched her just because, without expecting anything.

At the end of the afternoon, as the sun started to set, she helped clean up, still laughing about the game of dominoes she'd lost because she couldn't quite grasp the concept of the game.

Lucas left to check out the garden with his dad and uncles, something about a dying herb, and Julia found herself roped into bringing dishes into the kitchen. The whole house was painted a light blue color, with white doors and trimming around the ceiling. But the kitchen was bright, the cabinets a darker teal with gold handles, and a backsplash that was many shades of blue and green. It reminded her so much of Lucas's kitchen, it made her smile when she found herself walking in on Josefina and her two nephews washing dishes at the sink.

The three of them looked up when she entered, and Julia froze.

"I thought I'd come help you," she said, feeling like a dumbass. She handed them glasses, some empty, some still with beer in them.

"Benito!" Antonia called from the front of the house, and the boys rushed off, leaving Julia and Josefina alone.

"Thank you for having me," Julia said, hating that she was still trying so hard to make this woman like her. It wasn't like she'd done something wrong; she'd just shown up with Lucas. He'd say that Josefina's behavior had nothing to do with her, but she found that very hard to believe at the moment.

"Of course," Josefina said with something close to a smile, but not quite.

"Your cake was delicious. I can't really bake. Or cook very well."

Josefina's grimace almost looked like a smile.

"Yeah, the boardroom doesn't lend itself to learning such skills, I suppose," Josefina said derisively as she put away a glass.

Not altogether wrong, but it still bugged Julia. She wasn't ashamed of her past career. But she got the picture, and perhaps a bit awkwardly, she started to turn away.

"Thanks for everything."

She was almost at the door when Josefina spoke next.

"He doesn't bring people here often."

Julia froze, then turned back to look at Josefina, who was now leaning against the counter with her arms crossed.

"You must be very special."

Her first instinct was to get defensive, but she waited for Josefina to keep talking, as she obviously wanted to.

"Do you have brothers, Julia?"

"Two sisters." Julia shifted uncomfortably, afraid of where this was going.

"Then you know how protective a person can be about their siblings."

Julia took a couple of steps closer.

"I do," Julia said, and she drew herself taller. Josefina was tall, at eye level with Julia, even barefoot.

"Then you also understand that there's nothing I wouldn't do to protect my brother."

Julia bit down her annoyance. She wasn't going to end the night in a shouting match with Josefina, in spite of her nosiness.

"What I don't get is what you think you're protecting him from."

Josefina scoffed and huffed out a humorless laugh.

"Of course you haven't noticed. My God."

Julia froze, her mind failing to find any way to respond that didn't make her sound like a bitch.

Nosy older sisters were to be expected. She was one of those, after all. It was all concern, and she could at least relate to that. But her mind went back to the looks across the domino table as Lucas tried to explain how everything worked, and the way he held her close as he mouthed words of songs that terrified her at a cellular level. The look in his eye when he found her in a crowd. How it made her feel when he did, like her heart was glowing, about to burst with emotions she wasn't ready for.

"Why don't you just say what's on your mind, Josefina? I don't have time for games."

Josefina's face became a mask of anger. Terrible and beautiful. "Lucas being in love with you is not a game to me."

It was like Josefina had drilled a hole in her stomach and everything fell through it. Shaking, Julia braced herself against the corner of the counter, and every sharp word she would have used to put Josefina in her place died on her tongue.

One thing was knowing. Another was hearing it out loud. And an entirely different one was the way her own heart responded to it. Like it had the other night when she realized that she was irrevocably in love with him.

Her ears rang, and she couldn't move as Josefina stared her down.

"I know women like you. Rich princesses who don't give two fucks about getting in touch with their roots, until they're fucking a brown man to use as a prop."

"You don't know what you're talking about," Julia said, weakly.

"Oh, I do. You think I don't know who you are? The internet exists."

Shaking, nauseated, Julia had no words to deny it. To fight for herself. Chills ran up and down her body. How could she have thought they wouldn't know what a mess she was? Delusional's what she was.

Josefina came closer, and Julia saw that there were tears in her eyes.

"Lucas is the best person I know. He's good, and he's soft, and he's carried burdens you have no idea about with your privilege and your light skin."

"That's not what—"

"Not what?" Josefina interrupted. "Are you in love with him?"

The words got stuck in her throat.

Yes, she wanted to say. *Of course I love him. He is the best person any-one could know. He's been kind and gentle when I've been so hard to love.*

But as she stood frozen, Josefina shook her head sadly.

"You're not good enough for him."

Julia felt the blood drain from her face, and as Josefina left the kitchen, she fought tears of anger and grief.

There had been no lies in Josefina's cruel words, and even Julia could admit that. Her eyes filled with tears, but she ruthlessly pushed them back. A deep breath and she swallowed it all, every little fissure in her heart. So much of who she was had always depended on how people saw her, on how capable she was. Confident, independent to a fault, cool-headed. Dependable. But she could no longer be any of those things, not with how easily it was to break her like this. How Josefina's words mangled the little self-esteem she had built in the weeks since she'd been seeing Lucas, first as her teacher, then as her lover.

But later. She'd deal with it later, when she was alone and no one could witness how broken she still was, despite having thought she'd had some sort of breakthrough.

Outwardly, she was composed as she found Lucas outside. She pasted a smile on her face, a practiced one she'd perfected when expectations mattered more than how she felt.

Lucas smiled at her, his eyes warm, his hand soft as it took hers. Julia didn't look at Josefina, who ignored her pointedly as they said their goodbyes.

Pain in her lower back, she clung on to him as they headed back to his house. She should have pushed him away, but she reached for him instead. He kissed her deeply, like he always did, his mouth magic on hers, and she held him close. Closer than she ever had. But when their clothes were off, she realized she was bleeding. The pain in her lower back radiated to her abdomen, and tears sprang to her eyes. God, how could she have missed this too?

"Hey, it's okay," he whispered, pulling his boxer shorts on.

It wasn't okay.

She couldn't say anything as he helped her clean up. It should have humiliated her, but it didn't. He was gentle as he got her clean underwear from her overnight bag. She'd at least packed what she needed, since a girl could never be prepared enough for periods. When she had pajamas on, another one of his shirts and a pair of her own shorts, she met him outside the bathroom.

Lucas offered her a tiny vial of potion.

"It's the strongest thing I've got for pain," he said. "I'm not sure if it's strong enough, but it will at least take the edge off."

She looked up at him. She couldn't believe how this man could be a real person. And there it was in his eyes. A softness, an uninhibited way that he looked at her. Her heart tumbling, stomach sour, she took the potion and looked away before she did something she would regret.

In bed, a heating pad pressed to her abdomen, she closed her eyes, doing what was surely a terrible job pretending to sleep.

"Hey," he whispered, taking her face in his hands. "Look at me."

Close to tears, she opened her eyes and found his in the light of the single lamp they'd left lit. There was a question in them, and his mouth opened, but panicked, worried of what he'd say, she kissed him.

"Thank you," she whispered. His scent was all she could smell, his skin all she felt between his fingers. But she couldn't be the actress in those moments, couldn't show him the confident Julia. The one who had become uninhibited in his bed, the one that allowed herself to be caressed and brought to the edge of oblivion. Tonight, she let him hold her so close that he didn't see how her heart was breaking.

21

Something was wrong. Lucas couldn't put his finger on it, but Julia's energy had changed, and due to his personal philosophy of not peeking without express consent, rare anxiety had taken hold of him. His mind wasn't in his work, which today was helping Grey with deliveries.

"Finis communicationis," Grey murmured when the head of their last client of the day disappeared.

Glad to be done, Lucas helped clean up the two circles of salts and herbs he and Grey had concocted for deliveries. A larger one for the client, a smaller for trades and payments.

"Everything okay?" Grey asked as he took the large jar with the salt they would reuse the following week when more orders came in from witches all around the world.

"Yeah," Lucas said simply, but even he heard the lack of conviction in his own voice. Grey set down the jar where one of the salt circles had been just moments ago.

"I don't usually doubt your word," Grey said, "but that was a lie if I've ever heard one."

Lucas turned to his best friend in the world. Grey had been there for him ever since they met in college. Together, they had done things with magic that no one would even dream of. Thankfully, they didn't have to do some of those things anymore, but the man wasn't someone to lie to for no reason.

"I just had trouble sleeping last night."

Grey's facial expression didn't change much. His long hair was pulled to the top of his head, and weirdly, they were both dressed similarly. For the first time in ages, Lucas hadn't really felt like spending time picking out his clothes that morning, opting for old jeans and a simple rock band t-shirt that had seen better days.

"What's bothering you?"

Julia. The woman had buried herself under his skin so fast, his head had a hard time catching up, and the only other person who really knew how much was Grey. Lucas had even avoided talking to Helena too much, since she was becoming close to Julia and he didn't want the conflict of interest there.

"It's Julia, isn't it?" Grey kept cleaning up, so Lucas followed suit. He was driving himself crazy. This was why he took so much time to start dating after his relationship with Mariana had fallen apart. He'd always fallen fast and first. Every single time. And every single time, he was the one having to protect his overly-eager heart. With Julia, he'd known from the start that she wasn't available, and still, he couldn't help it but flirt endlessly with her. He truly hadn't been thinking when he'd decided to take her on dates to relax her. Lying to others was one thing, lying to himself was another.

Still, he couldn't bring himself to regret it. The woman was like a stick of dynamite, walking into his life and leaving every carefully placed brick in shambles.

In the pantry, he stopped.

"She's being weird."

"Weird how?"

"Same old. I think you'd know." Julia was convinced that Grey hated her, though that was far from the truth. Grey had tried so much in the past two years to connect with her, but she was in her head about everything. It was what made Lucas want to help her. No one was harder on themself than Julia.

Grey nodded solemnly. "Sophia's tried to talk to her about all this."

"She won't listen to anyone. I thought we were making progress, but things changed last Sunday." The moment they'd left the island, he'd felt the swift change, like she was retreating again.

They'd worked hard together, to help her get out of her head, but something was wrong. He could have asked, but she wasn't going to tell him. Julia hid parts of herself like a dragon its gold, all in trying to avoid getting hurt. Ironic that she always ended up hurt anyway.

"Did she have a good time at your dad's?"

"I thought she did. Everyone loved her. Maybe except for Josefina, but she doesn't like anyone at first." His sister was certainly someone who would benefit wildly from some self-work, but she refused, convinced she could handle it all on her own.

Grey grimaced, probably thinking about the first time he'd met Josefina and how rude she'd been. It wasn't until months later that Josefina finally warmed up to him.

"I'm sure she'll come around," Grey said as they finished wiping down the counters. Lucas took the broom, sweeping any debris left behind as Grey reorganized the potions they had left in the pantry.

"She usually does, right?" Lucas said, but he was unconvinced. It had been so long since he'd felt this level of anxiety about a person he was into that all he wanted was to get rid of it. But he knew better than to do that. It would just make everything worse anyway, so he steeled his spine and told himself he'd work through the uncomfortable emotion instead. Easier said than done, but he had to at least try.

His feelings for Julia had grown so fast, after that very first meeting when she'd looked up at him with so much trust she probably wasn't even aware she was giving him. And what could he say? He was attracted to her snappy attitude for reasons only his therapist could explain well.

After they were finished cleaning, he followed Grey out to the covered porch on the side of the house, which overlooked the ocean in the distance. They'd sat out there countless times before, contemplating life when they'd had to witness people let go of theirs.

Surprisingly, the void had brought them closer together, which Lucas could at least be grateful for.

It'd been a lovely day, sunny, clear, but his heart was not in the right place for him to enjoy it. Not when Julia wasn't responding to his texts.

After the third one, he'd stopped himself from calling her, to avoid overwhelming her any more than she already was, most likely. She hid when things were hard, and though all he wanted was to be her refuge, he couldn't—*wouldn't*—force it on her.

"I can ask Sophia, if you want," Grey offered, but Lucas was shaking his head before his friend was even done speaking.

"No, I don't want to put Sophia in that position." He was the man sleeping with her sister. Lucas couldn't make her go behind Julia's back and risk making whatever was happening worse.

Meanwhile, he'd have to force himself to relax, to allow things to develop on their own. Julia was a big girl—she could text him back when she felt like it, and he wasn't going to sit here pining.

That was a lie, he was definitely going to pine, but at least he wasn't going to be too obvious about it. They'd talk when they talked.

It was much later when he went home, already dark, after eating dinner with Grey since Sophia was extra busy these days, as the expansion to her club began.

He pulled into the garage and was about to get into the shower when he heard the knock. Immediately, he knew it was Julia. Heart jumping, he hurried across the house to open the front door. When he saw her, the bottom of his stomach dropped. She looked gray, like she hadn't slept since he saw her last, almost five days ago.

Unable to stop himself, he pulled her close.

"Qué pasó, mami?" he whispered as her arms went around his neck like a vise.

"I'm sorry I haven't responded," she whispered, her breath warm against his neck.

"What happened?" He closed the door and they stood like that, hugging in the entryway until she pushed away. Midnight and Opal bounded forward, aware of her energy. They were excellent companions for that reason. Lucas had seen it right away, when he'd gone to see them when they were born, and their instincts had only gotten better in the months since he'd had them. They wound themselves around Julia's feet, then his, making perfect little infinity tracks between the two.

"Has your power surfaced again?" The heat in his stomach rose to his throat, but he breathed to push it away. This wasn't about him.

Julia shook her head, but she wouldn't look at him. Still, he saw that there were tears in the brown depths. She looked like she wanted to say something, but her mouth opened several times without anything actually coming out. Finally, she settled on, "I just really wanted to see you." Her voice shook, though she tried to hide it.

A little fissure ran over his heart, so he kissed her forehead and poured every little bit of calm and comfort he had left in his energy reserves. He'd been struggling to do magic all day, not having slept, but he didn't care right now. Not when she needed him.

"I'm so glad you're here." He held her gaze so that she saw how serious he was. He wanted her to know that she didn't have to talk if she didn't want to, that he would be there for her anyway, and that she was safe.

Bending his knees, he scooped her up in his arms. The weight of her had become familiar, comforting. He could see it becoming his favorite thing in the whole world for the rest of his life. Oh, who was he kidding? It already was.

Her hands were in his hair now, and she was kissing him while he made his way up to the bedroom. Maybe he was avoiding the inevitable conversation they'd need to have, but in those moments, he didn't care. He wanted her to feel good, to take that sadness from her eyes. Dance with her every single day for the rest of their lives.

Upstairs, emotion building inside him, they only separated to remove their clothes hurriedly. She wanted control, so he gave it to her.

Her body was made of pure magic, so warm, so pliant under his hands. She kissed him hard, and it swelled inside him, that emotion he'd had trouble keeping at bay whenever she was around. And even when she wasn't.

"Julia," he moaned as her hips moved them both toward the abyss. The words started to form, but he saw it then, the panic in her eyes before she kissed him again. Still, as they came together, his eyes were wet, and it didn't escape him that so were hers.

22

Julia waited until he was asleep, hours later, before she slipped out of the bed and rushed to dress with shaky hands. He didn't move as she left quietly, only allowing herself to breathe when she was in the rideshare. Guilt gnawed at her for sneaking out like that without at least telling him why. She didn't need the conversation—wasn't sure if she could handle it. Coming here was a mistake. It would only torture him. She'd seen the look in his eye, how much he'd held in those clear depths. Everything she felt reflected there so she couldn't escape it.

She fought an intense urge to look back at the house as the car pulled away from the curb. It was better this way, she told herself over and over, stamping down every emotion until she couldn't even trace what they were anymore, swallowing every ounce of guilt.

But when the driver pulled up to the house, having battled with herself for too long, she couldn't keep herself safe from the onslaught of emotions that came over her when she saw the car parked on the side of the road. The black SUV she knew so well—entirely black, with tinted windows and black interior. It was like a hole of despair. She thanked her driver and practically ran up to the front door. Her fingers were shaking so badly, she failed to put in the code on the digital keypad. Panicked, she tried again. The door clicked and she stepped inside the doorway to see Harold walking up the driveway as calmly as if he were taking a walk in a park.

"There's no need to run," he drawled, but in a way that told her he was angry and holding back. How many times had she been on the other end of his anger or watched him be angry with someone else?

Julia could have shut the door in his face, but she was paralyzed. She stood right inside the wards of the house, watching him bound up the steps.

It was hard not to notice how beautiful he was. If only the inside matched, he'd be the perfect man. But, alas.

"What the hell do you want?" she asked as he came to the stoop, his fingers inside his jean pockets.

"Getting home a little late, aren't you?" And there was that smirk she'd like to wipe off his face with a chair.

"Don't you have a pregnant girlfriend to take care of?"

"Wife, actually." He grinned, showing her his shiny new silver band. "Just thought I'd tell you the news myself."

It was nice that she didn't actually care. There was no emotion, negative or positive, and she realized that growth had happened anyway. Even when she hadn't noticed it.

"Why are you here, Harold?" She held back a sigh of exhaustion.

When Harold laughed, there was no mirth in the sound or in his angry eyes.

"I just wanted to let you know in person," he said, but she heard the lie. He was here because he couldn't fathom that she didn't care anymore. "We were together for so long, I thought it was best if I told you instead of you finding out via social media. I mean, that's why you still follow us both."

Julia wouldn't explain that she was following them because, for some weird reason, she'd thought that unfollowing them meant she was losing. That by blocking them, she'd admit defeat when they'd gone behind her back and humiliated her. At first, it was a punishment, looking them up, allowing herself to be angry that they'd moved on like nothing happened. But now… she couldn't care less.

"You're not here to throw your new marriage in my face and we both know that." She looked at her wrist, at an imaginary watch. "So stop wasting both of our time and tell me why you're really here." She was proud of her tone, how it was steady.

The smile was gone in an instant, and in the lines of his face, she saw nothing but hatred. "That's always been your problem. That pride," he said. His tone changed, and it became less about gloating and more about being as cruel as possible. "You think just because your daddy made your career possible you're better than everyone else."

She went to close the door, refusing to let him see how his words affected her. Julia had put so much stock in her work ethic, in making her father proud, and the words stabbed her.

"How was Stephen, by the way?" Harold asked, and the doorknob slipped from Julia's hand. She couldn't look him in the eye, and he laughed, knowing that he had her in that weird spell he always had over her. "You thought I'd never find out, but Stephen's always been a sloppy drunk. Proof of how you got him to fuck you in the first place. And to get back at me? How pathetic."

Defense to his cruel words died before they ever came to her mind. She wanted to yell and rage at him, to explain so that he understood that her tryst with Stephen had nothing to do with what Harold and Kate had done. Even if Stephen's intention had been that, which she couldn't possibly know, it hadn't been hers.

"But I guess that guy you're letting fuck you now isn't that much better…" A pause. "Lucas, is it?"

The bottom of her stomach dissolved as her skin chilled. Her back broke into a cold sweat.

"I thought you were a little better than that," he scoffed, and heat flashed through her heart.

"Be very careful what you choose to say, Harold."

Harold's face split into a mocking grin, his mouth open and brows high. "Wow, defensive. Very interesting. Is he the one, Julia? The one who'll show you what the upbringing you loathe so much protected you from."

Julia's fingertips tingled.

"What the hell is that supposed to mean?"

"You know exactly what I mean, Julia. Conrad did right by you, by not allowing that… *colorful* lifestyle. Can you imagine?"

Her hands were shaking beside her, so she formed them into fists. Of all the despicable things he could have said, she never imagined Harold could stoop so low. "You need to go, Harold." Exhaustion weighed on her shoulders, and the sadness in her voice made her angry. Harold would think it was about his happiness with Kate, when she now couldn't care less. He'd used her emotions against her, ridiculed her need to connect with the culture of her ancestors, the witches she'd rejected for far too long.

"You were so perfect. What happened to you?" His awe was evident in his airy tone, but she would not go there. Yes, she was different now. She'd been torn so often, it was any wonder she was still standing.

"I guess I'm glad we didn't have kids together."

A laugh exploded out of her, complete with tears gathering in her eyes, and she snorted so hard her nostrils hurt. A terrible sound that mingled with anger and sadness. A storm of emotions that shouldn't have existed at the same time. Even Harold stepped back, his nostrils flaring with fear or anger or whatever the fuck. She didn't care.

"Do you really think I wouldn't have left you eventually?" she asked, uncontrolled, hysterical heaving bending her over. "I left before I even knew that you were fucking my best friend in my own bed. I had some dignity, even back then."

Harold bit the inside of his cheek. "Wouldn't have worked anyway."

"Yeah, you're getting it now."

He expelled a hard breath. "Not like you were even useful in that way. Off birth control and you couldn't give me the child I wanted so badly."

A child *she'd* wanted badly until she started to finally see who Harold really was. For six years, she'd devoted to a relationship that had always been based on manipulation and control.

"I didn't go off birth control."

He smirked. "You did."

"Harold, I didn't. I couldn't risk bringing a child into our lives. Our marriage was falling apart the moment it started." She couldn't have done that to a child. "A baby wouldn't have fixed our problems."

Harold stared at her for a while, his expression blank.

"Your assistant changed your pills at my request," he said, his voice pitched low. The laughter died, and time slowed as what he said registered. Back when she was so busy that she'd needed an assistant to do the smaller tasks of life that would otherwise slip her mind. Val had been an excellent assistant. He'd do everything Julia had no time for and was efficient and kind. It'd hurt Julia to let him go when her life fell apart.

"What are you saying?" she asked in a broken whisper. He couldn't possibly…

"I wanted a family so badly. And you were lying to me." He had the gall to sound angry as Julia stood there numb. "You left because I was angry about not being able to conceive. And now you want to use that against me, like I was the one who did something wrong."

Had he really convinced himself of that? Julia's feet were made of lead.

"When I had the pills changed, I thought it would make everything better. I'd get the heir I'd always wanted, and you would come to your senses. But then nothing happened, and I realized it then."

His blue eyes were almost colorless when she looked into them, shocked into silence and immobility.

"You were useless in the only way that mattered to me."

Julia heard her breathing in her ears, and she took a step forward, stumbling at the invisible barrier between her and Harold. Even the magic had picked up on it, how Julia wanted to allow the heat to rise inside her like a volcano. How she wanted to lunge at Harold and scratch out his eyes, how she'd use her magic on him and destroy him. She didn't even know if she could do that, but she'd find a way.

"You motherfucker," she ground out, her throat burning, her eyes full. It was made worse by that stupid look on his face, like he was offended, as if he hadn't just told her what he'd done to her. How he'd violated her and then made it sound like it was her fault. Of everything he'd ever done, his snide comments about her body, the manipulations, the flat-out hatred, this was the worst because he didn't even see how egregious it was.

She pressed a hand to her sick stomach.

"Get the fuck off my stoop." She felt breathless, spots dancing before her eyes. "Don't ever come back here. Don't ever contact me again, or I will ruin your life."

His face turned into an ugly mask of anger. "I fucked women our whole marriage. You did that. I loved you, and you made me stray with your condescension, as if you could do no wrong."

She went to close the door, but he continued, "And in the end, the mighty Conrad Montgomery, your hero, was nothing more than a criminal."

Julia paused before she closed the door, realizing that his words didn't hurt the way they used to. What Conrad had done was not on her, it never had been.

One last look at Harold's hateful face and she closed the door, walking away as he yelled profanities before she heard him leave.

Her legs gave up in the living room as a wail ripped out of her. It took her breath away.

She heaved, feeling the force of everything physically, her body heavy and aching. The heat grew within her, but it was familiar now, and when the power shot out of her, it wasn't uncontrolled as it had been before. The vase she'd gotten from Harold's sister as a gift flew off its side table and shattered on the wall. Julia covered her head as little bits of glass flew toward her, embedding into her skin. But she felt no pain, only anger; anger that was a path into awakening the serpent she'd rejected for so long. One that gave her power.

Julia's jaw tensed as she held back a scream, and a flick of her hand had the sofa crashing against a console table, which snapped clean in half. All the contents of the table exploded into nothing, leaving dust and debris behind.

It was all there, every emotion she'd denied herself for far too long. A vortex of pain made her vision black, though she was still aware, her magic swirling inside her, all over the house. It was like a tornado, lifting things into the air, crashing them into walls, destroying everything it could touch. Half blind, she rose on her knees, her arms spread wide, a hot breeze whipping her hair and clothes until her energy left her. As if it was sucked out of her, she trembled, her arms falling beside her, glass under her knees.

Julia collapsed on the debris-filled floor. She didn't know how long she lay there for, only thinking that for the first time in forever, her body felt light, if not exhausted. The house could be fixed, she would make sure of it.

Without the strength to get up after such a burst of power, Julia allowed her eyes to close, and everything disappeared for a while. Until her insistent phone kept making noise, and she sat up, moonlight streaming through the windows. Ignoring the terrible mess she'd made of Sophia's house, she reached into the small purse she still had strapped to her side, and picked up her phone. She didn't recognize the number and thought about not responding, but clicked the green button anyway.

She listened to the person on the other end, detached. Something about a fire at the house Julia refused to let Harold have. Made sense in a weird, fucked up way.

Knees weak, she thanked the officer, promising she'd come as soon as possible, and hung up to call the only person that made sense for her to call. But when she looked at his number on her phone, she stopped right before she clicked on his name and everything stilled.

Recently, Sophia had asked her if she was safe from Harold, and she'd said she was. Now, after Harold showed up here, telling her of the vile things he'd done to her, she wasn't sure anymore. Did she think Harold was capable of hurting Lucas? One side of her wanted to say no, that Harold wouldn't put his reputation in jeopardy by hurting someone. But now the house she'd kept out of pure spite was burning to the ground, and she knew it was his doing. No one else cared enough.

She never wanted to believe that she'd married someone who could do something like that, but she'd also never suspected her father was capable of killing someone.

Needing Lucas had become second nature. His presence, his voice, the way he talked to her and helped her understand things she'd never thought of before. Lucas deserved so much more than what she could give him.

Her heart squeezing painfully, she scrolled until she found Sophia's name and dialed. Her anger was gone now, dissipated into the air with the power she'd allowed free, and all that was left was sadness. Just as dark. Just as deep. Just as terrible.

"Hello?" Grey's deep voice came through, deep and sleepy.

"Grey?" Julia choked.

"Are you okay?" he asked, alert now. She convulsed, her mind trying to grasp why he was answering Sophia's phone.

"I need help," she told him. *In so many ways*, she added silently. After she explained what happened, he showed up, still in his pajamas, Sophia by his side. Together, they traveled to the posh neighborhood she used to live in, Grey behind the wheel of her car because Julia couldn't fathom driving. The concept of driving didn't make sense to her in those moments when everything inside her was unbearably quiet.

Julia sat on the passenger seat, Sophia in the back. She'd insisted on Julia taking the seat, and not having the energy to argue, she'd taken it. Grey kept throwing looks at her as they drove in silence down the dark highway. It was wet, like it had been raining in the time since Julia had come home from Lucas's.

Time didn't make any sense.

The gates were open when the three of them pulled up to the neighborhood. She could see lights flashing ahead, and the eye-watering stink of smoke hit her first when she got out of the car.

Talking to the cops and firefighters was a blur. Julia was thankful for Sophia and Grey's clear heads when hers didn't work. They asked all the questions, and Julia answered as much as she possibly could, even as her head swirled like a merry-go-round. A while later, having listened to the firefighters and cops talk to her about their suspicions of arson, she told them about Harold.

Time to stop being scared, Julia.

When she looked up at the charred remains of the house, she felt nothing. Not anger for what Harold had obviously done, and not grief over all the things she'd lost. In fact, she felt relief. That she didn't have to have this house she would have never lived in again, and that Harold would now be truly out of her life, along with his new wife and the baby he'd always wanted.

She couldn't bring herself to care about Harold and Kate anymore. Let them move on and live their lives. She would do the same, even if it felt impossible right then.

Grey and Sophia drove her home and walked inside with her.

"I'll pay to repair and replace everything," Julia said with a shaky voice as they stood in the wreckage she'd caused earlier.

"What happened?" Sophia asked, concern in her voice instead of the anger Julia had expected.

She tried to talk, but the words wouldn't come. Tears streamed down her face, silently at first, then with the kind of sobbing that stole her breath. Next thing she knew, arms were around her, so warm, smelling fresh and clean. It was Grey, right by her side, making soft noises. The kinds of sound someone would use to calm a small child, and it just made her cry harder.

"I'm so sorry," she cried, clinging to him. Her friend since they were little kids. Someone who'd suffered as much as she and her sisters had.

"There's not need for that," Grey said.

"Babe, take us home," she heard Sophia say. Julia closed her eyes, clinging to them.

The whirring in her ears got loud, unbearable, and her mind went with it.

Julia didn't notice the way Grey's brows were tight with worry, how his own eyes misted seeing her pain. And she didn't notice when he lifted her gently as he would a baby and cradled her against his body.

Julia was limp by the time they got to the house, and he laid her onto a bed in the guest room.

o o o

Hours later, she opened her eyes, not sure when she'd fallen asleep. She was boneless, like her nerves were completely numb. Sophia was sitting in an armchair in the corner, her hair a messy cloud of curls down her back. Darkness circled her hazel eyes, so much like their mother's that Julia felt like crying all over again.

Sophia gave a long sigh. "How're you feeling?"

Julia's nose prickled and she opened the covers for Sophia to climb into. Facing her sister, she found she had no strength left to stop the tears. They ran free over her nose and onto the pillow.

"I'm not okay."

Sophia held her close, their noses almost touching.

"I thought things were going so great for a while." Her voice was broken, her throat aching. "But I realized I was just pushing things aside by distracting myself with everything. The smoking, the dancing. The sex."

But it was more than just dancing and sex now. Julia was in love with Lucas. Irreparably.

"What happened tonight?" Sophia asked quietly.

God, she wanted to sleep for a whole year. She was so tired.

"Harold came over tonight." She told Sophia everything that had happened, what Harold had said about her pills, and how mean he was. How he knew about Lucas and it terrified Julia that he did

𝄢 : 242 :

because Harold was an awful person who could do anything. Or maybe that was Julia's anxiety talking, but who knew. Sophia listened with various shades of horror on her face until her mouth was open and her eyes were full of tears.

"That fucking asshole," Sophia spat. She hugged Julia, holding on to her tanktop as if she couldn't hold on tightly enough. Julia sobbed into Sophia's neck until her stomach and throat hurt, until there were no more tears left.

"I'll fucking kill him."

"No, you won't," Julia said, more tired than words could express. "I want to forget he exists." Let the police investigate him.

She wanted that part of her life in the past, though she didn't know how she was going to achieve it. It all felt so dark, so heavy, but there had to be a way she could leave it all behind. There had to be relief. No human could do this forever, and she was exhausted, ready to throw in the towel.

"You really think he could do something to Lucas?" Grey asked from where he stood by the door. Julia looked up at his tall frame, his hair falling in waves past his shoulders.

"I'd have said no two weeks ago," Julia said, "but after tonight…" She didn't have to finish that.

Sophia and Grey looked at each other.

"You understand I have to talk to Lucas about this," Grey said. Julia nodded. She wouldn't have it any other way.

"Please don't tell him about what you heard here," Julia told them.

"Julia—" Sophia started.

"Please." Julia squeezed her eyes tight. "I can't see him right now." Neither Sophia nor Grey argued, thankfully.

o o o

The following morning, Julia forced herself to call the insurance about the house and, afterwards, asked for an emergency session with Mariana. Talking about everything that happened with Harold felt like only half the truth when Julia knew who Mariana was in Lucas's life. But she couldn't bring herself to say his name out loud, and she left the session feeling more hollow and empty than she'd arrived.

"What if I can't have kids?" Julia had asked Mariana, who'd looked at her with pity in her eyes.

Julia didn't even remember how the therapist had responded.

Sophia and Grey offered Julia to stay with them while she did the next stretch of emotional heavy lifting. It could have been seen as stubborn, or hyper-independent, but Julia turned them down, deciding that it was best if she had her own space to care for her shit. This time, she wouldn't run, and she wouldn't numb her pain.

Days were long, too long, but when nights came, she breathed almost in relief, in spite of the depth of her depression. Darkness provided her almost a shroud of protection as she inactivated her social media profile. While she didn't block everyone, removing herself was best. No need to keep torturing herself.

But when Lucas texted and tried to stay in touch, she never responded. Maybe it was the wrong thing to do, but in those moments when she found herself in the prison of her mind, she knew that it was best this way. Her mom had sacrificed for her love, and Julia could do that too, if it meant that he was happy in the future. Even if it wasn't with her.

23

The distance was going to kill him.

He knew what Julia was doing, isolating, punishing herself, and he'd had to sit back and watch it happen. Forced himself to. It wouldn't be any help if he tried incessantly to get in touch with her when she wasn't ready to talk. He had to respect that, as much as it made him want to die.

He finished making himself a cup of lemongrass tea, which he'd never be able to look at again without thinking of Julia. Lucas hadn't missed being in relationships since Mariana had broken things off, had spent all that time moving on, finding himself outside of his relationships, only to be taken down by a gorgeous, pint-sized, grumpy woman. Her initial reluctance was so charming and painfully humorous, and then how she'd let her guard down, dancing until they were breathless with laughter and lust. Now that he knew what it was like to be with her, there was no way he could go back to what it was like before.

He loved her and wanted to be with her every day and night.

Lucas had loved before. Mariana had once been the love of his life, the one he thought he'd spend the rest of his days with, and for a while, so was Cole. But with Julia, things had always felt different. It was as if her spirit, the very energy of her soul, called to him.

He'd spend his whole life getting over her.

Setting the tea down on the little table in the patio, he laid down on the outdoor couch, a book on his stomach. He didn't know why he'd brought the book out—there was no way he'd be reading anything with how addled his mind felt. All he wanted was to talk to Julia, to ask her how he could help her, to do everything in his power to take the sadness from her. But he couldn't do that, so when he'd realized his texts would remain unanswered, he'd forced himself to stop. It wouldn't do any good to insist.

Grey knew something, but he wasn't sharing at Julia's insistence. Lucas both respected his friend and wanted to strangle him for not saying anything.

The kittens wouldn't stop hovering around him, obviously worried and making sure he was okay. Even now, they bounded out from the little side door he'd built for them and plopped on his lap, purring loudly.

Lucas stroked their soft fur as the smell of lemongrass wafted off the mug on the table. After a while, as the heat rose through the day and left him sweltering and miserable, though unable to move, the door to the kitchen slid open and Grey came walking out. His best friend was dressed in all black (shocking) and his hair was up.

"Haven't you heard about wearing light colors in the heat?" Lucas asked as he sat up, the cats jumping off to mewl up at the newcomer.

Grey grinned down at them and crouched to scratch behind their ears. They meowed as if they were complaining to Grey of everything they'd seen in the last few days, which consisted of Lucas lying around every time he saw himself without a client.

"I could make the same argument about your formal clothing, but I guess you're in worse shape than I thought," Grey said and sat beside Lucas.

Lucas looked down at himself. True, he'd been wearing the same linen pants for three days straight—they were his most comfortable lounging around pants that also looked fine for when he saw clients. At least he hadn't been neglecting his work, so there was that.

"I wasn't expecting you."

"I know," Grey said. "How are you buddy?"

"Terrible."

Grey didn't say anything, and Lucas gave into the urge he often had to stamp down when his friend came around.

"Have you seen her?" he asked.

"I have."

But Lucas knew his friend wouldn't really add much else. Being in a relationship with Julia's sister put him in a very particular position of loyalty to all sides, which meant he'd always choose not to speak too much lest he get in trouble with anyone. Lucas hated it.

"Is she okay?"

Grey didn't respond right away.

"You don't have to give me details," Lucas assured him, his tone pleading. "I just want to know she's okay."

Grey looked at him, his brows tightly furrowed. "I hate not being able to talk to you about this. Sophia's been spending a lot of time with her and Amy."

So she was safe. Lucas allowed himself to exhale. When he'd found out about what Harold did to the house, his first instinct was violence. Not often had he felt that way—he simply didn't think that physical violence was the answer to anything—but Harold Houghton got under his skin, from the first time Lucas had seen him at the club to the things he knew about him from Julia. And then burning the house to spite Julia… He was looking to catch a fist to the teeth.

"I wish she'd talk to me," Lucas said, realizing that what he needed was to talk to his friend about it. Helena, his other confidante, was close to Julia, and Lucas liked that. Julia deserved a friend like Helena, so he'd die of a broken heart before he did anything that changed that.

But he wanted to talk about her. What she was to him, how much he missed her. But inadvertently, he'd also been isolating to an extent, burying himself in work so he was too busy to think about her for the past ten days.

"Do you love her?"

Lucas deadpanned. "What do you think?"

Grey's was the face of sympathy.

"I thought it was going to be her," he added, also realizing how pathetic that sounded. Pining after her had been easy when they'd started seeing each other more regularly, when he saw her laughing as they laughed, and how the color had returned to her face over the weeks they'd been together.

Now, it was just torture.

"And what if she doesn't want to pick this thing back up?" Grey asked.

Then, he'd work his hardest to move on, even if it killed him because he didn't want to move on. But everything in life was temporary one way or another. If she never wanted him back, he'd eventually forget to be this sad, and he'd forget the way she moved, how she laughed when she relaxed, and how her body fit with his. Perfectly. He'd force himself to stop thinking about the way she looked when she slept, so peaceful on her side, curled with her hands under her chin.

"Sophia did the same thing when we found out about her dad," Grey said. She disappeared for weeks after they learned about Conrad and his crimes."

"So you're saying this is the way these women know how to deal with stuff."

"That, and she might come around."

"I don't know if I can have hope right now."

Grey patted Lucas's shoulder.

"Remember what you'd tell me if this were me."

Give it time. Right.

Grey left a little while later, after sitting together in mostly silence since Lucas couldn't talk as much as he really wanted to. Every word he wanted to say felt like he'd be talking in circles, and they would lead to no solutions.

The next few days, Lucas ran through the motions. He saw his clients throughout the day and checked his phone every time he had a second to spare. Nothing from Julia. So when she appeared on Sunday afternoon, as much as he'd wanted to feel hopeful when he opened the door, his intuition indicated something completely different. And his intuition hadn't failed him yet.

She looked as lovely as she always had, her hair a little messier than normal, tied into a knot on top of her head. But he loved this version of her just as much as he loved the put-together side, with her sky-high heels and expertly applied makeup. She wore sandals, shorts, and a t-shirt.

After he invited her inside, his heart a knot of nerves, they went to the sitting room and stood on opposite ends of the room.

"How've you been?" he asked when she obviously struggled to say anything at all. Her grimace spoke more loudly than her words.

"It's been hard lately."

He had to grip the back of the sofa to stop himself from taking her in his arms and convincing her that everything was going to be okay. How, he had no clue, but he'd try anything.

"What happened?" he asked softly, unable to look away from her face, though she was looking at everything but him. Even the kittens were nowhere to be seen.

She bit her lip, her brow furrowed.

"Do you want to sit?" He swallowed, struggling to keep the emotion out of his voice.

Julia shook her head. "I can't do this."

Yeah, his heart broke anyway, no matter how hard he'd worked to not make it about himself. The cracks were there from the moment Grey told him about the house and what they suspected Harold had done but had refused to say anything else.

He tried to swallow the lump that came into his throat, but it didn't move.

"That last night . . ." he started, then paused to think about what to say. "You knew it was over."

Of course she'd known. The way she'd shown up, without telling him she was coming over, and how she'd left while he was sleeping. He'd known she was gone before he opened his eyes.

"I'm sorry," she said and looked down, her face lined with grief and uncertainty.

"I wish you'd talked to me." He gritted his teeth. He wanted to be angry at her for running off like that, leaving when he was asleep, and then ignoring him like it meant nothing to her.

But he also knew that grief was not rational, and she was still grieving the life she'd once had. He couldn't fix things for her, couldn't do anything but stand aside and allow her to figure herself out. If that meant not being together, then he'd have to be okay with it.

Maybe it was for the best that it ended now.

"We both knew this was temporary," she said, but he had a feeling she didn't believe that either. "Maybe it was a mistake from the start."

"A mistake, Julia?" He couldn't help the question, how it came out, all soft and bruised around the edges. "All of it?"

Her lip trembled.

"I can't go there right now." She was breathing hard. "I came because I hated leaving like that and not responding. I don't do that. I don't ghost people who matter to me, and I did with you."

"I know what you're doing." It was his last attempt to help her see. Pride be damned, he had to tell her. "Julia—"

"I'm sorry for wasting your time."

But you didn't, he wanted to say. He wanted to kneel and beg her to stay, to help her see that she was lying to herself as much as she was lying to him. He felt his back curve at the pressure in his heart. And he said the words, even though they would change nothing.

"I love you, Julia."

Her eyes wouldn't rise from the floor, and that silence, that horrible silence that followed his declaration, expanded and swallowed him whole.

He leaned against the wall, watching her look so small and frail. All he wanted was to lock her in his room and feed her and love her until everything was right in her world again. His heart shriveled, for himself and for her.

It was torture, grieving someone who was still alive.

"I'm sorry," she whispered, turning abruptly and walking away. The door shutting behind her added a tone of finality, and it echoed through the house. Through him.

His eyes were hot when he dropped on the couch, and he stayed there in the dark all night.

24

Julia left his house like a coward, wanting so badly to say the words back to him. She was in a panic by the time she was outside. Her car waited for her like a hearse. She was dead—this was it. In her head, the words repeated over and over.

I love you.

I love you.

I love you.

Te amo.

Te amo.

Te amo.

She didn't cry, because if she started she would never stop. How did anyone get over the best thing that had ever happened to them?

He deserved everything, the whole sky, and she couldn't give it to him. She was barely keeping herself in one piece. And Harold.

Julia couldn't stop thinking about Will and what happened to him and her mom, even though everyone told her it wasn't the same. Lucas was a talented witch and could protect himself. But this wasn't just about him. It was about her. She'd become too dependent on Lucas, and there had to be a way for her to find herself amidst all the mess.

So instead of wallowing and crying until she dried out and hopefully died from it, she read the diaries that belonged to her mother.

Back when Sophia had discovered them, they had been blank, affected by a spell to keep Julia and her sisters away from magic. Now, Julia sat in bed with the first one, leaning back and fighting back tears as she read her mom's entries. Her handwriting was lovely, curly and clear. It almost looked like a font. And the ones that had written themselves with a spell her mother had created, like the genius she was, looked like the rest. As if they came from her hand because they came from her life. Her heart.

Over the next three weeks, she consumed every piece of writing she had the emotional capacity for; letters, magical recipes Sophia and Grey used so much, even the one with the cure for the disease that almost killed her. Sometimes she could read a few pages, and other times, a couple of lines sent her into a renewed wave of grief for the mother she'd lost too early.

Seeing her therapist three times a week was helping a little, even though she'd chosen to switch from Mariana to someone else. Julia had found that she couldn't handle seeing the woman Lucas had loved before her. She could barely concentrate in their sessions anymore, so she'd told Mariana it was time to move on to someone else and never came back. Mariana, of course, had been graceful and wished her the best.

But it didn't matter how much she talked about her pain; it stayed with her. She missed Lucas. Missed how he mouthed the words to songs while he danced, and how he closed his eyes when a lyric hit. And despite wanting to see him, even from afar, she'd avoided Nowhere at all costs. Maybe she'd be okay running into him at the grocery store one day, but watching him dance with other people might actually kill her. She was glad she was off social media, or she'd be stalking his profile like the lunatic she'd become. Or maybe he'd have blocked her for breaking his heart. It was the least she deserved for walking away like she had.

I love you, Julia.

His words haunted her, day and night. And they haunted her now as she sat still in the living room. Every time she'd done this, she'd been with Lucas, but it was time that she tried it on her own. There was so much she needed to work through, and slowly, she was starting to chip away at the biggest things. Julia understood that she couldn't change the past—her parents, Will, Harold and Kate… There was no use in suffering anymore.

It was night and she lay in bed after spending time with her girls. Sophia and Amy stayed behind while Helena and Victoria went home. Sleep came easy as she lay her head on the pillow, and the dream appeared swiftly.

Like last time, she was herself, walking into the past like she belonged there. Her mom hummed a whimsical tune while her hands were busy weeding the garden. Little Julia was on a swing, attempting to go higher and higher, to flip over the top of the frame, though her mom had always told her it was a bad idea.

Julia was suddenly in the body of her small self, and she jumped off the swing as it went forward. Her heart lurched and tumbled as she landed on her feet in the dirt, and then she ran over to her mom, who wore one of those signature dresses she liked so much. Her curly hair covered her back, despite the warm sun. Julia wanted hair like it, long and luscious and natural.

She knelt beside her mom in front of the garden beds.

"Can I help, mommy?"

Mommy's smile was warm and soft, her clear hazel eyes so full of love Julia felt it run through her body.

"Ven, mi amor," Mommy said softly, and side by side, they finished weeding, both humming the same tune, though Julia hadn't heard it before. Her mom was always making new music that sounded like it felt inside Julia's veins. Magical. Mommy gasped and pulled her hand back. There was a prickle of blood on her finger. Julia gasped too, and tears came to her eyes, but Mommy smiled gently, her eyes almost glowing in the late summer afternoon.

"It's okay, baby. Estoy bien."

"Does it hurt?" Julia asked, taking her mom's hand in hers and inspecting the wound.

"Only a little bit." Her mom reached for her chin and tipped her face so that they were looking into each other's eyes.

"It's okay to care, my sweet Jewel," her mother said gently, music in her voice. "But my pain is mine to carry, not your burden. Does that make sense?"

"Not really."

"We all have stuff we struggle with," she said, looking beyond Julia to the tall evergreen trees behind their home. "And we can help each other as much as possible. But ultimately, it's our job to care for our own problems, not the problems of others."

"Okay," Julia said, beginning to understand what she meant. But her dad always told her that she was his smart daughter, the one that was the most like him. And he always knew what people had to do. That was why he was the boss.

Julia watched that small version of herself from the side of the garden, where the flowers were singing and blue butterflies wriggled by, their wings vibrant. At that moment, she was all three of them. The current, adult version of herself, the child who sat next to her mother, and her mother too. And the sadness inside Silvana Candela punched her so hard in the gut that she felt the air leave her.

"Mom," she whispered in a strangled sob. From where she knelt, her white dress dusty, her mom looked up and found her standing there. She smiled, so beautiful and soft, and Julia lifted her hand, not quite understanding what was going on but also never wanting it to end. She wanted to be in this place where her mom was alive, where her own mind was still so pliable. Where she could learn every language her mom spoke, and where she could do magic. Like it had been when she'd been in a coma. She wanted that. Not this. Not what she had now.

She watched her mother stand up and approach the older version of Julia, the one who knew heartbreak in a way no one should, leaving little Julia kneeling by the flower beds. Julia was frozen to the spot as her mother came closer. Inside her, all feelings possible flashed through her, and she wished with all her heart that she could hug her mom one more time. That she could ask for forgiveness for the way she'd judged before she knew any better.

Twilight started to fall, and she could see it all fading away.

"Not yet, please," Julia begged as her mom took her face in soft hands dirty with earth. Julia shut her eyes at the contact. "I don't want to go yet."

Her mom smiled gently, her eyes filled with tears. "My love."

Everything quieted, even the ringing in her ears, when her mom pressed a soft kiss to her forehead. They were roughly the same height here, not tall like Julia had remembered her in her imperfect childhood memories. Julia closed her eyes and leaned in for the hug she craved, and she held on like it was a lifeline. Her mom smelled earthy and flowery, like cherry blossoms and petrichor.

"My sweet baby," Mom whispered as she stroked Julia's hair. "You wear my face, as I wear the face of those who came before me."

Her body erupted in goosebumps as her mom pulled back and smiled into her eyes.

"I love you, Mom," she sobbed, her face and neck drenched with tears. "I'm so sorry I blamed you for so long."

"There's nothing to be sorry about, my love." Another kiss, to her palm this time, and the twilight expanded. Rain fell softly onto her already wet face as the scene dissolved. And she might have been crazy, but the night smiled and whispered, *I love you, my Jewel.*

In the morning, Julia opened her eyes to find the house still dark and quiet. She lay there until the sun rose and she heard Amy and Sophia stirring. The dream had felt so real she could still feel her mother's hands on her face, the kiss on her forehead. Tears sprung into her eyes and she let them. The door opened, and there were her sisters, joining her on the bed and allowing themselves to grieve together. Julia told them about the dream and the last time something like it had happened. Amy was quiet, listening.

"That sounds like when I took the knowing potion," Sophia said. "It brought me back there in a way. It was like living it, but not."

Julia understood completely.

Later in the morning, they went together to their childhood home.

The house was completely empty, as they had gotten rid of all their father's things. It was a beautiful home, but so full of ghosts, so much pain in every corner. Big windows let in light, and a chandelier still hung from the ceiling in the circular entryway. Julia still didn't know what she was going to do with the house, as she was the executor, but her sisters had a say in all of it. There was no way any of them would ever live here, and hopefully, in the future, it would be a happier home for someone else.

To their right, their father's office, which had been added on to the house, was also empty. Julia didn't want to go in there. She knew the small space well, as she'd spent far too much time across from her father's desk, getting his instruction on how to run the family business she'd dedicated so much of her life to. The sunroom, just a few steps ahead of the entryway, used to look more like a greenhouse than a sunroom when her mom had been alive. Now, it was nothing but empty walls and dust. The wall of windows in there overlooked the large piece of land outside where the gardens used to be. They looked nothing like they used to back then. Her father had kept it well manicured and stylish after the death of their mother, but now, it was overgrown and unkempt.

Upstairs, the three of them paused outside the door that led into the attic, where their mom had done most of her magic. The place where she had died alongside the love of her life, William Constantine, after their father pulled out a gun in a fit of jealousy.

Julia took hold of the doorknob, which sometimes stuck, and pushed open the door. The wooden floors had a layer of dust on them, and there was zero furniture in here anymore. The bed that used to sit underneath the small window was sold, but the table that used to house a cauldron and countless bottles of dried herbs was now in Sophia's garage. Julia had even started thinking about using it herself, buying a house she could call her own and having a room for potions and magic. She had to start somewhere.

Holding hands, Julia, Sophia, and Amy went into the room. Why they'd needed to come in here, none of them truly knew, but it was cathartic in a way none had expected.

Sophia pulled out a bottle, a big one with a spray at the top, and she muttered little chants as she went around the room and cleansed it with whatever concoction Grey had prepared at her request. This house needed a good cleanse before they decided what to do with it. Starting with the room where all the tragedies had happened seemed like the right course of action until then.

As Sophia went around, the liquid looked like pure light as she sprayed it and continued to mutter. Julia watched her, awed at the things she'd learned about magic, knowing that she wanted to know too. Her mother would have wanted her to embrace this power she had been given, and for the first time since it had surfaced, she wanted it too. Amy's hand gripped hers as they watched Sophia in silence. When Sophia was finished with the cleanse, the three of them stood together, bathed in the stillness and newfound softness of the room. The heaviness that had once hung invisible dissolved like the smoke of the incense their mother used to burn.

Life was fickle, fragile in a way Julia had never considered before when she'd spent her days killing herself in an office. Now, it felt so urgent that she started living, though she knew that was her need to move on. It would take so much longer than a few weeks for her to put herself together, but she would someday.

They left when the whole house was cleansed, and outside in the circular driveway, they held each other again as it started to mist.

"We should sell it," Amy murmured, her voice thick. Her blue eyes were rimmed with red.

Julia and Sophia agreed.

Amy's face screwed up. "A part of me feels so good about all that." Amy gestured toward the house with her hand. "But it…"

"It hurts too." Julia held her closer still, feeling the same grief deep within her. "There's so much history here. The bad, but also the good."

"We take the good with us," Sophia said. "The place it happened in no longer matters."

"I'm glad we at least have the journals and photos," Julia said. The memories they had of Roselyn, their mom, Grey, Jeanette, and Will. It all mattered. Now they could write a new story and put this one to sleep once and for all.

25

Weeks later, with the wedding fast-approaching, everyone had lined up their travel plans, and life got busy. So busy that Julia didn't have time to think about anything other than her bridesmaid duties. Besides that, Julia had also taken up business duties for the expansion of Nowhere, which was officially announced and had received really good support on social media. She was happy to. Finally able to focus, and more regulated than she'd been in a while thanks to her new therapist, she was glad to take the reins of the business so Victoria and Sophia, her maid of honor, didn't have to. Especially since Victoria's in-laws had flown in from Korea to stay with them until the wedding in a couple of weeks. It was all a madhouse, and Julia loved it.

One of those nights, Julia got dressed for the bachelorette party, which was happening in tandem with stag night. Victoria had chosen a nice dinner at an upscale restaurant downtown, followed by going back to Nowhere. That part was nerve-wracking, since the men would end up there too, and Lucas had become close enough to Thomas now that he'd most certainly be at the celebration before they all left for the wedding.

God, she missed him, but reaching out hadn't really felt like an option. Not when she'd hurt him, leaving like that after he told her he loved her.

At least Harold hadn't made any more appearances anywhere he wasn't wanted. Julia suspected Grey had something to do with that, but she didn't ask and he didn't volunteer, so she chose to let it go. If it meant Harold stayed well away from her and her loved ones, she was fine with whatever spell he'd cast for it to be so.

The charred house no one was able to prove he'd burned down went up for sale and sold in less than a day, fire and all. Julia suspected it was Harold, of course, but she could happily say that she couldn't give a tiny rat's ass if she tried. She could have asked Sophia and Grey to use a potion, a spell maybe, to make Harold confess, but she'd realized she didn't care enough. It had never been about the house anyway.

"You look great." Sophia smiled in the mirror behind Julia, who'd chosen a red dress for the night because why the hell not. The past weeks had been good for her; had allowed her to grow a little, even if nothing was exactly perfect.

"Thanks, so do you." Sophia had on a black dress. Typical, really. She and Grey were dubbed The Blackertons, always wearing black if they could choose. "You good?"

"Nervous."

"Because of Lucas?" Amy asked, coming into the room. Victoria and Helena were somewhere else in the house, also getting ready.

"It's the first time I'm seeing him since . . ."

"I think you should talk to him," Amy said.

Julia breathed deeply. She'd never struggled with words; she was a businesswoman, for the love of God. If someone knew how to use words, it was her. But with Lucas… she couldn't bullshit her way out of having a meaningful conversation if she tried. He wouldn't do any less than that, and she wouldn't let herself do less than he—and she, for that matter—deserved.

While things had settled down for her, they were far from perfect.

Some days it was hard getting out of bed and brushing her hair, and other days she was on top of the world. Today, she was in a middle space between "I'm struggling hardcore" and "It hurts this horribly now, but not forever." A strange place to be, understanding it and not trying to rush to fix it. Like Lucas had taught her months before, feeling it felt harder, but it made it go away faster.

A soft mewl got her attention, and her heart softened as she focused on the tiny kitten she'd finally gotten. She was white with yellow patches and looked like a little daisy. Julia had called her Blossom. She picked the kitten up and allowed her to nuzzle into her arms. Blossom was the sweetest kitten, exactly what Julia had needed. Grey had been the one to find her for Julia, calling one night when a friend told him he had one kitten needing a home. It had been the right move. Julia had never had a pet before, as Harold hadn't really been a pet person, and she never had the time for one. The only pet she'd ever known had been Sunshine, her mom's cat.

"Hi, my sweet girl," Julia whispered.

"You've changed so much," Sophia said with a wistful smile.

Julia looked at her sister quizzically.

"Not so much, honestly."

"You have a pet," Amy pointed out, a makeup brush in her hand. "And you got a nose piercing."

Julia looked at herself in the mirror. She often forgot about the little gold stud she'd gotten two weeks before. Her girls had all gone with her.

"I kind of like it," she said, suddenly self-conscious. She had been making a lot of changes, but they were things she'd always wanted to do and never had the guts.

"It's adorable," Helena said, entering the bathroom with Victoria in tow. Julia was grateful their relationship hadn't suffered much after she dumped Lucas. Helena was fiercely protective of him and Grey, but she'd kept any comments about that whole thing to herself. "I'm glad you did it."

Julia grinned at her in the reflection in the mirror.

"I didn't say it wasn't cute," Amy protested, leaning forward to put some eyeshadow on her lid. Her phone went off on the counter, and Helena looked away as Amy tapped a message with a half-smile on her face.

"Who's that?" Julia asked. She had no idea what was going on with Amy these days.

"Oh, you haven't heard?" Victoria smirked. "Tom's back."

"Who the hell is Tom?" The name was familiar, but Amy dated a lot. It was hard to know.

"Remember the tennis instructor she was dating like two years ago?" Sophia said.

"The one who was dating a bunch of people without disclosing it?" Julia asked, and Amy looked up from her phone to roll her eyes.

"You're so judgmental."

"You're the one who was pissed when he told you he was dating around," Julia reminded her.

"It's casual," Amy simply said and put away her phone. "I'm not looking for anything serious anyway, and he's fun."

Julia looked over at Victoria, who was shaking her head a little.

"Our car will be here in two minutes," Helena said and moved out of the bathroom. Julia and the rest followed, Amy at the end of the line.

Julia sat sandwiched between Sophia and Helena, Amy and Victoria in the very back, chattering about their plans for the night. She couldn't stop thinking about the end of the night, when they went to Nowhere. Nerves about seeing Lucas made her quieter than normal. It wasn't guilt that she felt. She was well-acquainted with guilt, and this wasn't it.

Breaking his heart had only broken hers, but what else could she have done? She'd wanted to reach out more than once, but other things kept popping up. Not just Harold, but everything else. And after Harold came around and told her what he'd done, suddenly she feared the worst. Her possible infertility wasn't the most of it.

Soon, they left for the restaurant, where they met a few other friends of Victoria's. Champagne flowed along with the delicious food. Because Julia knew the chef, a close friend of Stephen's, he came out to greet them all and thank them for coming to the restaurant.

Ray was gorgeous, tall and dark, with a heavy Italian accent. And he flirted with Helena incessantly, revealing that he knew her from her time on the internet when she made music. She still did that, but had taken some time off to spend more time singing at Nowhere.

When Ray left to get back to the kitchen, he sent several bottles of champagne out, along with a card for Helena. She turned pink and put the card away.

After, tipsy and full of amazing food, they called another car to get to Nowhere. Julia's nerves were gone now, the alcohol giving her the courage she lacked sober.

Once in the club, they settled in upstairs on the private level, which had been reserved only for them and the men, who would show up any minute. Drinks flowed and Julia laughed, forgetting about her nerves as Sophia told stories about Victoria growing up. There was no timid giggling either, but full-bellied laughs that made her eyes wet and her stomach hurt. Victoria was radiant, her ever-glowing skin gleaming with happiness and her coily hair perfectly coiffed around her shoulders.

They toasted, talked about the wedding and every activity they'd do when they got to the island, and the DJ played songs that Victoria and Thomas loved all night. But when the doors downstairs opened, and Thomas walked in, Julia lost her steely nerves. He was laughing at something one of his childhood best friends was saying, but Julia's eyes searched for Lucas.

And there he was, laughing at something Grey had whispered to him.

The rest of the house cheered as the show started and Evan, the lead guitarist, took the stage. He said something, but Julia didn't hear words. There were cheers and raised glasses, which she followed, but her eyes were only for Lucas. And when they came upstairs to join the party, while Victoria and Thomas kissed deeply to the cheers around them, Julia's entire body was shaking.

Then their eyes met, and the entire crowd disappeared. It was only him by the bar, as far away from her as he could get in the small space.

"You okay?" Sophia whispered, coming closer.

"Yeah." She wasn't lying. She was okay, just gutted.

Maybe not okay then.

"I think you should talk to him." Helena leaned in. "He's miserable. Not that he says much to me about it these days, but I know him."

He didn't really look miserable as he chatted with people and drank from a glass of what appeared to be whiskey.

"You'll never know if you don't try," Amy said, and Helena threw her a scathing look, but Amy seemed to not see it. Or she was ignoring it.

Julia looked from one to the other, and suddenly, every single instance of Amy and Helena together flowed into her memories. There was no way.

But when Amy looked away, her nostrils flaring, Julia finally knew it. She opened her mouth to say something, but Helena shook her head almost imperceptibly, so she smacked her lips shut.

Amy and Helena.

Helena and Amy.

How the fuck had she missed that? It felt so obvious now.

Did anyone else know?

Yeah, she'd have to have a chat with both of them when she could, but that wasn't now.

"I agree with Helena," Sophia said quietly as the others chatted about travel plans. They'd all be flying; porting wasn't really an option since they were staying at a hotel. Finding places to port into privately could be a huge problem.

Julia looked at her sister. "I don't think it's a good idea."

"What's stopping you?"

"The fact that it's been weeks. Or Harold."

"Oh please, this has nothing to do with Harold, and we both know it," Sophia said, moving even closer so that no one could hear them. Julia watched Lucas chat with one of Thomas's brothers and Grey. "What Harold did was despicable, and you hiding it makes me think you're making yourself responsible for it."

Julia opened her mouth, but shut it before she said anything else.

"I don't want to push you into doing something you don't want to do," Sophia said. "But Grey doesn't have to tell me anything for me to see that Lucas is not happy either."

"If I tell him about Harold—"

"You'll have to convince Lucas not to kill him, yes." Sophia gritted her teeth. "I know I'm still having to hold myself back from hexing him at the very least."

Julia almost smiled. No, karma would do its job when the time came. Julia didn't want to interfere with the flow. She watched Lucas for a little bit longer, caught his eye briefly, and told herself that maybe being honest could be good. Even if it went nowhere with him.

Oh, who was she kidding? She wanted to do everything with him. She wanted him, his sense of humor, and the way he made love to her… She wanted to be with him. Steeling her spine, before she could convince herself otherwise, she got to her heeled feet. The bar felt a mile away, and Lucas was seated in the furthest corner. The space was pretty crowded now, many friends having shown up. The second floor wasn't a large area, so people were starting to move downstairs to watch the show as well.

She didn't know what she was going to say, or even if she should say anything at all. He looked like a movie star in his gray suit.

His hair, slicked back, was a little longer than she remembered, and even his scruff had grown out. He glanced up as she approached, and their eyes locked on each other. Julia had to force herself to keep walking toward him, as the friend he'd been talking to, one of Thomas's brothers, she assumed, was called away by someone else. His eyes slid over her figure, and they warmed. Grey, who sat on the stool next to Lucas, stood.

"I'll go find Sophia," he said with a brief smile for Julia. Things had been good between them. After her vision—dream—with her mom, she'd talked to him about everything. Sometimes, it was awkward still, but Grey was nothing if not accepting, so they were working on building their friendship once again.

"Hi," she said to Lucas, knees shaking.

"Hi." They were eye to eye, because he remained in the same position, like he wouldn't dare move. *God, please.*

Julia stood awkwardly, and he didn't say anything. Not a good sign. *Just out with it, Julia.*

"I owe you an apology," she said, starting to feel like this was all a big mistake.

"You don't owe me anything."

"I do, though. Not telling you what was going on was unfair, especially when you'd done so much to help me, and I regret it." Her hand rested on the edge of the bar, and she came closer still, to afford them a little privacy in the busy space. Thankfully, everyone was focused on Victoria and Thomas or the show below. "You brought me back to life when nothing made sense anymore, and I owe you so much. I'm sorry for hiding and not respecting you, us, enough to talk first. To let you know what made me hide."

Telling him felt like she was about to jump off a bridge with a bungee tied to her ankles; uncontrollably afraid, but called to the weightless fall.

"I thought I had my whole life figured out," she told him. "I excelled at everything, and I loved it. The recognition was like a drug. I took care of my younger sisters, and I was my dad's best friend. And when my mom asked me to be helpful, I took it to heart. I made it my entire personality to be the one who fixed everything for everyone. All because I felt like the key to happiness was to not think about the sadness I've carried around with me since I was a kid."

His eyes were sympathetic, and he looked like he wanted to say something, but he didn't.

"Everything in my life revolved around my mom's abandonment. The idea that she left us because she was in love with someone else made love seem like a waste of time to me. It felt wrong to love someone so much that you would do anything for them." Like she would do for him, she knew. She would kill anyone who hurt him. "Running is just easy for me, but I'm so tired of running, Lucas. I—"

"Julia—" he interrupted.

"Please just let me say it," she whispered, closing her eyes. "I kept you at arm's length because it scared me how you made me feel," she continued, because if she let him interrupt her, she would lose her nerve. "You looked at me like I was the only woman in the room, in the world, and I found myself leaning into you for comfort when life got too heavy. I just didn't know how to express that.

"I love you, Lucas. I'm so in love with you, even if you can't stomach the sight of me anymore. I love you, and I will always love you. And I'm a mess, I don't know what I want to do with my life anymore, but I know one thing for sure and it's that you brought me back to life. You showed me what joy was like when I'd never felt it before, and I'm sorry I sucked at showing you how much you mean to me."

Her heart was in her throat as she finished, but his brow was tight with worry, and when he didn't say anything right away she knew. Before he could utter a word, she steeled her back, but reminded herself that whatever he had to say, she would just have to take. No matter what it was.

Her stomach was so tight with nerves, she could barely breathe, as his mouth opened. She wanted to interrupt him, tell him about Harold and her fear that she couldn't have kids, but it felt wrong. She knew that if she told him everything, it might work in her favor. Might make his face turn into the happy expression she'd fantasized about when she thought about seeing him again. It was a manipulation that she wouldn't inflict on him.

"Julia." He sounded like she felt. Absolutely fucking miserable. She wanted to run from the feeling because she knew what was coming, and she didn't want to hear the words because it would shatter her. It would destroy her. But she stayed. Because she didn't run from her problems now, as much as she wanted to.

"You know I love you," he murmured. "That hasn't changed."

Her heart started racing with something akin to hope, despite her resolution to not let it get to her.

"I just don't . . ." he swallowed, at a loss for words.

Her stomach unraveled and the bottom fell out, leaving her suddenly empty and cold.

"I really want you to be happy," he said. "I want you to find everything you want, but I just don't think I can . . ."

For a long time, she just stood there waiting for the sentence to end because it felt like an unfinished thought. But she knew what he was saying, and finally, she nodded, refusing to look into his eyes where she would see the truth of how much he did not want her anymore. In their amber depths, she would never find the warm desire she had come to love so much. How when he looked at her she felt sexier than anyone else on the face of the earth. How when he touched her, he ignited her. How when he kissed her, when he was inside her, he consumed her so thoroughly.

Lucas had decided to move on, and it wasn't with her.

"I understand," she whispered, and at the same time another, familiar voice came.

"Lucas?"

Julia turned to see Mariana standing there, smiling quizzically at Julia.

"Oh my God, Julia," she said with a brilliant smile. "It's so good to see you."

Julia couldn't react. Her entire body felt frozen on the spot, looking at Mariana move in slow motion. She looked as lovely as ever, but wearing a green dress that was reminiscent of the dress Julia now treasured from her first time with Lucas.

Kicking herself into action, she pasted a smile on her face. The actress was back.

"Hi, Mariana. You look great." Her voice didn't even belong to her anymore. Mariana's smile was dazzling.

"A little different than at the office," she giggled and looked at Lucas, who had stood and hovered behind Julia, who was afraid to look back now. "What a small world that you two know each other."

Julia could only nod, her smile trembling with the effort of keeping it on her face. "I'll leave you to it."

The tears were coming, hard, but she kept her chin high, even if she wanted to curl into a ball and die. Blind, Julia made her way through the crowd, toward the stairs that would allow her to go outside and leave this all behind. Her heart was in pieces, and as she reached the bottom of the stairs, there was Sophia.

"Jules?" she murmured, concern on her face.

"I'm going to go home, okay?" she said thickly, and as Sophia nodded, she headed toward the employee door. She picked up her purse from the office, chest heaving with the force of her grief, and continued on to the back. Only when the door was open and she was out in the cool night did she let herself break.

Tears slid down her face as she pulled the app on her phone and ordered the ride, hands shaking. And when the ride was ordered and she had to wait the two minutes that it would take for them to get there, she was leaning against the wall as sobs snapped through her. By the time the car showed up, she had eyeliner and mascara running down her face, snot everywhere. Thankfully, the woman handed her a little pack of tissues and didn't ask what was wrong, because that would have been the last straw. The night lights were a blur as they passed, and when she was finally home, the flood really came. If the tears had been hard before, they were worse now that she allowed herself to slide to the floor right inside the door and feel the magnitude of this pain. It almost broke her in half.

"Julia," came a voice, then several knocks and more yelling of her name. She opened the door to find her sisters, Victoria, and Helena still in their pretty dresses, looking disheveled from the night of drinking and partying.

Julia was engulfed in a group hug, and she dissolved into sobs again until she couldn't cry anymore.

Later, in the living room, mostly in the dark, they sat around in the way they did so often. The difference was that Amy was the one sitting at the window with the joint while Julia lay across Victoria's lap, who smoothed her hair gently.

For the first time since she was a child, she allowed herself to be held.

26

The day before Victoria and Thomas's wedding, Lucas spent time in Puerto Rico with his father. He'd been meaning to visit, but kept putting it off because he knew the conversation would inevitably turn to Julia, and he really didn't want to deal with it.

After seeing her at Nowhere, when she'd declared her love for him, every instinct screamed at him to take her in his arms and fold like a wet napkin. Damn pride, damn hurt. And then Mariana had shown up and he knew Julia had misinterpreted it. Mariana had texted him when she thought she saw him, and he'd told her he was at the club, where she also happened to be.

Now he didn't know what Julia was thinking, and despite the impulse, he'd decided not to reach out. Part of him thought it was best this way, that they move on from each other, and part of him hated himself for hurting her. The pain in her eyes when she realized what he was trying to say, though the words didn't even finish leaving his mouth, cut him deeply.

Outside, it was warm and overcast, humid as hell, and he worked beside his father in the garden. He was sweating like a horse, but the exertion was welcome. His sisters were showing up for dinner any minute, and he looked forward to seeing them, even if he had little energy for the nosiness that would surely come with it.

Simply put, he was in a shit mood.

"Hijo, siéntate," Dad said, handing him a cold glass of lemonade. Lucas dropped onto the ground and drank the whole thing in one go. "What's going on with you?"

Here we go.

"I'm struggling with something."

"Maybe I can help."

Lucas didn't doubt his father had nuggets of wisdom that would help, but he wasn't sure if he even wanted to hear any of it. He was the one who fucked up when he didn't run after Julia like he'd wanted to the other night.

"Is this about the young lady you brought home?" Dad asked.

"We broke up." *Never really started, to be completely truthful.*

His dad hummed, slowly getting himself on the ground next to Lucas, a big acerola tree above them.

"Do you love her?"

Lucas looked at his dad. "I do."

"Then why aren't you fighting for her?"

"She needed time apart." *Until she confessed her love and I was too stubborn to beg her to be with me.*

"Is she with someone else?"

"No." But when she did find someone, he would actually die. He'd never get over her. "It wasn't about that."

"I won't ask because it's not exactly my business, but you are." An arm went around Lucas, and he leaned in, feeling again like a kid. "I hate to see you sad."

"Sadness is necessary to grow."

"Yes, but sadness for the sake of sadness doesn't help anyone. Are you learning from it now?"

"Not a damn thing."

His father nodded sagely.

"You'll figure it out. You're like your mom—nothing escaped that woman. Had a solution for everything."

True. Constanza Marrero had been a formidable woman, fiercely protective of her family until the very end. An even better witch, too.

"I can't use magic for this," Lucas told him.

"If there's a chance," his dad added as noise came from the front of the house, "then don't go out without a fight."

Karla was the first person outside, and Lucas hugged her, then Antonia, and finally, Josefina.

"Where are the boys?" he asked Antonia, who usually had her kids in tow.

"Con el pendejo del padre hoy," she said in an annoyed tone that made Karla cringe away.

"Y tú?" Josefina asked as they went to the kitchen and began preparing dinner. He would leave in the morning for DR, though the wedding wasn't until the day after that, but there were activities he'd been asked to attend.

"Nothing. What are you up to?"

She smiled. "Not much. Going out with my boyfriend later."

Lucas raised his brows. "Boyfriend. Very nice."

"It's new, but it's exciting. He's great."

"I'm very happy to hear that."

Josefina was peeling garlic as their sisters and father prepped the rest of the food. The kitchen was small, but held all of them comfortably.

"And your girlfriend? I assume she's in DR for the wedding now."

"She's not my girlfriend."

Something about his tone made Josefina stop peeling.

"Did something happen?"

"They broke up," Karla said. "Seriously, you never check the group chat now that you're into Pedro."

"Your boyfriend's Pedro?" Lucas inquired. Pedro was a good childhood friend, who hadn't mentioned anything about dating Lucas's sister last time they talked a week ago.

"I guess she took my words to heart, then," Josefina said and pursed her lips, going back to the garlic.

Sure he'd heard wrong, Lucas stopped cutting up plantains and turned to her.

"What do you mean?" he asked way more calmly than he felt inside now.

Josefina looked up at him and shrugged.

"Ay Dios mio," Antonia muttered from the other side of the kitchen, and Lucas threw a brief look at her.

"You want to tell me what you mean, or should I just force it out of you?" Lucas asked, the storm inside him gathering pressure. He wasn't going to force anything, even though he could, but Josefina obviously needed a nudge to start talking.

"I talked to her when you brought her here," Josefina said. "We were cleaning the kitchen, and she came to help. I told her that she better not hurt you."

As calmly as possible, Lucas put down the knife on the counter and glared down at his sister, while everyone else went completely silent. Josefina only looked up at him with the defiant set of her chin he knew too well.

"What the fuck did you say to her?"

"Language!" Karla, the religious one in the family, said.

Lucas turned to her, a thunderous expression on his face.

"Tú no te metas, Karla." Out of his business is where he wanted all of them. His heart was racing and he was starting to shake.

"Ey, a mi no me hables en ese tono."

"Karla," their father warned, and Karla snapped her mouth shut. Behind her, Antonia's eyes were wide as saucers, but she said nothing.

"What did you say to her?" Lucas asked, turning back to Josefina.

She turned red. "I only told the truth. That she wanted to slum it with a brown man until her whiteness came to bite him in the ass. She didn't disagree, you know."

Lucas ran his hand through his hair and closed his eyes, doing everything in his power to stay calm. It wasn't working. It was no wonder Julia had been different when they left that day. How quiet, even though she'd tried to seem like everything was fine. He should have known.

"You have no fucking right, Josefina."

"I have every right!" Josefina yelled. "You're my baby brother, and it's my job to protect you from those succubus women. The last one didn't exactly treat you nicely."

"I'm thirty-two years old!" Lucas exploded, and Josefina flinched. He didn't lose his temper often, but Josefina was one of the only people who plucked at those strings like no one else could.

"I don't fucking care how old you are."

"Mira, Josefina . . ." he growled through teeth clenched so tightly they hurt. There was so much more he wanted to say to her, to yell and rage for putting shit in Julia's head when their relationship had already been fragile. "No te metas en mi vida, Josefina. I swear to God, I will never speak to you again if you pull anything like this again. You did it to Mariana, to Cole, to everyone I've ever brought here, and I'm fucking tired of it."

"Oh, forgive me, sir, for wanting you to be happy."

"What? By chasing away anyone I love? No one's ever been good enough for you, and it's not your life so stay the fuck out of it."

"Lucas, hijo," said his dad softly, taking Lucas by arm and leading him out of the kitchen.

"No, why don't you leave him here to keep yelling at me?" Josefina's voice wobbled, but their father turned around to regard her angrily.

"Josefina, ya cállate."

Josefina turned back to the garlic and used the knife to chop angrily while Lucas followed his dad's lead and went to the little orchard in the back.

"Mírame, hijo," Dad said, and Lucas met his father's eyes. He couldn't remember the last time he'd been this angry at one of his sisters. It was cute when they were younger, but that shit had real life consequences now. It wasn't simple kid stuff anymore. Julia was the woman he loved, who he wanted to spend the rest of his days with, and though her responses weren't Josefina's responsibility, his sister had no right to butt into his relationship like this.

"Lucas," Dad said to get his attention. Patient like a damn saint, the old man. Lucas looked at him again, his eyes hot and wet.

"No sé qué hacer." What if she didn't forgive him? He was, of course, going to beg and grovel.

"Hijo, Josefina was wrong," he said, "but if someone being rude made Julia pull away, then it was bigger than just the words."

Yes, he knew that, but it was so much easier to blame everything on someone else. And he had every right to be pissed at Josefina too, but all the anger deflated. All he wanted was to go to DR and find Julia.

"Don't make any decisions until you're clear-headed."

Lucas closed his eyes and breathed in deeply. His dad was right. He would go to DR tomorrow, as he had planned, and he'd find a way to talk to Julia then. Get her to listen to him. Beg if he had to. What he'd do if she refused, he didn't know and didn't want to think about at all.

27

Julia had been busy the moment she arrived on the island, bustling to make the wedding happen without a hitch. She didn't have to do any of it, but she wanted to take care of anything she could so Victoria didn't have to worry. So far, her friend was getting her hair done by Jeanette, makeup by Amy as requested. The previous night, they'd had dinner with everyone who'd come to the wedding, and not that she'd been looking, but Lucas wasn't there. Not concerning at all, of course. She didn't care if he showed up or not.

A lie, but she was willing to do that until she actually believed it.

She found out later that his flight had gotten delayed due to weather, and she hadn't breathed in relief because, again, it didn't matter.

The staff to the venue, a gorgeous building on the beach, were on top of everything, but Julia supervised anyway. The flowers were in place, and the chairs were decorated with lace and greenery. Outside, on a platform straight on the beach, a round arch matched the decor of the chairs. The venue's wedding planner, a tiny plump woman with dark skin and straight hair, directed some of her staff into laying out the white rug between the two groups of chairs. Seeing that things were under control, that the sun was shining above her, bright and hot as hell, she followed Amy when she came out to tell her it was time to get dressed. They were both in their bridal party robes as they headed down the hallway. Julia smiled and greeted the staff.

Julia had been meaning to talk to Amy about Helena, but there was never a good time. She wanted to be careful how she approached it, because though Amy was an open person, she'd never dated a woman. Not that Julia knew.

"Victoria's very calm, which worries me," Amy said as they walked down a brightly-lit hallway.

"It's good that she's not freaking out," Julia said.

"You weren't freaking out and ended up throwing up before the ceremony."

"That's because my body was rejecting Harold and I didn't even know it." Julia shivered and opened the door to the wedding suite. It was a wide room, with a wall of windows overlooking the Caribbean Sea. The dresses were hanging off hooks above the windows, almost glowing in the sunlight.

Julia had already done her hair, leaving it as wavy as she could manage without it turning frizzy.

Sophia was already pulling her dress on with the help of Helena, who was ready.

In front of a large mirror, Victoria talked to Jeanette, who was doing her hair. While Jeanette was dressed in her long white gown, Victoria still wore her bridal robe. She was glowing, and their identical green eyes met in the mirror as they spoke. Julia watched them for a moment, her heart so full of joy for her family, these women she loved so much, doing the things Julia would have wanted to have with her own mother when it was her time to get married again.

Turning away, Julia reached for her dress. Amy helped her, adjusting it so it hugged Julia's body just right. It was an absolutely stunning dress, and it fit her perfectly.

"You're so talented," Julia told Amy as she finished zipping the dress.

Amy beamed but said nothing, and Julia wanted to push for a response. For some reason, Amy shrunk away from praise with her own designs. Julia thought that Amy could take her store to the next level by offering her designs instead of carrying other people's, but Julia had kept it to herself. She didn't want to meddle any more than she had to.

She put a hand to her stomach, which was fluttering with anticipation; for Victoria and Thomas, but also at the thought of seeing Lucas. The last time they'd talked hadn't quite gone the way she wanted it to, but now she was ready. It was okay if she couldn't be with him—she would treasure the time she spent with him anyway.

Feeling sexy, she put on simple gold earrings and observed her own reflection, pleased to see the color back on her cheeks and the few pounds she'd gained in the last weeks.

Julia had chosen a sexier makeup look, her eyes smoky, and her lips more natural. At her throat was a simple gold necklace, which matched the thin, long earrings and the bracelet.

Jeanette, green eyes bright and surrounded by smokey black, stood at the front of the room as Sophia and Helena finished helping Victoria with her dress and lace cape. She looked like an angel.

"It's time," Jeanette said just as a knock came on the door. It was Victoria's father, big and tall, in his dapper white suit.

"Sounds like we need to get out there," he said in a booming voice.

"We are ready." Jeanette grinned at him, and he grinned back.

"Oh my god," Amy said in a wobbly voice when they were all standing in a circle. "You look amazing."

Victoria's eyes misted, becoming brighter than usual.

"No crying!" Sophia shrieked and looked at Amy with a mutinous expression. She rushed forward with a tissue and made sure no tears dripped. Victoria's makeup was subtle, but tears would ruin the beautiful eyeliner work Amy had done.

Victoria turned to look at herself in the mirror for a few moments, and everyone went silent to allow her a moment that ended with a shuddering breath.

"Holy shit, this is finally happening," Victoria breathed, and everyone laughed.

Two years ago, this wedding almost didn't happen due to the spell Sophia had inadvertently cast. Now, here they were about to walk out.

"You're marrying the love of your life tonight," Jeanette said, smiling. "Right here on this lovely island, with this lovely weather, and everyone who loves you cheering you on."

Victoria nodded, her eyes misty again, but no one yelled and no one moved this time.

"Do you see anything, Mom?" Victoria asked Jeanette, who smiled even more as her eyes went faraway somewhere. Julia held her breath as magic filled the room, and anxiety festered in her stomach.

"The future's fickle, love," Jeanette said. "It can change according to your every decision."

Victoria nodded, and Jeanette hummed.

"I see the number three. Not necessarily children, either. Women birth many things, and you will do that, in more than one way."

Victoria's smile bloomed, bright, happy. "Thank you, Mommy," Victoria said softly, then turned to everyone else. "Let's get married!"

Julia cheered alongside her sisters and friends.

"Now get me some fucking tequila or something. Jesus Lord, I'm so nervous," Victoria squealed.

"Right away," Amy piped, lifting a bottle of tequila blanco as if she'd been waiting for someone to ask. Julia snorted, and when Victoria took a swig straight from the bottle, barely making a face, Sophia burst out laughing. She grabbed the bottle next, taking a drink herself. Everyone else in the room followed suit, even Julia, who could barely swallow from laughing.

There wasn't anything really funny about it, mostly a happiness in the air that they all felt deeply and it spilled into the world. The room had gone from being filled with nervous energy to turning calm and filled with anticipation instead. As Julia walked out, Helena right in front of her, it dawned on Julia.

"You did that," she said, taking Helena by the arm. Her blonde friend said nothing, just smiled faintly and kept walking, as she was singing while the wedding party walked out. "I wish you could teach stuff like that."

"You never know," Helena said. "I just facilitated relaxation. Nothing major."

Julia laughed. Sure, nothing major.

Helena continued walking, and Julia followed. Right inside the doors to the platform where the wedding was taking place, Julia accepted the bouquet of asters, baby white roses, and various fragrant green leaves, and stood beside Thomas's older brother, Tae. She put her hand through the crook of his elbow, slightly taller than him in her heels. He was gorgeous, with dark hair like his brother's and deep brown eyes.

He smiled at her, and she smiled back as Sophia moved forward on the arm of the best man, Thomas's other brother.

It was as if the weather had conspired to be absolutely perfect. The few clouds that hovered about them were bright pink, orange, purple as the sun started to set.

As she walked out, she saw Jeanette at the arch, waiting for Victoria and Thomas.

The ocean was a gorgeous backdrop, with all those incredible, warm colors reflected on the bright turquoise waters and the guests.

Off to the side, Helena sang a love song. White curtains moved in the breeze and flowers adorned the aisle and altar.

Julia grinned as she walked on the arm of her companion. She hadn't realized how much one could love a wedding, when it was so full of happiness and everyone she loved in it.

Including *him*.

Lucas sat just off the aisle, with a cousin of Victoria's on one side, Grey on the other, and those luminous eyes were right on her. His mouth opened in a silent gasp that she felt all the way through her. But she kept walking until Tae left her on her side of the aisle and took his. Everything else went in a blur. Thomas walked down the aisle with both of his parents, Victoria by her father shortly after. They were married by Jeanette in a short but sweet ceremony filled with loving words and the wisdom only years and experience could bring.

Some words were exchanged between the bride and groom, and tears were shed—from Thomas mainly since Victoria was taking not ruining her makeup rather seriously—and finally a kiss. The entire ceremony, Julia fought looking over at Lucas, and every time she ventured a look, his eyes were on her. Thrilled, she kept her smile to herself. It had to be the dress. Or that he loved her still. She'd rather have the latter.

They'd done photos a couple of days before, in Seattle and on the island, so there were only candids being taken tonight as the reception progressed. It was a party, with loud music, low lights, and an open bar. She danced with her sisters mostly, trying to ignore the tingling on the back of her neck. She wouldn't turn to see if Lucas was looking at her from where he was chatting by the bar with Grey. It could be because the last time she'd tried he'd turned her away, but as the night progressed, Julia found it more and more difficult to approach him. She'd wanted to so many times throughout the night.

Roped into dancing with both of Thomas's brothers, she lost track of Lucas, and when she saw him again, he was dancing with Victoria's cousin, who hung around him way too much.

She was with Tae, who wasn't much of a dancer, but he was trying so hard to keep the beat. It was adorable. He was adorable and sweet, and she had a genuinely good time chatting with him. After the first three songs, she slipped off her shoes, and Tae grabbed her again. She laughed, snorted even, when he took her around the entire dance floor as if they were waltzing to reggaeton.

Victoria's cousin (Laney, Julia thought) laughed when they came across each other at one point. Julia couldn't look up at Lucas. It was like looking up at the sun.

"You guys are so fun!" Laney yelled over the music, her pretty brown face shiny with sweat.

Julia smiled at her, the energy contagious, but when she looked up at Lucas, his eyes glinted.

She looked back at Laney. "You have the best dancer here. Enjoy."

Laney grinned up at Lucas, whose jaw worked.

"You should show me how good you are," Laney said, her smile turning sultry.

Julia gritted her teeth. Served her right for being a dumbass.

No. She wasn't talking to herself like that anymore. Lucas had every right to dance with Laney, and of course the woman was into him. He was Lucas Dolores, after all.

She couldn't take her eyes off Lucas now, but she still danced with Tae, who kept trying to keep the conversation going. Somehow, along the way, she stopped paying attention and felt horrible. Maybe she wouldn't get to talk to Lucas at all, and that had to be okay, but disappointment still lanced through her at the thought that they could be in paradise together but apart.

"I'm not much of a dancer." Tae laughed suddenly. "Maybe you'd like to get a drink with me and just chat?"

She accepted, trying to forget about Lucas and Laney, and drank a tall, frosty glass of local beer, which was golden and bubbly. As far as beer went, this was excellent, and Julia was not a beer person.

But she didn't forget. In fact, her eyes kept going to where Lucas was dancing with Laney, then Helena, and a couple of other women who approached him, from Thomas's family.

Tae was so cute, with adorable dimples and smooth skin, but she couldn't do this. Not when her mind was on Lucas, so acutely aware of where he was, that she could focus on nothing else.

Her mind went to every moment she spent dancing with him, how it led her to finding pieces of herself she'd long lost. How dancing had led to so many moments she would never be able to forget.

She knew that getting over Lucas would be something she would never fully be able to do.

And suddenly, understanding for what her mom had gone through crashed inside her. She felt like she'd been struck by lightning, thinking about her mom and Will, and how a love could last until your last breath.

She looked up at Tae, her stomach shivering uncomfortably.

"I'm sorry, Tae, I need fresh air," she told him, trying not to sound as breathless as she felt.

"Would you like company?" he asked, but she reached for his cheek.

"I think I want to be on my own right now," she told him. Oh, she felt terrible, but she couldn't stay in that loud room for much longer or she might throw up.

"You good?" Sophia asked as Julia walked past her.

Julia turned back to her sister, who was by Grey, the love of *her* life. And Amy who had this thing with Helena for sure because they were gone from the party, probably convinced no one noticed.

"Yeah, just going to step outside for some air," Julia said in a rush, grabbing the green bottle of local beer from a bartender. "This okay?" she asked him, walking out without waiting for his response. Rude as hell, but the overstimulation had gotten to such an uncomfortable place, she nearly ran out. The moment the doors closed, the music was muffled and she felt relieved. She took gulps of cool sea air. A maze of hedges and tall palm trees decorated the big garden. Blissfully barefoot, the paved ground was cool against her skin as she took off down a path. There were stone benches all along the way, and lights shone overhead. Julia took deep breaths, the icy bottle gripped tightly in her hand. One sip of cold beer and the panic calmed significantly, but her eyes still wanted to fill.

She hadn't been having many panic attacks, but sometimes she still felt pulled apart. Her therapist, Dr. Jones, said it would calm down with time and practice. She believed him—it was the same thing Mariana had often told her—and she did feel a difference now.

Her feet hit sand, and the sounds of the ocean calmed her more than the alcohol could, so she tipped her head up to the starry sky and breathed sea air as deeply as her lungs would allow.

"Julia."

Julia didn't turn.

"I want to be alone, please," she said, hating that her voice shook.

But Lucas didn't leave. Instead, he came to stand in front of her, looking down at her with those x-ray eyes. She could get lost in there forever.

"I talked to Josefina before I flew here," he murmured.

To wet her suddenly dry throat, she drank deeply from the bottle. She'd forgotten about Josefina, if she was perfectly honest.

"Why didn't you tell me?"

Another long pull of beer. Thank god it was one of those half-liter bottles. "I didn't think it was necessary."

He frowned. "Not necessary to tell me the horrible things she said to you?"

She looked up at him finally. "And what, Lucas? Start a fight between you and your sister?"

"Yes," he snapped. His voice softened when he added, "You should have told me—"

"*That* would have gotten your sister on my side, for sure," she scoffed.

"So you let her intimidate you. Josefina hates everyone when she first meets them," he said, sounding rather annoyed. "Was it that easy to give us up?"

She heard the hurt, but it still irritated her.

"Don't talk to me about easy. You have no idea the hell I've been in."

"Then tell me."

"I can't tell you. Last time I tried, you told me you didn't want to be with me."

"I was being a prideful prick," Lucas said, his jaw working. "You hurt me, too."

"So you wanted to retaliate?" She thought of Mariana. *Did she go home with you?*

"It wasn't like that."

She bit her lip, trying to find the words. To allow them to leave her so he understood her better.

"Maybe it was partly because of Josefina, but it's not about her," she said, looking out at the darkness of the ocean. "I felt unworthy of love my entire life, and it's taken all this shit to happen for me to realize it. Josefina only reminded me of that."

"She was wrong."

"She wasn't wrong. She was cruel because she's afraid for you, and that's not okay, but her words were true."

"So what does that mean?" he asked quietly.

"I don't know," she told him truthfully. She didn't think she could take another heartbreak. His fingers reached for her wrist, and she didn't have the strength to pull away. "What are we doing here?"

"Please, I just want to talk to you."

"Is there really much more to say?"

"So much." He took a step closer so his scent was all she could register now. "I love you, Julia. I've been miserable for the last few weeks. And when Josefina told me what she'd said, all I wanted was to come here and find you."

Her heart was racing, hammering so hard against her chest now. He thought her hesitation was because of Josefina, and maybe it was wrong, but she felt the urge to tell him.

"Lucas, it's not just Josefina," she told him. "I don't know anything for sure, but I might not be able to have kids."

She had a doctor's appointment when she got back to Seattle, but while she had no idea, she wasn't going to keep her hopes up.

"I asked Grey to not say anything, but I found out some stuff that last night we…" she trailed off, embarrassed, and her face heated. She told him about Harold and his confession, and watched several emotions cross over his face, finally slipping away when she was finished. His expression was blank, but his eyes were misty.

"Julia, that's vile," he ground out.

"I know. Then he burned down the house, and it scared me." Now that she was talking, she couldn't stop. "I thought about my dad and how I could have never fathomed him doing something so horrible, and I was afraid."

"That Harold would come after you? Are you scared of him?"

"Of course I'm scared of him," she said. "This wound I have with my dad won't let me think otherwise."

"I will fix it," Lucas said, his mouth pressed into an angry line.

"No, we're staying away. Believe me, Sophia wanted to hex him, but I just want to forget about Harold and Kate. I don't want to retaliate, and I don't want to hear about them or talk about them. I'm so over them."

Lucas's breathing was fast as he looked out at the ocean. He took the beer from her hand and took a deep swig.

"I really wish you'd told me."

She looked up at his profile. "I should have."

Exhausted, she slipped to the sand and sat, her feet all the way in front of her. He did the same, and she realized he also didn't have shoes on. He didn't have the jacket to his suit anymore, and she couldn't blame him when it was so hot and humid. It was, thankfully, cooler out here on the dark beach.

The beer bottle between them, they sat in silence for a while. She thought about every step that had led her to this moment; her out of control powers surfacing again, talking to him for the first time. The days when he'd taken her out just to get her to relax. Falling in love with him so hard and so fast she was still reeling. And it could be that she'd grown from her ordeals, or maybe it was because she was a little tipsy, but when she looked at him again, she said, "I'm sorry I didn't tell you."

It cost her—pride was not easy to let go of—but she was glad to say it anyway.

"I'm sorry about Harold."

A silent sigh left her, and her body finally relaxed.

"I want you, no matter what," he added, twisting so he was close to her, leaning over her. She shivered as her eyes slid up to his.

"And what if I actually can't have kids?" she asked. She suspected she'd be fine, but she couldn't ask him to compromise a family if he wanted one.

"Julia, there are so many ways to be parents," he said. "We can choose any of those if the traditional way doesn't work out. And if we decide not to have kids, I will be okay because all I want is you. I love you."

Julia closed her eyes, letting his words seep into her.

"Please, Mami, don't shut me out." His forehead came to rest against hers. Her breath stuttered. "Yo me muero por ti. I want everything, the good, the ugly, all of it. I only want to be with you. Tell me it's not too late."

She felt wrung out, gooey like a hot cookie.

"I missed you," she whispered, fingers slipping into his hair as she held him close, bright moonlight bathing them.

"God, I missed you," he murmured, his lips close. "I don't know how I survived."

Her heart hammered, quickened, melted, and finally, he kissed her. She went weeks without this; without his lips and his scent, and the way he loved her.

Like coming home after a long trip, Julia relaxed into him. She wasn't sure how long they were there for, Lucas pushing her back so she was laying on the sand, their mouths glued together. A sigh escaped her, and he drank it like he was dying of thirst. She tightened her arms around him, pressing her body to his like she'd craved for weeks.

His clever hands were everywhere all at once, and all she could do was grip his hair tightly. Mostly because her dress was too tight and she couldn't put her legs around him like she wanted to.

Public place, Julia. Relax.

She could die a happy woman with his arms so tight around her, his tongue licking her lips, his teeth biting her gently, a promise of what he would do when they could be in a more private place. A private place she wanted to go find immediately, and she almost suggested they get the hell out of there (no one would miss them) when a giggle drifted in the wind toward them.

It was like trying to unglue herself. She wanted nothing less than to stop kissing him, but Amy and Helena had appeared from somewhere in the dark beach.

"You two, get a room," Amy called. They snorted, laughing, and disappeared toward the garden.

Julia and Lucas laughed, him now leaning on his elbow so he could hover over her.

"Likewise," Lucas snorted.

"They think no one knows."

"I didn't for a while, actually. Made me feel stupid when it dawned on me."

"Hey, same."

More laughter, more kissing. Finally, he helped her up to her feet. He adjusted himself, trying to hide the evidence of his desire. But she only had to look him in the eye to know. His gaze was molten on her, sincere, loving.

They walked hand in hand toward the building, pausing a few times to kiss and sway together to the muffled music in the distance.

Inside, they found the party in full swing. Sophia was giggling as Grey twirled her around with no rhyme or reason. She had also removed her shoes, and there was a merriment now, a harmony Julia allowed herself to receive. It rushed through her, that energy of her people laughing. Victoria was dancing with Jeanette, their foreheads pressed together despite the faster rhythm of the song. It was devastating in a way it hadn't been before. It wasn't jealousy, but a yearning that buried itself into her bones. If she married Lucas someday, she wanted that, and she knew that Jeanette would freely give it.

They danced like idiots, sweating and breathless, their arms and legs wild, causing some of the employees to look at them like something was wrong with them. Julia laughed more that night than she had in a whole year.

And drunk with love and champagne, Julia followed the crowd when Amy suggested loudly that they get in the ocean.

Her feet hit the sand again, Sophia and Amy beside her. They ran into the ocean with matching shrieks. Dresses would be ruined, but when you were surrounded by everyone you loved, those things didn't matter.

She screeched when her sisters pushed her around, forcing her head under the warm Caribbean water.

It had been a very long time since they'd acted like kids, careless and free, and it was welcome. Craved. Celebrated.

But she wasn't laughing anymore when Lucas reached for her, turned her, and kissed her salty lips.

They were shuttled to the hotel, and Julia and Lucas made out the whole way there, seated at the very back of the van. Carrying their shoes, they stopped often on the way to the elevators. Neither remembered the ride up to the top floor, or walking along the hall-ways to find her room, which they passed twice before they forced themselves to pay attention. Breathless with laughter and lust, she opened the room. They undressed slowly, a struggle since their clothes were still wet and clinging to their bodies. The lace stuck to her and left imprints of the design on her skin, but standing naked in front of him, the sliding door open to the sounds of the ocean, it was the best she had ever felt. Her cage was gone, and she was free to fly now.

Epilogue

J ules, could you pass me those pins over there?" Amy asked, pointing at a tiny plastic box on the counter. Julia went to move forward, but because she was practicing her power as much as she could, she instead waved her fingers toward the little box. It floated toward her, only spilling a tiny bit, which meant she was improving in her stability.

The past eight months had been good to her, even during hard days. Her magic was now second nature. Almost.

"Thank you," Amy said without looking up, and pinned the dress so that it lay correctly on Helena's body. Helena and Sophia were both singing tonight, Sophia choosing to debut her first song in Spanish. She, Julia, and Amy had been taking Spanish lessons at a local language school, so this was all kinds of exciting for everyone involved. Julia was so proud of herself and her sisters for all they'd accomplished and how far they'd come in the last year.

There were dancers getting ready for the show too, and the chatter was excited, the cloud of hair products fragrant and just a little too much. Julia fucking loved it.

Victoria spoke into her earpiece. She looked a little green, but it seemed like her morning sickness was starting to subside, thankfully. It'd been precarious there for a minute, when poor Victoria could barely take a sip of water without throwing up. Now, at thirteen weeks, she seemed to be feeling much more like herself. She was, of course, glowing, but there was nothing new about that.

"I have to go out front," Victoria announced, smoothing her hands over her pencil dress. She wasn't showing at all. "I love you all, break a leg. It's going to be an incredible show."

The dancers cheered and Julia joined in.

"I'll come with you," Julia said, blowing kisses at Sophia, Helena, and Amy as she followed Victoria out the door. "You look amazing."

Victoria beamed. "So do you. Moving in with your hunky boyfriend's agreeing with you."

Julia laughed. Two months ago, she'd finally given in and moved into Lucas's house with him. She'd spent most of her time there and had taken half his closet anyway, so her hesitation to make the jump didn't make much sense. Dr. Jones said it was normal to feel that way after everything she'd gone through, and he'd convinced her that there was nothing to fear. The happiness in Lucas's face when she asked him if they should just do the damn thing had been the highlight of her life.

"He's a pretty great roommate," she said as they walked down the hall.

"I'll bet."

Julia giggled, opened the door, and walked into the ecstatic energy of the club.

She stood at the edges of the room, where Evan was now taking the stage and starting the show. The dance floor was filled with tables and chairs tonight. Victoria went to the front to greet Thomas with a kiss, promising to meet her at their table. Those two were adorable.

But Julia wanted a different kind of adorable. A man so beautiful it almost hurt to look at him. A god in bed, a cinnamon roll who sang to her in Spanish and sometimes cried when they made love. Lucas sat at their usual table, which overlooked the stage at the perfect angle. Julia moved forward, ignoring everything and everyone else. He had a glass of whiskey in one hand, balanced on his knee. In his other hand was a cigar, unlit since there was no smoking of any kind at Nowhere.

"Hola, Papi," she whispered into his ear, then bit the lobe softly. He turned his head toward her, and there it was. Her stomach erupted in butterflies as that look he gave her. Warm and molten. Pure honey.

He bit his lip before she kissed him deeply. The entire room was gone, the music distant. He pulled her to sit on his lap.

"Food's coming," Grey said, and Julia pulled back to realize she'd completely ignored him.

"I hope you ordered my favorites." Julia narrowed her eyes at him.

"You mean everything Caribbean on the menu? Because yes," Grey deadpanned. Julia laughed.

She sat on his lap almost the entire time as they watched the show. It was gorgeous. Helena and Sophia enchanted them all with their lovely voices. Julia could swear she knew the moment Sophia's singing turned into color in the air, even if she couldn't quite see what Sophia did. Still, she felt the shift.

Lucas's hand rested on her thigh, just underneath the short skirt she'd opted for tonight. He kissed the spot under her ear, sending warmth down her body, to her feet.

When they left the club to head home, he held her hand, bringing her knuckles to his lips every so often. She tried to remain calm, but her insides were dancing. Butterflies. Always butterflies with him. But this time, it was more than that. Anticipation because she knew what was coming. They'd discussed it plenty of times. He played music softly as they swayed together in the dining room when they got home, the house quiet around them. Their three cats were probably upstairs in their bed.

"Te amo, mami," he whispered, leaning forward to kiss her. "Amor de mi vida."

Her throat constricted.

"I want this, you, every day," he continued, his eyes hooded as he looked down at her. All the love he felt for her was in his features, in his warm eyes that were like the whole universe contained in one place. "Forever and beyond that. Marry me, baby."

Without letting her go, he reached into his pocket and pulled out a little box. Julia's breath shivered in and out of her, her eyes misty and warm. They stopped swaying so he could open the box as he knelt in front of her.

She didn't stop the tears as they came. The ring was gorgeous, a deep green stone sparkling on a simple gold band. Lucas looked up at her expectantly, his eyes bright and pleading.

Julia beamed, pulled him up to standing again so she could kiss him silly.

"Sí, mi amor," she said between kisses, and after he put the ring on her finger, they continued to dance.

THE END

Acknowlegments

I'd be remiss not to thank the various writing groups I belong to. My people make my job so much easier.

My betas: Katrina Mendizábal, Monica Rai, Kass O'Shire, Kelsey Fausett, and Wren K. Morris. You guys saved my butt. Thank you so much for the hard work and dedication to reading this and leaving me feedback I cannot put a price to. Special thanks to Bex Deveaux for the late night writing sessions and the chats and the advice. I appreciate you.

To the NaNoWriMo team in BWOY: You made it so fun to dive into this story, and the support and love I experienced is unmatched and will forever stay with me. You're a lovely group of people. Allie, Kassie, Ash, my cheerleaders in this project. You guys made this part so much fun.

To my editor, the lovely Lisa. You're freaking awesome. I don't know what I would have done without you.

To my friend Jesse, for always finding the fun in the fuck.

A very special thanks to Stacy for always reminding me why we chose this career, and for talking me out of the most intense bouts of self-doubt I've had in forever.

About the Author

Carolina Castillo was born and raised in the Dominican Republic. When she's not writing, you can find her reading, singing, dancing, and rewatching all her favorite funny shows and movies. Occasionally, she goes outside.

For more from Carolina, you can find her on TikTok and Instagram @Creatively_Unwritten.

To sign up for her newsletter and for more about her books or what she's been up to, visit carolinacastilloauthor.com

Also by Carolina Castillo

Purchase anywhere you get books, including the author's website, where you can find signed copies and other bookish goodies.

Stay tuned for Helena and Amy's story.

For more information on Carolina's books, as well as playlists and other fun stuff, visit carolinacastilloauthor.com